PRAISE FOR AMY LILLARD

"Lillard's evocative prose, well-drawn protagonists, and detailed settings result in an inspirational story of romance, faith, and trust."

—*Library Journal* for *Caroline's Secret*

"Lillard is skilled at creating memorable characters with enduring faith, and readers will look forward to the next installment."

—*Publishers Weekly* for *Marrying Jonah*

"There are family and friends, interesting characters, lots of angst and problems, sadness, sorrow, death, anger, insecurity, fear, jail time, reminiscences, tears, disappointments, stubbornness, secrets, laughter, happiness, romance, loving, and love."

—Romancing the Book for *Loving a Lawman*

"This story was so funny and fast-paced, I had a hard time putting it down."

—Coffeetime Romance and More for *Brodie's Bride*

"Amy Lillard never disappoints! Her writing is always fun, fresh, and fabulous!"

—*USA Today* bestselling author Arial Burnz

"Amy Lillard weaves well-developed characters that create for lovers of romance a rich fabric of love."

—Vonnie Davis, author of A Highlander's Beloved series

ALSO BY AMY LILLARD

MAIN STREET BOOK CLUB MYSTERIES
Can't Judge a Book by Its Murder

OTHER MYSTERIES

Unsavory Notions
Pattern of Betrayal
O Little Town of Sugarcreek
Shoo, Fly, Shoo
Stranger Things Have
Happened

Kappy King and the
Puppy Kaper
Kappy King and the
Pickle Kaper
Kappy King and the
Pie Kaper

CONTEMPORARY ROMANCE

Brodie's Bride
All You Need Is Love
Can't Buy Me Love
Love Potion Me, Baby
Southern Hospitality
Southern Comfort
Southern Charm

The Trouble with Millionaires
Take Me Back to Texas
Blame It on Texas
Ten Reasons Not to
Date a Cop
Loving a Lawman
Healing a Heart

AMISH ROMANCE

Saving Gideon
Katie's Choice
Gabriel's Bride
Caroline's Secret
Courting Emily

Lorie's Heart
Just Plain Sadie
Titus Returns
Marrying Jonah
The Quilting Circle

A
Murder
between
the
Pages

A Main Street
Book Club
Mystery

Amy Lillard

Poisoned Pen
PRESS

Published by Poisoned Pen Press, an imprint of Sourcebooks
P.O. Box 4410, Naperville, Illinois 60567-4410
(630) 961-3900
sourcebooks.com

Library of Congress Cataloging-in-Publication Data

Names: Lillard, Amy, author.
Title: Murder between the pages / Amy Lillard.
Description: Naperville, Illinois : Poisoned Pen Press, [2020] | Series:
    Main Street Book Club ; book 2
Identifiers: LCCN 2020018072 (print) Subjects: GSAFD: Mystery fiction.
Classification: LCC PS3612.I4 M87 2020 (print) | DDC 813/.6--dc23
LC record available at https://lccn.loc.gov/2020018072

Printed and bound in Canada.
MBP 10 9 8 7 6 5 4 3 2 1

I'm always asked if I make characters who are representative of real people in my life. Well, yes and no. Most times, the characters come to me with their own set of quirks and baggage, but there are occasions when I add a little something to reflect people I know. Camille's handbag is one such incidence.

My best friend's mother always carried a handbag with remarkable things inside. Need a tissue? Mary's got it. Fingernail clippers? Just ask Mary. Lotion? Lipstick? Three-eighths socket wrench? Mary. And the most interesting thing about her handbag is she never set it down. Even when she was at my friend's house! She would have it sitting primly in her lap, as if guarding its secrets.

Her family always swore that if anything happened to her, they would call 9-1-1, then dig through her bag to see what all was in there while they waited for the ambulance.

Then this past year something did happen, and her family forgot all about that vow. Until later, that is. So what was in Mary's handbag? It's a secret that I will take to my grave. But if you want an idea, watch Camille and see what she drags out of her bag, for her character was inspired by Mary. So it is to her that I dedicate this book.

1

"Let us come too. Please..." Fern lifted her chin, sensing what was coming next.

"No." Arlo's voice was clipped as she set down the stack of books she had been shelving and made her way over to the reading area where the book club ladies held their daily meetings. She knew Fern was only trying to drag her into their conversation, and she had taken the bait, but ever since the book club started meeting at Arlo and Chloe's Books and More, she'd been forced to keep them all in line. "You are not going out to Lillyfield mansion and bothering Mrs. Whitney under the guise of me picking up a donation."

"But—"

"No," Arlo repeated. "I have to collect a box of books, but that doesn't mean I need any help." Or distraction.

Book club. She almost snorted at the title. It had become a hen party, plain and simple, but there was no way she was telling them they couldn't meet. Not only had they helped solve Wally Harrison's murder just a few months before, but one of the members was her guardian. Well, at least she had been back when Arlo had needed a guardian.

"Elly," Arlo started, using the special name she had for Helen. Her plea didn't work. The ladies were already in full let's-solve-a-mystery mode. And their latest centered on their most recent book club read.

"But what about the book?" Camille asked.

"There's no mystery to be solved there," Arlo said as gently as she could. Behind her, Chloe Carter, her best friend and bookstore business partner, slammed a cabinet shut in the coffee bar that sat opposite the reading nook.

"Sorry," she mumbled, still loud enough for them to hear. Whatever. She wasn't fooling Arlo. Chloe had made the noise to camouflage her own laughter. She thought it was brilliantly funny that Arlo had to spend most of her time these days making sure the book club members didn't get in the way of the police and their real investigations. Well, it had been when they were trying to uncover who killed Wally. This time they had simply made up a mystery. Or rather, Wally had.

Wallace J. Harrison was the closest thing Sugar Springs had to a celebrity. More so now that he was…well, let's just say that he was even more popular posthumously. Not even Mads Keller, current police chief and former running back for the Sugar Springs Blue Devils, could touch his celeb status. And Mads had spent years playing for the San Francisco 49ers. Wally was a writer. Had been, anyway. He had written a runaway bestseller before his death. *Missing Girl* had spent many weeks at number one on the *New York Times* bestseller list and even longer in the top ten.

"There most certainly is." Fern nodded her head

emphatically, while Helen and Camille mimicked the sentiment.

When Arlo had put out the notice that she was starting a Friday night book club, she had hoped to get the young and hip citizens of Sugar Springs to come and chat. Okay, maybe not hip, but at least people who weren't decades past retirement. Instead she had gotten three of the oldest and most unique residents who were now determined to actually solve mysteries instead of reading them.

There was Camille Kinny, who had never managed to lose her Aussie accent though she had been in America for longer than Arlo had been alive. She had taught English at the high school to almost everyone in town. And she had forgotten more about books than most people learned in a lifetime.

Helen Johnson, who owned the Sugar Springs Inn, had become Arlo's guardian when Arlo's hippie family had decided that six months in Sugar Springs was more than plenty. They had liked the town well enough; they just didn't like staying in one place for too long. While Arlo's brother, Woody, loved the lifestyle, Arlo had had enough. She dug in her heels and demanded she get to stay. She had been sixteen at the time, old enough, her parents decided, to make up her mind about such things so that's exactly what she did. And she had been in Sugar Springs with Elly ever since.

Then there was Fern Conley, who was as grumpy as Helen was welcoming, but Arlo loved her all the same. There was a freshness about Fern. She didn't sugarcoat things, preferring the direct route. Sometimes her words came out harsh, but they were always the truth. Or at least, the truth as she saw it.

"In fact," Fern continued, "it's the biggest unsolved mystery in Sugar Springs."

"You cannot go out to Lillyfield mansion and bother that poor woman," Arlo insisted.

"You're going," Camille pointed out.

"To pick up a box of books they want to donate to the store." Arlo kept a case of used books in Books and More, classics and donations mostly, but it did offer a variety for the readers in town. And she was always willing to sift through donated boxes for anything acceptable. "I was invited."

"It's been a month since her stroke," Fern protested.

"A month is not nearly long enough for someone to recover," Arlo returned.

"Every stroke is different," Helen chimed in.

"The internet says six months to two years. But after about six months a person has gained back all the mobility and skills that they most probably will." Camille had looked up the information on her phone.

"See? Judith Whitney has not had time to recover properly. Which is exactly why you should remain here and, gee, I don't know...talk about the book." Arlo frowned. "You are a book club, remember?"

Helen glared at Camille. "Thanks a lot."

"We *are* talking about the book," Camille explained sweetly, ignoring Helen's sarcasm. She shifted her purse in her lap but never made a move to set it on the floor. Or anywhere for that matter; the square white handbag was always solidly perched on her knees. The ladies had already told her that if she ever collapsed, they were looking in her purse before they called 9-1-1. No one knew what all she had in that mysterious receptacle of hers, and once she started digging around inside, only heaven knew what object she would unearth or what repercussions might follow.

"Asking Judith Whitney about a disappearance that happened forty years ago—"

"Fifty," Helen corrected.

Arlo sighed. "Fifty years ago is not talking about the book."

"It is if said disappearance is the subject of the book," Fern countered.

Arlo might as well face it. Her arguments were pointless—at least when Helen, Camille, and Fern were involved. She moved around the couch and plopped down next to Helen. "Seriously. How do you reckon that Wally's book is the same as the case of Mary Kennedy?"

"Here, kitty, kitty, kitty," Faulkner, Arlo's African gray parrot, squawked from his cage. He preferred to be let out as much as possible, but with the book club meeting and the fact that Auggie, Chloe's cat, was still staying upstairs in Sam Tucker's office, Arlo thought it best to limit his free time.

Helen leaned over toward the cage. "Gimme a kiss," she crooned to the bird. She pursed her lips as Faulkner gently nipped at her with his beak.

Arlo rolled her eyes. She had told Helen too many times to count that the move was dangerous. One day she was afraid that Faulkner would bite too hard and Helen would be lipless.

When she said as much to her guardian, Helen would just laugh and wave away Arlo's concern, stating that she would rather live life on the edge.

Arlo had no argument to that.

"It's A to B," Camille explained. "There's a missing girl in the book. You know...that's probably why he named it *Missing Girl*. And there was a missing girl here."

Arlo closed her eyes ever so briefly and even managed to bite back her incredulous sigh.

"And the last time she was seen, she was leaving Lillyfield after giving Baxter Whitney a piano lesson," Fern added.

Sugar Springs folklore. Arlo had heard the story before; everyone in town had. How the woman, Mary Kennedy, piano teacher and organist at the First Baptist, had simply vanished fifty years before. Her car went missing, and there had been no sign of her since she had driven through the gates of Lillyfield mansion. The mansion had always had the large iron gates, but they hadn't always had security cameras. And once she was out of sight, she was gone.

Just like the lady in *Missing Girl*.

Arlo shook her head. "There are differences between the case and Wally's book. A lot of them."

Fern waved off her protest with a "bah" and a flick of one hand. "It's fiction."

"*Right.*" Arlo felt as if she were reasoning with a brick wall, or maybe a two-year-old. Same difference. "If it's fiction, then it's not true."

"Not all of it," Fern reasoned.

This was getting her nowhere fast.

"Hey, ladies." Sam Tucker greeted them from the doorway that led to the third floor staircase. "What are we talking about?"

"Sam!" All eyes turned to him.

The second floor was filled with shelves and comfy

chairs, but Arlo and Chloe had decided to rent out the top floor in order to help make ends meet. Never in her wildest dreams had she imagined that Sam Tucker, her old flame, would set up shop there. He picked up Auggie, who had wandered down at his side, and carted him over to the sitting area.

"Here, kitty, kitty," Faulkner crooned.

"I thought you were keeping him upstairs," Arlo admonished. The words sounded ridiculous. Auggie wasn't even Sam's cat, but he had stayed with him a few weeks before when Chloe went to jail during the Wally Harrison investigation. Chloe was worried about moving him again so soon and had asked if Sam could keep him a while longer. It was a fine plan except for Faulkner. He and Auggie saw fit to attack each other on a regular basis. They didn't come across as outright enemies, but they tussled around enough to worry Arlo that their play could turn dangerous.

"You know Auggie."

She did. And the ginger-striped feline seemed to do whatever he pleased. Wasn't that just the way with cats? She wouldn't know. She had never had one. Her family's nomadic lifestyle had never allowed for one, and when she moved into Helen's inn, it had always been a health and allergy worry. Faulkner was the closest she had to a childhood pet.

The bird began to chatter and whistle.

"Take him back upstairs, please," Arlo said, with a nod in Auggie's direction. "I don't want to have to cover Faulkner's cage."

"Are you trying to get rid of me?" Sam pouted when he asked the question, but his eyes twinkled. Those baby blues had once been the very reason Arlo had believed they could have a future together. The wishful thinking of a naive eighteen-year-old. And yet there were times when she still wondered…

"Of course not." Arlo didn't have to answer; Helen, Camille, and Fern did it for her. Though she would have said the same thing.

"Put the cat back upstairs, then come tell Arlo how we really need to go out to the mansion," Fern instructed.

Sam chuckled, then scooped up Auggie once again. He disappeared into the stairwell, then reappeared seconds later, sans the cat. "I'm not sure I can do that."

It was a miracle they were even *thinking* about listening to Arlo. Ever since she had started the book club, she had been the voice of reason, an oftentimes ignored voice. And all she was supposed to be was a host. Instead she felt like a babysitter of juvenile delinquents. Okay, maybe it hadn't been that bad. But in the few short weeks since she posted her flyers about the club, they had certainly had their adventures.

"You read the book," Helen said. "Wally's book."

"Yes." Sam had joined their little group for a while and had read *Missing Girl* right alongside them.

"Is there or is there not a similarity between the Mary Kennedy case and the missing girl in the book?"

He shot Arlo an apologetic look before answering. "Well, yeah."

Fern gave a satisfied nod. "See?"

"Missing—missing," Arlo said. "Of course there are similarities, but that doesn't mean that you have to bother a me—an elderly citizen of our community without true provocation." She had been about to say "mean old lady" but stopped herself just in time. Judith Whitney might just be the meanest person in Sugar Springs, as well as the wealthiest, but there was no reason to be rude about it.

"But if she knows something…" Fern pressed.

"I heard that she can't walk, talk, or even write," Helen added. "Whatever she knows could be locked inside her mind forever."

"Elly." Arlo chastised her, managing to contain most of her protest over her guardian's dramatic statement.

Arlo took a deep breath and tried again. "If that's the case, there's no use going out there at all."

"Pah." Fern waved a dismissive hand. "Rumors."

"That was from the beauty shop," Camille reminded her.

Camille and Helen managed to go to the beauty parlor every Friday. They said it was to keep up their hair, but Arlo was certain it was to find out Sugar Springs's latest gossip. Though in all fairness, she knew it was hard for Helen to maintain her fire engine red ends.

They mulled it over for a moment, each taking in what they knew and piecing it together.

"How ironic that she hired a nutritionist to improve her health, then turned around and had a stroke not a week later," Fern mused.

"Too little too late." Camille nodded, though her mouth was turned down at the corners.

"Money can't buy you everything," Arlo pointed out.

"Just someone to take care of you when need it the most," Helen said.

They all nodded at that one.

Sam sidled closer to Arlo. "Did I miss something?" he asked.

"Nope. Sometimes they're hard to keep up with."

"But if she can't talk," Camille started again. "She probably has another way of communicating."

"Maybe, but why would she know anything at all about Mary whoever, anyway?" Arlo interjected.

All three of them turned and stared as if she had lost her mind. Two heartbeats passed before they turned away.

"They think you're crazy," Sam murmured so only she could hear. His small chuckle took any sting from the words.

"Don't you dare laugh," she warned him, though her mouth twitched at the corners.

"I really need to go out there and talk to Haley too." Fern said with a nod.

"*We* need to talk to Haley," Helen corrected.

"That's what I said," Fern grumped.

"Why do *we* need to talk to Haley?" Arlo asked, ignoring Sam's muffled sniggers. He was enjoying this way too much.

"She asked us to," Helen said by way of explanation.

"Haley asked you to come out to the mansion."

"That's right," Camille said.

"Haley Adams whose sister works here part-time asked you to come out to Lillyfield where she works to talk about something?" Arlo asked. "What?"

Fern gave her an innocent look. "It seems she might have a mystery she wanted us to help her solve."

"And she would have contacted you why?" Arlo pressed.

"Maybe because we've gotten a reputation for being good at solving mysteries," Camille said with a whimsical smile.

"Street cred," Fern said in backup.

Arlo was speechless, but it was a good thing. As Fern

spoke, the bell over the door rang, and all eyes turned to the newcomer.

"Hey, Mads." Chloe was the first to greet Sugar Springs's chief of police as he entered. "You want a coffee?" She asked the question but was already making him his favorite before he answered.

"Thanks." He caught Arlo's eye. "Can I talk to you for a minute?"

"Sure." Something in his tone told her he wanted to keep whatever it was private, so she moved toward him even as she felt all eyes on her. They might have been something back in the day, but there was no need for gawking. Still she knew they were. All of them. Right down to Sam. Okay, maybe he had the right to be interested. After all, hadn't she thrown Mads over for Sam, only to have Sam leave town to pursue his career after high school?

But that was over. Years now. Mads had gone on to play football, Sam had gone to college and whatever school to become a private eye, and Arlo had stayed in Sugar Springs and opened a bookstore. Life goes on.

"What's up?" she asked just as Chloe passed him the to-go cup of mocha java.

The buzz of his phone cut short his reply. He unclipped it from his belt, surveyed the screen, and sighed. "I've got to go. Okay if I come back by later?"

Arlo nodded. "Sure. Be safe."

"Thanks for the coffee."

"Anytime," Chloe replied. Then he was gone.

"I wonder what that was about," Camille mused.

Arlo knew one thing it *wasn't* about: the missing piano teacher.

She turned to find Sam studying her, his eyes unreadable. Could he feel it too? That small rise in tension when the three of them were together? Or was she letting her imagination run away with her? After all, prom night was ten years behind them now. They had grown up. Life goes on. Still his expression... She only had a moment to contemplate the look before the ladies' chatter started up once more.

"I say we drive out there and just see," Fern said. She held up the keys to her Lincoln limo. Okay, so it wasn't really a limo, but it was the longest town car Arlo had ever seen. In fact, she was certain there were limos with less space inside. "Arlo can pick up her books, and we can talk to Haley and see what's up with Judith. Three birds. Who's game?"

Camille and Helen immediately raised their hands.

"Let's do it," Helen added. "I've got all sorts of time before I need to be back for supper."

"I am not going to Lillyfield," Arlo said as they started gathering their things. Purses and book bags, even the umbrella that Camille liked to carry when the sun got too hot.

Arlo needed to pick up the donations, but she felt it particularly important to do that alone. Or maybe with Chloe. Certainly not with the three elderly sleuth-wannabes.

If only there was something Arlo could say that would convince them to stay away from Lillyfield. If only.

"You better go with them," Chloe said when they were almost out the door. Her tone spoke volumes. *Here we go again.*

Arlo sighed. "I'll get my purse."

Fern, Camille, and Helen cheered.

They all climbed into Fern's Lincoln with room to spare.

Arlo briefly wondered what it cost to fill the beast with gasoline but pushed the thought away and got down to business. The business of dissuading the ladies from bothering Judith Whitney. Like any of Arlo's efforts had proved fruitful to date. You couldn't blame a girl for trying.

"Do you really see a connection between Mary Kennedy and *Missing Girl*, or do you just want to solve another mystery?" she bluntly asked.

"I can't believe you would ask us that," Helen harrumphed from the front seat.

Fern nodded as she caught Arlo's gaze in the rearview mirror. From the slant of her eyes alone, Arlo could tell that Fern was frowning. "I think you don't want to see the similarities because you don't want to have to worry about us trying to solve the case. You worry too much, you know."

"Hear, hear," Helen said.

"Of course, discovering who actually killed Wally was sort of thrilling," Camille admitted.

Which told her everything and nothing. She knew there weren't actual similarities between the book and the case besides the general inspiration Wally used to write a great story. But she also knew the book club ladies would do anything to make a mountain out of a molehill when it came to finding a new crime.

"If you want to go digging around and trying to figure out who killed Mary Kennedy, that's fine I guess." Arlo tried to make her voice sound as dull as possible. As if finding out who murdered Mary Kennedy would be the most boring thing ever.

"It's a free country," Fern reminded her. As if she had forgotten.

"And we don't know if she's even dead, love. Just missing." Camille gave her a sly smile. "But if she is dead, don't we owe it to her to find her body and lay her to rest?"

"I suppose." Arlo sighed. "But I don't think bothering one of Sugar Springs's most upstanding citizens is the best way to go about it."

"Lillyfield was the last place she was seen alive," Camille reminded her.

The others nodded.

"Fifty years ago. And you really believe Wally's book holds the answers to her disappearance?" Her tone did its best to convey that she thought it entirely unlikely.

"Yes!" the three ladies said simultaneously.

"How?" Arlo challenged. "And I'm talking more than just the word *missing*."

Helen turned in her seat to better look at Arlo as she spoke. "You've read the book. All the things he mentions. The diner."

"Name me one small town without a diner," Arlo demanded.

But Helen wasn't listening. "One stop light in town. The Red Devil high school mascot."

"We're the Blue Devils," Arlo reminded her, but Helen was lost in her own reasoning, ticking off the similarities as she saw them.

"The old cemetery, the theater in town. Even two rival grocery store owners."

"Those are details that could have come from anywhere." Most all the writers she had ever talked to used bits of their personal lives to embellish their stories. A different kind of *write what you know* scenario.

"But they came from Sugar Springs, love." Camille patted Arlo on the knee.

"That's what I'm saying. Just because those things are part of Sugar Springs it doesn't mean that the rest is."

"It's too much of a coinkidink," Fern interjected from the front seat. "Because those things are part of Sugar Springs, and we have ourselves a missing girl here. Well, it just stands to reason."

Round Two to the Book Club.

"And when we get to the house, let me do the talking," Fern instructed.

"Why do you get to do all the talking?" Helen and Fern seemed to constantly be locked in a battle of who ran the book club. As far as Arlo could see, the power was really Camille's.

"You're too tall," Fern stated. Helen was a very tall woman. "An intimidating business owner. I'm just an aging housewife."

Who probably worked for the CIA at its inception.

"And what are you going to say?" Camille asked, her lilting accent a little stronger with the excitement of solving a new mystery.

"I'm going to ask whoever opens the door if Mrs. Whitney is available and if we could possibly speak to her." Fern's car slowed as she neared the large iron gates that blocked the winding drive to Lillyfield. The gates remained closed as the ladies waited for someone inside the mansion to open them.

"You will not," Arlo demanded.

"I hope it's not that same girl who came into the bookstore." Camille made a face.

A new Lillyfield employee had come into the store a few short weeks ago. She had wanted a book and had been put out that Arlo didn't have the exact one she was looking for. Arlo had ordered it of course, but not without getting a dressing down on the importance of having a customer's needs in stock. Arlo had smiled politely, nodded understandingly in all the right places, then gently escorted the woman to the door, praying all the while that it would be the last she would see of her.

"Won't be," Helen said with confidence. "She was here cooking for Judith, but I'm guessing she's gone now. Not much to worry about when everything is pureed."

"I suppose you're right," Fern said. "But she was"—she searched for a word—"forceful."

Got it in one. The cook/nutritionist that Judith had hired could have doubled as a bodyguard. She rivaled Helen in stature, but unlike Helen, this woman wore a perpetual frown to go with her suspicious eyes.

"What was her name?" Helen mused.

"Pam," Arlo supplied with certainty. It wasn't a name she was likely to forget anytime soon.

"What's taking so long?" Camille asked. She peered around the front seat to get a better look around the gates and up the drive leading to Lillyfield.

"Pam?" Fern asked. "She didn't look like a Pam."

Camille shrugged. "I'm sure she hasn't always looked the same."

"True." Helen nodded. "The gates are open." She nudged Fern, who was half turned in her seat in order to talk to Camille.

Fern whipped back around and drove the car up the winding drive to the mansion.

Lillyfield was the biggest antebellum home in Sugar Springs. Built by Colonel Eustace Lilly in the 1840s, it was a rambling structure with several additions tacked on over the years, though no one in the Lilly family would attest to such. As with all proper antebellum homes, it was painted a soft, clean white with large black shutters and Corinthian columns that stretched from the portico to the half-moon balcony on the second floor. With two more stories stacked on top, it was an impressive structure to say the least.

"Now remember; I'm doing the talking." Fern locked the car and pocketed the keys.

Helen frowned, and Camille rolled her eyes, but neither one protested.

"*I'm* here for a promised donation," Arlo reminded them. "*I'll* do the talking."

Together they marched toward the double doors of the mansion.

Fern used the large brass knocker shaped like a lion's head to summon someone to the door.

This time Helen rolled her eyes. She stepped forward and pressed the bell. The chimes could be heard even where they stood.

"That should do it," Camille said. They waited for someone to answer their call. After what seemed like much longer than necessary, the door finally opened.

"Yes?" The young girl was dressed in black slacks and a white shirt. She had a small white apron tied around her waist in what Arlo supposed was the closest to a maid's uniform that still existed these days. Her long blond hair was pulled back into a ponytail, and if Arlo was guessing correctly, she was in her late teens/early twenties. Maybe even the same age as Haley, who also worked as a maid in the mansion.

"I'm Arlo Stanley," she said. "From the Books and More in town. I got a call last week about a donation of books."

"Oh, hi," she said and stepped back so they could enter. "It has been a busy day for visitors."

The women exchanged greetings with the young girl, and Arlo got down to business.

"I believe I talked to Robert," Arlo said.

"Roberts." The girl nodded. "He's the house manager."

"Sort of like a butler?" Fern asked.

The young maid smiled. "Sort of."

"Is Haley working today?" Helen asked. "Haley Adams?"

A shadow of a frown crossed the girl's face before her smile returned. "She's around someplace. Do you need to speak to her?"

"No." Arlo shook her head. "Her sister just works at the Books and More." She gave a small shrug.

"Yes, please," Fern said, shooting Arlo a withering look. "We would love to talk to Haley."

"Oh." The maid paused as if waiting for any other questions they might have. When none came, she sucked in a deep breath and expelled it quickly. Her smile widened just a bit as if realizing she might have been acting rudely and she wanted to make up for it. "Y'all can wait here, and I'll go get Roberts. And Haley."

Before the book club ladies could start to question her about Judith and any connection to Wally's book, the young girl disappeared down a hallway tucked under the wide, winding staircase.

Arlo rocked back on her heels and waited for the inevitable.

"I wonder where Judith is?" Fern mused, looking up toward the second floor.

"We did not come here to bother Mrs. Whitney," Arlo said, wondering how many times she would have to repeat herself before anyone paid her any mind.

"If she can't walk, how did she get up the stairs?" Fern asked.

"Someone could have carried her," Camille replied.

"Or she could be down here on the first floor in a guest suite or something," Helen said.

"Are there any guest suites on the first floor?" Fern asked.

"No idea." Helen gave a shrug.

"There's probably an elevator," Arlo supplied.

"You know what?" Camille started. "I do believe you're right. I think I read something about that in one of those pamphlet things that they give out when they host the annual barbecue."

"Probably not going to be a barbecue this year," Helen lamented.

"Probably not," Camille agreed. "I haven't seen any flyers for it in town. And it should be coming up here pretty soon."

"You would think that girl would at least have seated us in a parlor or a receiving room." Fern looked around at the foyer where they stood. There were no chairs, and Arlo figured visitors were supposed to stand until told otherwise.

"It's nice here though," Camille added.

And it was nice. Shining marble floors, gleaming mahogany staircase, and polished oak paneling. There were small, obviously antique tables scattered around, pushed close to the walls and usually situated under a painting of some sort or another. The paintings themselves were in heavy gilded frames with small lights glowing from above them. The largest table was in the middle of the floor in the center of the star pattern made from two different-colored marble inlays. A large vase sat on the table, tall stalks of gladiolus—peach, white, and red—reached toward the ceiling. The remainder of the tables held bronze statuettes and other assorted treasures.

"Look," Fern said, making her way to one such table. "They need to clean in here."

A perfect circle of gleaming wood shone through the thin layer of dust.

"That table is closest to the door," Helen said. "It's harder to keep knickknacks by the front door clean. Too much traffic in and out. The dirt just blows right in."

"There are no knickknacks there," Fern said.

"There was at one time," Arlo pointed out, then silently chastised herself for entering into such a ridiculous conversation.

"Whatever it was," Camille added. "It's gone now."

"Maybe someone took it to clean it," Fern said.

"Ms. Stanley?"

The four of them turned as a man in a suit glided toward them. He carried a cardboard box as if the contents might actually do him physical harm. The odd tilt of his nose suggested they possibly smelled foul as well.

"That's me." Arlo gave the man a smile and a small wave.

He thrust the box toward her as soon as he was close enough to relinquish his hold. "Here is the donation you were promised."

Arlo took the box and bit her tongue. It wasn't like she had called for the donation. They had contacted her. This

Roberts person acted as if he was doing her a favor by giving her books. Okay, maybe he was, but again, she didn't beg for a freebie. "Thank you," she finally managed.

"I trust you have a tax receipt for us."

"I—no," she said. "But I can mail you one just as soon as I get back to town."

He gave a stern nod. "The rest of the boxes can be picked up at the service entrance."

"The rest of the boxes?" Arlo asked. If there were more, why was he bringing her this one?

"That's right. There are several more boxes around back. Surely you didn't think I would call you out here for one—" He waved his hand toward the box she held in her arms.

Arlo wasn't sure how to answer that and was saved the trouble when a large clatter sounded from above. They turned their attention upward just in time to see a person at the head of the stairs topple. Arlo had only a minute to register that the someone was a female, wearing black pants and a white shirt like the maid who had let them into the house. Her blond hair had escaped her ponytail and floated around her face as she tumbled. She didn't make a sound as she fell, hitting the wall and then the banister before coming to a stop on the polished marble floor.

"Oh, my stars!" Arlo gasped. She dropped the box and rushed to the girl's side. A tumble like that could be fatal.

Arlo dropped to her knees next to the maid and brushed her hair back from her face. But it wasn't the maid lying on the cold marble floor, her breath gone forever. It was Haley Adams, the very person they had wanted to see.

2

THE HOUSE REMAINED A FLURRY OF CHAOS RIGHT UP TO the moment Mads and Jason arrived. Jason Rogers, Mads's chief officer, was as scattered as Mads was efficient. But his heart was in the right place. Most folks just smiled when his name was mentioned. *At least he tries.*

Thankfully, Sugar Springs wasn't typically a hotbed of crime. So, Arlo figured it balanced out in the end.

But today…

They all watched quietly as Roberts covered Haley with a pale yellow sheet. Camille, Helen, Fern, and Arlo stayed in the foyer while the other maid—Sabrina they had learned her name was—called 9-1-1 for help, though no one knew exactly what sort of help they needed. There was no *helping* Haley. Did one call an ambulance or go straight to the funeral home? When did the coroner get involved? Did he even need to be involved? In the end, they asked for Mads and an ambulance, and decided to let him sort it out when he arrived.

In those long, precious minutes that it took the police to

arrive at the mansion, different workers trickled in to witness the scene. Though truly there was nothing to witness; it looked like Haley had simply fallen, probably tripped on her way down the stairs. From there, she tumbled to her death, most likely breaking her neck on the way down.

Simply. Tragic.

And even without the gore or horror—other than a lifeless lump under a plain sheet—Lillyfield employees still made their way through the foyer to get a glimpse of the body.

"Is that Baxter?" Helen nudged Arlo in the side.

She looked up to see a short man in a suit with jet black fringe around a gleaming bald spot and overlarge glasses. Baxter Whitney, Judith's adopted son, stood near the edge of the room, though it looked as if he had gained a good thirty pounds since Arlo had last seen him. His hair appeared unnaturally dark—had it been that light-sucking black before?—and of course there was a little less of it than there had been the last time he had been in Sugar Springs, but it was undoubtedly the Whitney son returned to Sugar Springs.

"I'd heard he and Anastasia were back in town." Camille said with a small nod in his direction.

Anastasia Whitney was Baxter's daughter, too old to be living with Mummy and Daddy but never away for long. She had been married a couple of times, if all the rumors around town were true, but neither one had been successful.

"Because of Judith's stroke?" Arlo asked.

"Because of Katherine's"—Helen coughed—"indiscretions. But it's just a rumor."

"What?" Fern took that time to join in the conversation. "Baxter's wife had an affair? With who?"

"I don't know," Helen replied. "I don't even know it's true."

"And she didn't come back to Sugar Springs?" Fern frowned, a little put out, a lot thoughtful.

Camille shrugged. "Not as far as I know."

"Where did you hear something like that?" Fern demanded.

"You would hear stuff too if you'd let someone do your hair from time to time," Camille told her. The tone she used was gentle but chastising all the same.

Fern sniffed. "A waste of money if you ask me."

"But good for information."

Arlo half-heartedly listened to their banter. It was the same story, different day.

As Mads and Jason commandeered the foyer, they instructed Arlo and the group to remain there until one of them had a moment to talk to them. So far, they had interviewed almost every mansion staff member, leaving the book club waiting. She had called Chloe and told her the condensed-condensed version with promises to fill her in once she got back to the store, explaining that it could be some time before she was allowed to leave.

Instead of listening to the ladies bicker, Arlo watched as, one by one, the interviewed and then dismissed employees scurried off, peeking in from time to time from entryways, before quickly ducking out once again. Soon enough, it was only Arlo, the book club, and Pam the nutritionist left standing in the foyer with police.

Pam, the same woman who had rudely chastised Arlo at Books and More, had rushed down the stairs just after Haley's fall, immediately barking orders to call the police and an ambulance. She stood over the body like a mother tiger protecting her injured young and wouldn't let anyone near until Mads and Jason arrived.

When the police got there, she appeared helpful and concerned, though Arlo found her attentiveness somewhat annoying. In the long run, it didn't matter who called the police, who called the ambulance, or even who witnessed the fall. Haley Adams was still dead.

"I don't understand what's taking so long," Fern grumped. "It was just an accident."

"There are a lot of people to talk to," Camille said, her voice as patient as ever. "I suppose they have to make certain it was an accident."

Fern's eyes grew wide. "You don't think she was pushed."

Helen scoffed. "Of course not. Who would want to push Haley down the stairs?"

"But the police have to be thorough," Camille added. "I saw it once on *CSI.*"

"Arlo," Mads said, moving toward her.

She turned her attention to the chief of police.

The coroner had already come and taken the body away, and Jason was over talking to one of the kitchen workers while another officer interviewed one of the gardening staff. There had been a time when the mansion had employed twice what it appeared to today, but Arlo supposed things were tough all over.

"What a mess, huh?" she said by way of greeting.

He nodded. "Can I talk to you a minute?"

"Of course." When she remained standing in the same spot, he grabbed her elbow and pulled her closer to the staircase.

"Can you tell me everything you saw when you came in?"

Arlo frowned. It was weird to see Mads in full *cop mode*. "Nothing really. The maid—Sabrina—let us in and said she was going to get Roberts."

"The butler," Mads confirmed.

"I think they prefer *house manager* these days."

"And which direction did the maid go when she left this room?"

Arlo pointed to the doorway under where the staircase became the second-floor landing.

"She didn't go up the stairs." It was nearly a question, but not quite.

"No." Arlo shifted, a little uncomfortable with all the questions. Or maybe she was just fried after standing for hours while they waited to be questioned as the lifeless body of someone they knew had been hauled away.

"Go on," he prompted. "Then what happened?"

"So, we were waiting for the house manager, and then Haley fell." And that was all she could remember.

"Did you see anyone else come through the foyer? Go up the staircase?"

She shook her head.

A rumble sounded, and Arlo looked up to see where the noise was coming from. Then the ornate panels behind Mads opened. Two men stepped out. One was Roberts, the house manager, followed by another man short enough that Arlo barely got a glimpse of him as he turned into the doorway and left the foyer behind. All she could see was his bald head and tattooed arms before he was gone.

"I told you!" Fern hollered. "There is an elevator."

Arlo sighed but didn't see the need to correct her. She turned back to Mads. "Is there anything else you need?"

"Why were you here in the first place?"

"We came to get a donation for the bookstore." She pointed to the place where the ladies stood. The one box that Roberts had brought to her was sitting at Helen's feet.

Mads gave a curt nod. "Well, sorry to tell you that the books will have to remain here for a time."

"Really?"

"We're in the middle of an active investigation," Mads explained. "Nothing in or out until we find out exactly how Haley died."

....

"She fell." Fern tossed her handbag into one corner of the couch and flopped down next to it. When they had finally been allowed to leave the mansion, they had headed back to the bookstore for their own debriefing. "What else does he need to know?"

"Welcome back," Faulkner squawked. He was sitting on top of his cage, watching for their return.

"Tell me everything," Chloe said, rushing Arlo as she came in the door.

Camille sat down in the armchair and placed her handbag primly in her lap. "Unbelievable."

"Can we get some coffee first?" Arlo asked with an apologetic smile. "It's been a long day."

She could tell that Chloe was a little disappointed, but her friend was nothing if not patient. "Of course," she said. "But after that…"

"I will tell you everything," Arlo promised.

Chloe headed back behind the coffee bar and started making drinks with Indy 500 speed.

"I just can't believe that took so long," Helen said.

"I can't believe that young girl is dead," Camille countered.

Everyone went silent. Having to stand in the foyer of the mansion for nearly five hours was nothing compared to the fact that Haley Adams was gone; a young and beautiful girl with her entire life in front of her was now dead.

"The butler did it," Faulkner chirped. "The butler did it." The ladies ignored him.

Arlo wondered if some bright pet company made muzzles for mouthy parrots. She might have to check into that.

"Come and get it," Chloe called.

The ladies filed up to the counter and grabbed a cup. Chloe motioned for Arlo to sit back down and brought her coffee to her. Then she settled down on one of the couches next to her. "What happened?"

They all started talking at once, each recounting the tale in a different order. Finally, Chloe held her hands up. "One at a time," she pleaded.

"You tell it," Arlo said, looking to Helen.

She tossed her braid back over her shoulder and retold the tale, how they had arrived at the mansion and, quickly after, Haley had fallen down the stairs.

As complicated as it seemed and as long as the afternoon was, the whole thing was summed up in just a few short sentences.

"Unbelievable," Chloe breathed.

"That's what I said." Camille nodded in agreement, fidgeting with the strap of her bag.

Helen slowly shook her head. "And poor Haley."

"Poor Courtney," Chloe clipped.

Camille gasped in response. For a moment they had all forgotten that this would affect her as well.

Chloe sighed and stood. "I guess we'll have a little extra work to do in the upcoming days."

"I can help," Arlo assured her.

Chloe smiled. "I think we're going to need it."

....

The phone was ringing first thing when Arlo got to the Books and More the following day.

"Arlo and Chloe's," Chloe answered, shooting Arlo a look that told her without words that the phone had been ringing nonstop all morning. Books and More might not open officially until nine, but Chloe propped the doors open early, baked muffins, scones, and other tasty treats, and sold them and her unique coffee drinks to anyone who happened by before then. Mostly the customers were other Main Street store owners and a few from the side streets.

"Courtney," Chloe breathed into the phone.

Arlo immediately stopped unloading her bag and joined her business partner at the coffee counter. She raised her eyebrows and waited patiently for Chloe to give her some clue as to what Courtney was telling her.

"We heard, hon," Chloe said. "I'm so sorry."

Arlo pointed to herself, and Chloe nodded. "Arlo too. We're just sick about what happened." Once again, she waited for Courtney to say something on the other end of the line. Arlo could hear her voice but couldn't understand the words. It didn't matter though; her sorrow and tears were coming through in her tone. Surely that was the reason that Chloe didn't tell Courtney that they had been there when Haley had spilled down the stairs. There was no sense in upsetting the girl further.

Courtney had started at the Books and More before they even opened their doors. She had helped paint, stock shelves, and decide which couch should go where. She was kind and dependable, and had been a lifesaver when Chloe had been arrested. She had to be taking the death of her sister hard. Courtney and Haley had been as close as sisters could be.

"No, no," Chloe said gently. "Don't you worry about it. Take all the time you need, OK? Just keep us posted when you can, and spend this time with your family. Your folks need you now more than ever."

A few more sentiments and one teary goodbye, then Chloe hung up the phone. She wiped the tears from under her eyes and shot Arlo a rueful smile. "I knew I should have worn my waterproof mascara today."

Arlo went around the coffee bar and hugged her. They had been through so much together. Best friends since tenth grade, when Arlo first moved to Sugar Springs. Going into business together. And more recently Chloe being arrested. It had been a long haul for them.

"I don't know what we're going to do about her shifts."

Arlo nodded. "We'll figure something out."

"I guess I can just work longer. Or maybe not come in as early."

Arlo laughed. "I think everyone would revolt if they couldn't get their morning coffee. Maybe you could teach me how to make the drinks."

Chloe shot her a look. "Remember how that went last time?"

Disaster was too kind of a word.

A bookstore might have been Arlo's dream, but Chloe had always wanted to run a little corner café like she had seen in Paris. The coffee shop part of the Books and More wasn't exactly like those in France, but it was good for Sugar Springs. And maybe one day, they could add a few wrought iron tables and chairs to the front and give the place that *Ooh la la* feel. Until then, coffee and books in comfy chairs would just have to do.

Arlo held up her hands as if in surrender. "Fine, fine. You win. We'll come up with a different plan."

"I do appreciate it," Chloe said. "But I guess I can stay late." She gave a heavy sigh. "I just keep thinking about it," she said. "Haley. She was so young. She had the whole world ahead of her."

Indeed she had. Haley Adams had been a premed student at Ole Miss, planning to be an obstetrician. She'd had a handsome boyfriend—also premed—that she had dated since junior high. It appeared she had the world by the tail. She was sweet, pretty, and smart. Then to just die like that in a tragic accident. Well, it didn't seem fair. But as Arlo's dad had always said, fair was where you went to get cotton candy.

"Really sad," Arlo agreed.

The bell rang over the door, and she looked up to see Mads coming in.

Chloe wiped her eyes once more and gave a huge sniff, then managed to pull her face into a look of greeting. "Hey, Chief. The usual?"

He shot her a grateful smile. "That would be great. Thanks." He turned his attention back to Arlo. "Have a minute?"

"Of course. What's up?"

She eased onto one of the barstools, and Mads followed suit. He adjusted his gun belt. "Did you know that Wally's book is being made into a movie?"

"I had heard it was a possibility."

"Well, the producer called me a couple of days ago. Seems they want to have a premiere here in Sugar Springs."

Arlo nearly swallowed her tongue. "Here?"

"I know."

"At the old Coliseum?" It was the only place big enough to hold such an event. And of course, other than the drive-in, it was the only place to show a film in Sugar Springs. When people wanted to take in a movie, they drove to Corinth.

"Yep."

"Isn't it haunted?" Chloe asked, sliding his mocha java in front of him.

"The producer thought that added to the charm." Mads sighed. "It's going to be a security nightmare. I tried to talk them out of it, but they are adamant. Of course there will be an official opening in Hollywood, but they wanted to show the film here too."

"Because the town in the book and the mystery of the missing girl took place here?" Chloe asked.

Mads shrugged.

"Do you really believe that?" Arlo had heard all the arguments from the book club, but she wasn't convinced. Sure, there were a few similarities—a small Mississippi town, a missing girl, a missing car, and all happening in the 1970s, but it still wasn't enough. But Arlo couldn't be sure if the book club really thought they were the same story or if they were using the few similarities to poke around and nose into other people's business.

"I don't know, but the movie company thinks it would be good publicity and all with Wally having grown up here."

"And having died here," Chloe whispered.

"Yeah, maybe."

"We can do it," Arlo said with more confidence than she really felt. The idea was starting to grow on her.

"I'm talking to everyone on Main Street. It'll affect all your businesses if we bring in so much Hollywood. There will be people all over."

"Most will stay in Corinth," Chloe said. "Or drive down from Memphis."

"I disagree. I think they are going to want the whole experience of Sugar Springs," Mads said.

Arlo couldn't help herself. She laughed until she snorted. "Yeah, 'cause Sugar Springs is so happening."

"You live here."

"The lack of bustle is the exact reason why I live here."

"But you'll do it?" Mads asked. "You'll help get this town ready for a movie premiere?"

"Of course we will." Chloe answered for them both, but Arlo didn't mind.

"It'll be another six months or so."

"Have you talked to Helen?" A crowd of that sort was bound to affect the Inn.

"I tried to call her yesterday, but then this murder happened."

The one word stole Arlo's breath away.

"Murder? What do you mean, murder?" she gasped.

"Murder?" Fern screeched. They had been so busy talking they hadn't heard the bell ring telling them Fern had arrived early for the daily book club "sesh," as she liked to call it.

"Haley was murdered?" Chloe asked.

Mads shook his head. "I shouldn't have said that."

"But you did," Fern pressed. She set down her book bag and made her way to the coffee bar. "Sweet Haley was murdered?"

"Hit in the head with a blunt object," Mads admitted. Then he held up one finger before Fern could continue. "That's all you're getting from me right now. We have an ongoing investigation, and I'm doing my best not to alert any potential suspects."

"But we were there," Arlo protested. "We saw her fall."

"Apparently she was already dead before that."

"What sort of object?" Fern asked.

"How's that even possible?" Arlo shook her head.

"We don't know. We're working on it," he said to Arlo. He turned to Fern. "And we don't know. It's missing." Then he stood and reached for his wallet, intent on paying for his coffee.

Arlo laid one hand on his arm. "Your money is no good here."

Fern shot her a look. "You always make me pay."

"And you do nothing about keeping the peace. In fact, you seem intent on shaking the peace until its teeth rattle."

Mads chuckled. "Thanks for the coffee." He nodded at Chloe and Arlo in turn. "Keep that information under your hat."

"Will do," Arlo replied. She stood and walked Mads to the door.

"And if you hear anything..." he said.

Arlo nodded. "You'll be the first to know."

3

"THE KILLER COULD HAVE BEEN ANYONE AT THE MAN-sion yesterday," Helen mused.

The book club had gathered for their noonish meeting, and Fern had nearly tripped over herself to tell them that Haley had been murdered.

"*We* were at the mansion yesterday," Camille reminded her.

"We know one thing," Fern said. "It wasn't Judith. Not if she's as incapacitated as all the rumors are saying she is."

"It was probably someone on staff," Helen said.

Arlo was half-listening as she rearranged the cookbooks by diet and specialty. She was doing her best to stay busy and not allow her brain to think too much about witnessing Haley fall down the stairs, already deceased from a blow to the head. Overkill? She shook her head at her bad pun, thankful that it had only been in her thoughts.

"I don't know," Fern replied. "How many staff members does Judith have on these days?"

"Let's see," Camille said. She ticked the positions off on her fingers. "There should be an upstairs maid, downstairs maid. A cook and a butler."

"I think he prefers house manager," Arlo reminded them.

"The butler did it," Faulkner said again.

Fern snorted "Nope. But I do think you've been watching *Downton Abbey* too much, knowing every staff position in a manor house."

"No such thing," Camille protested.

"*Downton Abbey*. Don't forget to watch *Downton Abbey*." Faulkner finished his reminder with a shrill whistle.

Helen glanced over to Arlo. "Where does he learn these things?"

Arlo merely shrugged. Faulkner's memory was akin to a sponge, though he seemed to absorb the most annoying phrases to repeat.

"Who do we know that works at Lillyfield?" Fern asked.

"They keep to themselves mostly," Camille said.

And it was true. They had their groceries and other essentials delivered. Arlo wasn't sure where she had picked up that tidbit, but she knew it to be true. Judith never seemed to come down off her hill to mingle with the little people.

"I'm sure there are a couple of maids and a cook," Fern said.

"I met him once," Helen said. "The cook."

"What about that Pam person?" Camille asked.

"I don't think she actually cooks," Helen said.

Camille frowned. "She doesn't?"

"She just tells the cook what to cook," Helen explained.

Fern raised her brows and twisted her mouth into an incredulous frown. "It's good work if you can get it."

"And there's Betty Carson," Helen continued. "She cleans for them part-time. Ever since her husband died."

"Is she the upstairs maid?" Fern asked.

"How do you have one upstairs maid when there are four stories?" Camille mused.

"I have no idea," Helen replied, but Arlo didn't know if she was talking to Fern or Camille. Or if it even mattered.

"There's the blond girl," Fern said. "Sabrina."

"Isn't there basement? What about an attic? Do they have people to clean those too?" Camille asked.

"And I would know this how?" Fern grumbled.

"I don't know. TV maybe?" Camille raised her brows in question.

"What about the gardener?" Fern continued.

"Why would he be in the house?" Helen asked.

Fern shrugged. "That's a lot of people if there's someone special to clean each area."

"Then it could be a number of people," Helen clarified.

The wispy memory of the bald-headed man she had seen walking with Roberts brushed through Arlo's mind, but she let the thought drift away. She had never seen him before, she was certain, and it was nothing to her as to why he was there and if Mads had questioned him. Nothing to her at all.

"And it seems like the police have it well under control," Arlo added, reminding them as well as herself. The book club might only be going over all the people they had seen themselves yesterday at the mansion, but that was as far as it needed to go.

Chloe shot Arlo an encouraging smile, then gave her a thumbs-up. Yes, an A for effort. At least she had tried to curtail the book club ladies and their tendency to nose around in other people's business. Of course, Chloe might still be in jail if they hadn't bothered to get involved with matters that didn't pertain to them, but that was another story altogether. Still, if Mads and Jason were going to do their job and find out what happened at Lillyfield, then it would be best for everyone involved if Fern, Helen, and Camille stayed out of their way.

"You should concentrate your energy on Mary Carlyle."

Chloe shook her head. "Blew it in one."

"Kennedy," Fern said. "Mary Kennedy."

Arlo nodded. "Right Mary Kennedy."

"But we get the point, love. You want us to leave Haley out of it."

"Maybe we should," Helen mused. "We're awfully close to Haley's case. It might cloud our judgment."

Arlo looked to Chloe. That was the worst part about bad news in a small town. Whoever it was, you knew them.

"Mary Kennedy, it is." Fern gave a definitive nod and picked up her copy of *Missing Girl*.

Arlo slid onto one of the barstools at the straight edge of the coffee counter. At least they weren't talking about Lillyfield any longer, as they speculated over Mary Kennedy and where she could have ended up—dead or alive.

"Sam came down twice while you were gone," Chloe said with a knowing look.

"Twice? I wasn't gone that long." She had just run over to the florist to order flowers for the Adams family.

"Yesterday, I mean. When you were at the mansion. With everything happening, I forgot to tell you. Anything I should know about?" Chloe started to rearrange the muffins in the front of the display case. The blueberry always sold out before any other flavor, to such a degree that Arlo wondered why Chloe made anything else.

"Nope." Arlo shrugged.

"Don't give me that. I've seen that look on his face before and—"

"And what?"

She shook her head. "I don't know. He just seemed so intense, like the old days, I guess."

"The old days are long gone," Arlo said.

"Yeah." Chloe seemed like she wanted to say more, but she was interrupted before she could.

"Arlo, are you coming to discuss this book with us or not?" Fern grumped.

Arlo smiled at her best friend. "Duty calls."

"Want a coffee for reinforcement?"

"Please." Arlo slid from the barstool and made her way to the reading nook.

"As I see it," Camille started, "the necklace is a key point."

Arlo sat down on the couch next to Helen and picked up a copy of Wally Harrison's *Missing Girl*. "Necklace? I don't remember any necklace."

"Not in the book," Camille gently chided. "Mary Kennedy. In the book it was a tiara."

The tiara. Arlo had almost forgotten about it. Or maybe she had read Wally's book a little too quickly. It was a difficult read. Written in a stream of consciousness style, it was a bit highbrow for some.

"That's right," Fern agreed. "Mary was accused of stealing a necklace from the mansion when she was out giving Baxter his piano lesson."

"I remember that," Helen said on a short breath. "But no one ever found the necklace. Is that right?"

Fern nodded. "Some folks say that she took the necklace and left town, using it to start over somewhere exotic."

"Like Pontotoc?" Camille asked. She shifted in her seat and adjusted the straps of her handbag.

"Like Biloxi," Fern corrected.

Arlo didn't bother to say that she didn't find either town to be particularly exotic but at least Biloxi had a beach.

"I think he killed her," Helen said. She closed her copy of *Missing Girl*, one finger between the pages as to not lose her place.

"Aren't we supposed to be talking about the book?" Arlo asked. But she was too late. The ladies were on their tracks.

"Who?" Fern asked.

"Weston," Helen replied.

Fern cackled. "You think Weston Whitney, Judith Whitney's husband, killed Mary Kennedy?"

"Obviously, you don't." Helen sniffed.

"Well, no. I mean her husband…" Fern trailed off. "Anyway, everyone knows it was her husband. Mary's. If she's dead at all."

Camille nodded. "What was his name?"

"Jack," Fern said, then shook her head. "No, Jeff. Yeah, Jeff Kennedy."

"He used to lay his hands on her," Camille continued.

"Like a faith healer?" Arlo was really confused.

"No, like a boxer." Camille doubled up her own fist and pretended to punch herself in the face.

"Really?" How was one supposed to respond to that?

"Well, back then people didn't talk about it like they do now," Helen explained.

"And you think he was the one?" Arlo shook her head at herself. Once again she had gotten sucked into the vortex that was her Friday-night-turned-every-day book club.

"Seems logical to me." Fern gave another shrug.

"Maybe if they had been able to find his diaries," Helen added.

"*The Diary of Anne Frank*," Faulkner squawked. "Read the classics."

Helen pinned Arlo with a sharp look. "He got that one from you."

"Guilty," Arlo said with a smile.

"The butler did it," Faulkner said again. He moved his head up and down in his traditional bird dance. "He's guilty."

"Jeff Kennedy kept diaries?" Camille asked. "How do you know this?"

Helen shook her head. "Weston Whitney kept diaries. Or whatever you want to call them. These little sketchbooks he carried with him everywhere."

"Oh, I remember." Camille nodded. "But I always thought he was writing poetry and whatnot."

"He was always a queer sort."

"Fern," Arlo admonished.

"What?"

"That's not something we say," Arlo gently explained.

Fern shrugged. "Why not? It's true."

"It may be, but—never mind." Arlo sighed. Political correctness was lost on this over-eighty crowd.

"What's wrong with writing poetry?" Chloe had finished making Arlo a coffee and had joined them in the reading nook. She propped her bottom on the arm of the couch and waited for an answer.

"Nothing if you're Longfellow or Thoreau," Fern replied.

"Thoreau! Thoreau! Thoreau! Don't Thoreau the books!" Faulkner squawked.

Chloe rolled her eyes at the bird.

Arlo ignored him.

"You can't go around doing things like writing poetry these days and get away with it," Helen said as if the rule was written in stone at the courthouse.

"You can't?" Arlo had missed the memo on that one.

"Not unless you want someone to think you're limp in the wrists," Fern continued, her nod seriously emphatic.

And PC flew right out the window. Arlo wasn't even going to try and field that one.

She caught Chloe's look and had to turn away. She wasn't sure whether to laugh or to cry.

"But this was fifty years ago," Helen said. "Things were different then."

"Fifty years?" Chloe nearly choked. "I thought this was at least in this decade."

"Listen to that," Arlo said. "You're trying to solve a fifty-year-old cold case."

The ladies shrugged in eerie unison. They were all nearing ninety. What else did they have to do?

"Maybe he was having an affair with Mary?" Helen mused.

"Weston?" Fern scoffed.

"If he was..." Arlo flicked a hand in the air but couldn't bring herself to say the words. "Wouldn't he have been having an affair with...someone from his team?"

"Church softball?" Helen asked.

"No," Arlo said gently. "A man."

Chloe stifled a laugh, then pushed up and made her way back to the coffee bar.

"I don't think he was gay," Helen explained.

"But—" Arlo was having a hard time keeping up.

"He was merely sensitive," Helen continued. "Not at all a strong person like Judith."

"She ran roughshod over him till the day he died," Fern elaborated.

They all agreed.

"But if we could get our hands on one of his little note-books…" Helen started.

"Diaries?" Arlo asked.

Fern nodded.

"Then we would know for certain," Camille finished for her.

"Who knows if they even kept them?" Fern asked. "Those little books could be at the bottom of the landfill by now."

"We don't have a landfill," Camille pointed out.

"And what exactly does this have to do with *Missing Girl*?" Arlo asked.

"Well, it's the same," Helen said.

"Exactly the same," Fern backed her up.

Not exactly if there was no necklace. "The missing lady in the book comes back to town." Years later, but she does return. That was a major difference.

Camille waved a dismissive hand. "Oh, that part's a little different. But the rest is the same."

"Well, she wasn't a piano teacher in the book either. She was just a visitor at a party," Arlo reminded them.

Helen nodded. "But she disappeared after leaving the mansion."

"Which is not Lillyfield," Arlo pointed out.

"Maybe not by name, but by every other standard," Helen argued.

"And her car was never found in the book," Camille said.

"Just like Mary Kennedy," Fern added. "See the similarities?"

They were still no more apparent to Arlo now than they had been before. And even if they were there, maybe Wally had simply patterned his mystery after the disappearance of Mary Kennedy. He might have heard the stories as a child while he sat at the feet of his grandmother and ate home-grown watermelon. Or maybe it was just a coincidence entirely. Who knew?

Chloe leaned in close. "What would be the harm in letting them go on about this?"

Arlo thought about it for a moment. All the players were gone, she supposed. Maybe it wasn't a terrible idea to let them try and solve the mystery of the missing piano teacher, especially if it kept them away from Lillyfield and out of Mads's hair while he investigated the tragedy that had just occurred there. "What happened to her husband?"

"Judith? He died years back," Helen replied. "I thought everybody knew that."

"No," Arlo said. "Mary."

"Prison, I heard," Fern replied.

"For?" Arlo asked.

"Murder," Camille said.

"Whose murder?" Arlo asked.

Fern shot her a look that said she really wished Arlo would keep up. "Mary Kennedy."

"But if... I mean, she was never... I don't understand," Arlo admitted. Was it possible to have a murder without a body?

"Things were different back then. He went to prison for a few years. And that was that." Helen gave a small shrug.

"So, he's out now?" Arlo asked.

"Maybe," Fern said. "I don't know."

"He doesn't have any family around here that I know of," Camille answered. "If he's out, there's really no reason for him to come back."

"I suppose not," Arlo murmured.

The bell over the door rang, and a customer came in. Tiffany, the young mom who hired a teenager to look after her toddler for one hour in the afternoon so she could have a break at the bookstore.

Tiffany's arrival meant the slow time was over. The kids would be getting out of school and heading down Main to their favorite stores before starting home. Arlo had a crowd that came in for coffee each afternoon. She supposed that was as good a reason as any, and maybe having them so close to the books would spark a love for them as well. She could hope anyway. Still Arlo and Chloe's Books and More could hold its own against the drugstore's old-fashioned soda counter and the arcade games Phil next door let them play for a quarter a turn.

Arlo waved but didn't get up. Chloe was already on her feet.

"Unless he took the necklace and has hidden it somewhere, biding his time until he can cash it in." Fern raised her eyebrows in an encouraging way, once again trying to get everyone in on the mystery.

"Wouldn't he have done that like thirty years ago?" Arlo asked. "Cashed it in?"

Fern shrugged. "Prison time moves differently."

"How do we get back in?" Helen asked.

"In where?" Arlo demanded.

Fern rolled her eyes. "Lillyfield." If she had been seventy-five years younger she would have finished with a "duh."

"You don't need to go to Lillyfield." Arlo looked to Chloe for help, but she was behind the counter making Tiffany one of her almost-famous coffee drinks.

"Plus it's crawling with coppers."

She didn't have time to answer Fern as someone else came in the front, the bell going off again.

"Arlo?"

She spun around. With the conversation swirling and the traffic trickling in through the front door, she hadn't heard Sam come down the stairs from the third floor. "Sam." She pressed a hand to her beating heart. All this talk of murders and missing people had her a little jumpy. Or maybe it was knowing that she had been out to Lillyfield when someone had died. Accident or not, that was a little unnerving.

"Did I scare you?"

"A little." She shot him a forgiving smile.

"Sorry." He didn't really look sorry, or maybe that was just those dimples playing tricks on her.

"What's up?" she asked, pushing all thoughts of his dimples aside.

Sam, normally so confident and cocky, shifted from one booted foot to the other. He was dressed as he usually was in faded blue jeans and a button-down shirt. Today's was denim as well. His version of a Canadian tuxedo. "I was just wondering..." he started, then shifted again. "I mean, if you're not busy and you're free on Friday night. That maybe..."

Arlo waited. This was so unlike Sam. "Are you okay?"

He nodded. "Want to go to dinner on Friday night?"

It might not have been the very last thing she had expected him to say, but it was definitely in the top five. "Dinner?"

He shifted. "You know food. At the steak house. To catch up."

She nodded in return. They'd had plenty of time to catch up, but neither one had made the effort. It might be good to sit down and clear the air. Just as friends.

"Is that a yes?"

"Sure." The word surprised her. Yes, she did want to have dinner with him, and yes, she did want to talk. The thought took her off guard. But at the same time, it didn't. Sam had been a big part of her life back then and continuing on today, seeing as how he was in her shop almost as much as he was upstairs in his office.

He smiled, his shifting stopped, and it looked as if the tension left his shoulders. Was it such a big deal that they were having supper?

She turned to find all eyes on her. At least the ones belonging to Chloe and the book club members.

Okay. Maybe it was a big deal. But it was just as friends. Right? Or was it more? Did she want more? She didn't know.

....

"I just don't get it," Helen said as she came into the Books and More the following day at noon. She set her Crock-Pot on the coffee table in the reading nook and placed her hands on her hips. "Who would want to murder sweet little Haley?"

"Jealous lover?" Fern asked, coming in directly behind

her. Close enough that Arlo suspected they had ridden over together.

"She was twenty years old." Arlo sighed.

Fern shrugged. "You never know with kids these days."

Helen shook her head. "Not Haley. She was one of the good ones."

"What'd you bring?" Arlo asked.

"Sausage Ro-Tel dip." Helen set the Crock-Pot on the coffee table and reached into her tote for a bag of tortilla chips.

"Yum." Fern rubbed her hands together in anticipation.

"Where's Camille?" Arlo looked around as the two ladies settled in and started munching on their midday snack.

Helen rolled her eyes. "On a date."

"A date?" Arlo and Chloe asked at the same time.

"A date," Fern confirmed, her mouth half-full of chips and cheese.

"With who?" This was good stuff, and Arlo moved around the couch to sit down next to Helen. It didn't hurt that it put her that much closer to the food. She hadn't had lunch yet.

"He's a keeper," Faulkner squawked. "A keeper."

"Some man she met on the internet." Helen rolled her eyes and dredged another chip through the dip before popping the entire thing into her mouth.

"Chaser," Faulkner continued.

"Wait," Arlo said, loaded chip halfway to her mouth. "Camille was on the internet?"

"She's ninety," Fern said. "Not living in Outer Mongolia."

"I think Outer Mongolia is very modern these days," Chloe added. Like Arlo, she had moved around to be closer to the food, but she didn't settle herself into a seat. She propped her rear against the arm of one and reached for the bag of chips.

"You know what I mean. She's smart enough to work a computer."

"Beater," Faulkner continued. "Might be a beater."

"I know he's a bird and all, but what if he's right and this man hurts Camille?" Chloe asked.

"Or he could be a scammer," Arlo added.

"Where'd she meet him?" Chloe continued. The bell over the door rang. Chloe grabbed one more chip before heading back to the coffee bar to take care of the customer now waiting there.

"Golden Years," Fern supplied. "It's a dating site for people over seventy."

"I had no idea such a thing existed," Arlo said in awe.

"Neither did I," Helen said. Not surprising, seeing as how Helen hated electronics. "Why would she want to go on a dating site anyway?"

"To find a man?" Arlo asked.

Helen shook her head. "Why she wants one of those is beyond me."

But Arlo understood. Helen had constant company. There was always someone staying in the inn, and half the bachelors in the county came to eat supper with her. She was one of the finest cooks in Northeast Mississippi. But with so many people around, it was easy to forget that you had no one special. But Arlo went home to an empty house. Every. Day.

Maybe that was why she accepted Sam's offer of dinner. It was one more evening she wouldn't be alone.

She hated the words as they floated around in her head.

It wasn't that she was always lonely. She loved her life. She loved her store, her job, her friends, she even loved the ladies in this ridiculous book club. But there were times…

"Did she check into him before she met him?" Arlo asked.

"How should I know?" Fern grumbled.

"She's your friend," Arlo pointed out. "You could have asked her."

Fern shook her head. "She messaged me on Facebook and said she was going to meet him for coffee in Corinth."

"Why didn't they meet here?" Arlo asked.

Fern shot her a look.

"Right," she said. Camille wouldn't have gotten any peace if she had met the man here and they would have grilled him with questions until he ran off screaming into the night. Or afternoon, whatever. "I wish she had told you his name."

"Jack," Fern said with a quick nod. "James. No, Jack. Wait. Joe."

"Joe?" Arlo asked.

"It was definitely Joe."

"Joe what?"

"Joe Mama." Helen snorted.

"Will you take this seriously?" Arlo did her best to keep her tone level, getting upset wouldn't do any good. But these ladies, they were almost like children when it came to the internet. They didn't understand the dangers that lurked on their innocent-looking laptops.

"Sorry." Helen sobered up and waited for Fern to continue.

"Does this Joe have a last name?" Arlo asked.

"She didn't say," Fern replied.

"And you didn't ask." It wasn't a question.

"She is a grown woman."

Arlo couldn't argue with that, and she had talked to them about the dangers on the internet. No sense beating a dead horse. "This man could be anybody," she tried again.

"I suppose." Fern gave a small shrug. "Still not sure what she wants with a man anyway. My Charlie was as useless as tits on a boar hog."

Arlo closed her eyes. She had heard the expression her entire Mississippi life, and every time it stopped her in her tracks. "We're not talking about Charlie," she said as patiently as she could. "We were talking about Camille."

"Well, you know Camille. She'll charm him with that Aussie accent. He won't be able to refuse."

Refuse what? Arlo wasn't going to ask.

"And if that doesn't work, she can tase him."

"Does she carry a Taser gun?" Arlo wouldn't be surprised. Camille seemed to have everything else in that magical handbag of hers.

"More like shoot him with a .357," Fern corrected.

"Please tell me she doesn't carry a gun." Arlo closed her eyes against the thought.

Fern shrugged. "Mississippi is a constitutional carry state." Which meant anyone could carry a weapon without having to obtain a permit for it.

"Lord, help us all," Arlo breathed. The last thing she wanted to do was go visit Camille in jail because she had shot some man she had met on the internet. "Do you know what time their date is supposed to end?"

"I guess when they decide it's over," Fern replied.

"You know, you're not being much help here," Arlo said with a sharp look in her direction.

Fern just shrugged again. "She's fine."

"I hope so," Arlo whispered.

"But this deal with Haley," Helen said.

Arlo supposed that since Camille was gone for the morning, they weren't going to discuss *Missing Girl* or even Mary Kennedy.

"It's so sad," Fern agreed. "Who would do that?"

"I thought your vote was for a jealous lover," Arlo said.

Fern frowned. "Seriously. Who?"

They all thought about it for a moment. Who would do something like that to Haley, a sweet girl who seemed to have the world at her fingertips? How could someone so young make an enemy that cruel?

"Poor Courtney," Helen said.

"I suppose she's taking some time off," Fern asked.

Arlo nodded. "We told her to take all the time she needs."

"What about the afternoon shift at the coffee bar?" Helen asked. "You're not going to hire someone to replace her, are you? That wouldn't be right."

"No. We're not hiring anyone to replace her. Chloe's just going to work late. Or I guess I could try my hand at coffee drinks again." They had made it okay these last couple of days. They could hold on a while longer.

"Lord, please no!" Helen threw her hands up in the air in an overly dramatic gesture.

"Hey!" Arlo protested. "I can run the Keurig."

"Faulkner can run the Keurig."

"Make me a cuppa, sweet thang," he squawked.

"Seriously," Fern said. "You are not allowed behind the coffee bar for anything but brewed cups."

"Sweet thang," Faulkner continued.

Fern turned to Chloe. "And you're not allowed to work overtime."

"Not sure how that's going to work," Chloe murmured.

"I'll make the coffee," Fern said. "All you have to do is show me how. I'm a quick learner."

Chloe looked to Arlo. She just shrugged. "We pay Courtney a little over minimum wage. Sound good?"

But Fern was already shaking her head. "Don't want to do all that and have to worry about taxes and such."

"You want cash?" Arlo asked, not sure how that would affect her taxes and such.

Fern's eyes twinkled. "I want coffee."

Chloe grinned. "Deal."

"I sure wish Camille was here," Helen said. "She's going to love it when we tell her about the movie premiere."

"So much," Fern said. "And maybe..."

"Maybe what?" Helen asked.

"Maybe with all that publicity on the story, we can get Mads to reopen the case on Mary Kennedy."

Arlo wasn't a hundred percent sure that it had been closed. "Can they close it if she's never been found?"

Fern nodded. "Yeah. They sent her husband to prison."

"That's right." Helen snapped her fingers. "So it has to be closed."

"But if we can get some new evidence, then we can have him reopen the case."

"And if Jeff Kennedy is still in prison, then they would release him."

Fern gasped. "Just like the Innocence Project."

"He did it," Faulkner squawked. "The butler did it."

"And the West Memphis Three," Helen said.

Arlo looked to Chloe, who shrugged. Once the women got on a roll like this it was hard to get them off it. And she surely wasn't wasting time informing them that the West Memphis Three got out of jail on an Alford plea. Which basically said they were guilty, but they didn't do it and had served enough time for their crime. It was the perfect way for the government not to have to take responsibility for locking up three innocent men for two decades.

"Are you sure it's the same story though?" she asked. Deciding it was time to come back around to *Missing Girl*, the real reason why they were there.

"Positive," Helen said with a firm nod.

"See, there are things about stories," Fern said. "Things that make them satisfying. If Wally had left the missing girl missing, he wouldn't have had a novel, just a recounting of part of a tale that happened fifty years ago. Readers want for the missing girl to be found."

"And you know this how?" Arlo asked.

"Camille told us."

Camille, the retired English teacher.

And the worst part of it all was she was right. There were certain elements that made a story satisfying, and for all of Wally's rambling writing style, he had hit them all.

"I say we go tomorrow," Helen said emphatically.

"I'm in." Fern gave a decisive nod.

They both looked to Arlo.

"Go where?" she asked.

"To the police station to talk to Mads about reopening the Mary Kennedy case."

She shook her head. "Y'all can leave me out of this one."

4

"YOU HAVE GOT TO DO SOMETHING," CAMILLE SAID THE following morning.

As threatened…er, promised…the day before, the book club ladies had met early in order to come as a group to the police station and talk to Mads about reopening the Mary Kennedy missing person/murder case. Of course they had started at the Books and More and left Arlo no choice but to trail behind like an annoying little sister.

She followed them down Main, into the station, past Frances Jacobs's desk, and into Mads's office without so much as a by your leave.

Now they hovered around Mads while Frances lurked in the doorway and Arlo wished she was any place other than there.

"I have to?" Mads asked.

Arlo was pretty sure he didn't like to be told what he had to do, and any doubts were squashed by his deepening frown.

"It's imperative," Camille continued.

"I would gladly do something," he started in a tone that clearly conveyed his apathy. Yet even then he managed to come across as a caring public servant. At least to Camille and the other ladies he did. "But without new evidence, my hands are tied." He held out his hands as if to show them the invisible ropes.

"Here's your new evidence." Fern slapped a copy of *Missing Girl* into his open palms.

Mads had no choice but to accept the tome or drop it. "This is not new evidence." He tried to hand it back, but Fern's arms remained stubbornly at her sides. He looked to Arlo for help. Like she had any control over the book club.

"Have you read it?" Helen asked.

"I have." Mads nodded.

"Then you've seen the evidence," Helen continued.

"I don't recall—"

Fern scoffed. "Wally's book is full of new clues. You just have to read between the pages. So to speak."

Mads shook his head. "A fiction story that is possibly based on a cold case is not enough to reopen that case. I'm sorry." Once again he tried to hand the book back to Fern. She didn't take it.

"Maybe you should read it again," Fern said.

He opened his mouth to say something, then sighed and set the book on his desk. For a moment, Arlo was certain he was going to explain the difference between clues and evidence—which would have saved her the trouble, even if the book club wasn't known for their superior grasp of logic and would probably ignore every word—but he didn't. Which meant she would have to eventually.

"So?" Camille asked.

"So what?" Mads asked in return.

"Are you going to reread *Missing Girl*?" Camille demanded.

Mads looked from the retired English teacher to Arlo. Their gazes snagged and his eyes asked what he should do.

Arlo nodded as surreptitiously as possible.

"I suppose," Mads said, taking her unspoken advice.

"Good." Fern nodded, then stepped forward and snatched the book off his desk. "Get your own copy. This one's mine."

. . . .

"He has to be the most stubborn man I have ever met," Helen harrumphed as they made their way back into the Books and More.

Faulkner flapped his wings and tsked in response.

"The most stubborn," she said again.

Considering the amount of male traffic Helen had in and out of the inn, that was saying something, though Arlo decided it was best to leave her commentary out of the conversation. Helen was pretty wound up after their encounter with Mads.

"At least he agreed to reread the book. Surely that will help." Camille's optimism was in full swing.

It was Fern's turn to harrumph.

Faulkner tsked again.

"We'll just have to solve the Case of the Missing Piano Teacher without his help." Camille patted Helen's hand.

"I don't think that's the best name for the case," Fern said.

"I like it." Camille gave a firm nod. "It makes it sound like Nancy Drew—"

"And you read all of them when you were a child," Fern cut her off. "Yes, you told us."

Camille nodded. "That's right."

"Are you going to tell us about your date?" Arlo asked, doing her best to change the subject. As soon as the ladies had gathered at the bookstore, they had marched down to talk to Mads. This was the first real opportunity Arlo had to ask about it.

Camille shifted in her seat and picked at a spot on her slacks. "It was fine."

"Fine?" Arlo asked. "That's all?"

Camille looked up and smiled. "It's enough."

"New evidence, he said." Helen snorted. "How much new evidence do you need?" She held up a copy of Wally's book. Little pieces of paper and transparent tabs in a variety of colors stuck out in various places among the pages. "It's all in here."

"Evidence," Faulkner chimed in. "Gotta have the evidence."

Arlo glanced over at Chloe, who only shrugged. These days Chloe had become Switzerland, leaving Arlo to run interference with the book club. Babysit. Whatever. "You still haven't proven that the book is about the missing piano teacher. What was her name?"

"Mary Kennedy," Fern supplied. "And it's close enough."

In for a penny, in for a pound, Arlo always said. "Explain this to me." Arlo eased down into the armchair and looked at each of the ladies in turn.

"We wanted to explain that to Mads," Helen huffed. "But no. I tell you what, Arlo. I don't remember him being such a testy boy. Was he like this when y'all were dating?"

"I honestly don't remember." But that was honestly a

lie. She remembered almost everything about him from that time. He had been the same back then as he was today: thoughtful but maybe not as stern. And these days there was an air about him of sadness. No, that wasn't right. It was more of a loss, like he had come so close to having it all. Maybe he had. Though she thought that it had less to do her with and more to do with his football career cut short.

"Well, he wouldn't even listen," Fern complained.

"Tell me," Arlo requested. Not bothering to try to explain that Mads was trying to solve a recent murder that had the whole town in a tizzy.

"We've been trying to tell you for a week now," Camille shifted her handbag in her lap but still didn't place it on the floor.

"Sorry." Arlo shot them a smile. "Tell me again. Now."

Fern frowned but started. "Mary Kennedy was a nice lady."

Arlo nodded encouragingly, though she was certain they could have left out that part and still completed the story. She had promised to listen, so that's exactly what she would do.

"I didn't know her that well." Helen shrugged.

All eyes turned to Camille. "Don't look at me. All I know of her is she taught a lot of my students piano. They seemed to like her well enough. I mean it was fifty years ago, but I don't remember anyone complaining about her. In fact it's a miracle that anyone remembers her at all. She was very average."

"That's right," Fern said. "We went to church together."

"You went to church?" Arlo couldn't stop her mouth from dropping open at that one.

"Very funny," Fern said. "I'm going to let that slide and

tell you that she had an average voice, she didn't sing in the choir, and she was always dressed nicely enough. I mean, her husband was a delivery man, and she taught piano. They weren't exactly rolling in the dough."

"Children?" Arlo asked.

"None." Fern shook her head.

"So, the two of you were friends?" Arlo nodded.

"Not really. We just went to church together."

Arlo shook her head at that one. "I just can't get over that."

"Well, try," Fern snapped. "I wasn't always as enlightened as I am now."

Camille frowned. "Does that mean you don't believe in God?"

"I don't believe in church," Fern replied.

"Aren't they the same thing?" Arlo asked. She hadn't been raised in church. Her parents were hippies, not staying in one place long enough to find the cheapest grocery store much less a church home. She had gone a couple of times since then, but she never felt God there. Only when she was outside and alone did she feel the presence of a higher being than herself. Call it what you will.

"Not in the slightest." Fern drew in a deep breath obviously preparing for a lengthy speech on the topic, but Camille cut her off.

"This has nothing to do with Mary Kennedy," she reminded them.

"Right," Arlo said. "So, Mary Kennedy..."

"She would come to church with marks on her from where her husband grabbed her and probably shook her. I remember this one time when the air conditioner went out in the sanctuary. Lord, it was hot in there. She was wearing a sweater over her dress. She took it off. Bruises all up and down her arms."

"And no one did anything about it?" It was unfathomable to Arlo.

"Things were different back then." Fern shrugged one shoulder.

"I find it hard to believe," Arlo said.

"That no one would say anything?" Fern asked.

"Yes, this poor woman was being abused. It's ridiculous that it was just allowed to happen."

"Ri-dic-u-lous," Faulkner enunciated.

"I agree," Helen said. "But times were different."

"Different times," Faulkner said. "Different strokes. Different folks. Different—"

"Hush," Arlo told the bird.

"I love you," he said in return. She might have to reconsider her decision to not to take him home with her. It seemed he was lacking for attention during the evening hours. At least that was the only reason she could think of for his loquacious attitude of late.

"I know for a fact several women from the church tried to talk to her," Fern added. "Not all at once, mind you, but at separate times. They needed her to admit that something was wrong. Once she had done that, we could have stepped in to help her, but until she came forth…."

"That is something I will never understand." Arlo shook her head.

"Different times," was all Helen said in return.

"Different times," Faulkner repeated. "Different strokes. Different folks. Different colors. Pick a rainbow."

Arlo rolled her eyes. "You just had to say it, didn't you?"

Helen merely shrugged and leaned over toward the bird. "Gimme a kiss," she said. He obliged by nipping at her pursed lips.

Arlo shook her head. "So she didn't come forward, and he continued to abuse her."

"Yes, until one day she disappeared." Helen gave a negligent shrug.

"She was driving home from giving Baxter Whitney his piano lesson," Fern jumped in.

"Baxter." Camille shook her head. "Trying boy."

"Mary had been going out there for a while," Helen said.

"How do you know that?" Arlo asked.

She shrugged again. "I dunno. Probably beauty parlor talk."

Which meant it might be true, but it might not. And considering it was a fifty-year-old memory…

"The character in the book," Arlo started. "Millicent Andrews. She wasn't abused."

"But she disappeared one night after driving home from the largest mansion in the area. Her car was never found."

"Okay," Arlo said. "Let's take this one thing at a time and compare each item."

"Can we get one of those big dry-erase boards like the police on TV use?" Camille's eyes sparkled with excitement.

"No," Arlo said. She was hoping that by giving their ideas an audience she would appease their sense of adventure. And that they would see that the two stories had very little in common. It was worth a shot, anyway.

"We could set it up right there in front of the used bookshelves. You don't sell that many used books, do you, Arlo?"

"No."

"See then? It'll be perfect."

"I mean no, you can't set up a dry-erase board."

"Bugger," Camille grumbled. "That's no fun."

"I'll write it down," Fern volunteered and took a notebook from her book bag. Camille had already beat her to it. She had a steno pad from her magical handbag in seconds, out and ready to go.

"Write that down," Helen instructed. "Mary was abused and Millicent wasn't."

"That's a similarity right there," Fern exclaimed. "Their names both begin with the letter M."

"Their last names begin with different letters," Arlo protested. "That is not a true similarity."

The bell rang, and a customer came in. One of the regulars who stopped by as much for a coffee as they did to browse the shelves. It didn't matter to Arlo as long as they came in.

"It is," Fern countered. "I saw a special on CNN about aliases and most people choose an alias that begins with the same letter as their real name."

"Mary didn't pick that name. Wally did."

"Mary had a little lamb," Faulkner interjected. He must have been feeling a bit neglected. He rarely resorted to nursery rhymes in order to gain attention.

"I still think we should write it down. His name for her could be considered an alias."

"No," Arlo said.

"Already done." Camille smiled.

Helen chuckled.

She was seriously outnumbered here. "Millicent wasn't a piano teacher."

"But she played the piano in the book. Remember? She plays the baby grand at the beginning of the party."

"'And as I watched, the lady in the flowing red dress settled herself onto the piano bench and began to play, the melody sweet and poignant sending pangs of longing through me of memories best forgotten.' Page fifty-two," Helen stated.

"It's still different." Arlo wasn't sure why she protested; they were going to override her anyway.

"Close enough," Helen chirped. "Write it down."

"And the narrator of the story," Camille added. "He's in love with Millicent."

"Like?" Arlo prompted.

"Well, I believe Weston Whitney was in love with Mary Kennedy," she continued. "That could be something."

"But the narrator in *Missing Girl* kidnaps the girl to have her for his own." Arlo thought it was a valid enough point of difference.

"Kind of like *Lolita* without all the underage stuff going on," Helen mused.

"We don't know the age of the woman in the book. It could be just the same," Camille protested.

"Nah," Fern interjected. "They would have said something in the story. That was the cutting edge of *Lolita*."

Once again the conversation was getting way off subject.

"But we know that Weston didn't kidnap Mary," Arlo did her best to steer them back on track.

"Do we?" Helen said.

Arlo would have thought better of her guardian. Helen didn't normally act as crazy as the other two. But something about this story had her jumping all over the place. At least Arlo hoped it was the story and not something serious. Helen was getting up there in age. They all were. And though Arlo knew it seemed as if they had all their faculties, a person had to wonder at times like this. "Weston Whitney did not kidnap Mary Kennedy."

"He might have. He could have snatched her up and stashed her in the basement at Lillyfield," Fern said.

Arlo sighed.

"It could happen," Camille protested.

"Especially in a house the size of Lillyfield. Lots of places to hide," Fern added.

"And you know the uber-rich," Helen said. "Very eccentric."

"I wouldn't call Judith eccentric. She's just mean," Camille said.

"Weston was eccentric," Fern added.

"But he wasn't the one with all the money. He only got that when he married Judith." Helen pointed out.

"A person can become eccentric. That's what money does to you," Fern said.

They all nodded in agreement.

"Another book club meeting?"

"Sam!" The ladies all called his name and stood, each having to give him a hug as if they hadn't seen him in years instead of just a day.

"So, handsome, when are you going to come back and join us?" Camille pouted.

"When my case load eases." He smiled. He was a skunk, Arlo decided, using the ladies for innocent attention. After all, who didn't want to be told they were handsome, smart, and fun?

"How much is there to do in little ol' Sugar Springs?" This from Fern. Her pout was almost as good as Camille's.

"You'd be amazed at the work you can do on the internet."

"Helen maybe, but we've been trying to solve this Mary Kennedy case the old-fashioned way."

He looked to Arlo.

Don't ask, she mouthed in return.

He nodded. "If you need any help—"

Arlo shook her head in warning.

"—let me know."

Too late.

"Well," Helen started, looping her arm through his. "There is one thing."

Arlo shot him a semiapologetic smile as he was led away. She had tried.

Forty-five minutes later, he found her shelving books in the cooking/homelife section.

"Why didn't you warn me?" His words were accusatory, but his smile was still firmly in place.

"First of all, you know how they are from your own personal experience, and secondly, I tried, but you just plowed on in. 'Just let me know if you need any help.'"

"Did you know that they—"

"I know," Arlo interjected. "I even went with them."

"Son of a gun." Sam shook his head in disbelief.

She placed the last book on the shelf and turned to fully face him. He was as handsome as ever today in one of the endless pairs of faded jeans he owned. The wear made her wonder if he'd had them since high school. Possibly. He hadn't gained any weight over the years, just a few more laugh lines around his eyes and mouth. But the shadow of worry still hung around him. "How's your mom?"

"The same." He sighed. "She says she's all right, but you know how it is. She doesn't want me worrying."

"Of course not. But you do anyway." Who didn't worry when their loved one had cancer?

He smiled. "You know it."

A small moment passed between them. It was silent and comfortable, the warmth of old friends.

"Did you know that Haley Adams was murdered?" he finally asked.

"Yes. How do you know?"

"I'm a private dick, remember?"

"I thought we had agreed that you wouldn't be telling people that."

He chuckled. "It's not my fault that your mind is in the gutter."

Arlo shrugged. "So, who told you?"

He shrugged in return.

"You went to the barbershop, didn't you?"

He raised a hand to his perfectly sun-bleached shaggy hair. "What does that have to do with anything?"

"Gossip. Dye Me a River is the same way. You need to know anything in this town that's the place to be." Always had been, always would be. "Wait a minute. You didn't go to Tony's; you went to Dye Me a River."

"Maybe, but I don't' see—"

"And got highlights!" She almost screeched the words.

"Lowlights," he said, moving closer to her. "And not so loud. You'll ruin my reputation."

"With the ladies?" She nodded toward the reading nook where the book club was still going on full strong though the topic had turned from Mary Kennedy to Martha

Tubbs's hummingbird cake recipe and whether or not it was really her grandmother's or if it came out of *Southern Living* magazine.

"All the ladies."

"Maybe I don't want to go on a date with you after all."

He looked crushed, but the expression was exaggerated, put-on. "You wound me."

"I just didn't know I had agreed to go to supper with such a Lothario." She raised her brows and pursed her lips as if to say, *prove you aren't.*

"Now I'm really hurt." He hung his head, mockingly defeated.

She shrugged. "I calls 'em likes I sees 'em."

"I thought we were going as friends."

Her heart gave a dull thud in her chest. Was that what she wanted? Or was she disappointed. She didn't know. Maybe a little of both. "Are we?"

He chuckled, but the sound rang a little nervously to her. "Of course. What else?"

What else indeed?

And if she wasn't such a big chicken, she would ask him outright. But she was out of dating practice. She had spent the last two years building the store into what it was today, and that hadn't left much time for anything other than work, books, and Monday night supper with Helen. Though these days, she hadn't even saved time for that. But she *was* a big chicken, so she let the moment slip away without questioning him.

"Did you hear about the movie?" she asked instead.

"*Missing Girl*?" he asked. "I did. Pretty amazing, huh?"

"Really amazing. Who would have thought we would have our very own movie premiere right here in Sugar Springs?"

"Crazy."

"Of course, that's got the ladies working double time to solve the murder of Mary Kennedy." Arlo nodded toward the reading nook, where they were still hard at work, marking passages in *Missing Girl* and discussing things they had already noted.

"There's no actual proof that she's been murdered," Sam said.

"What do you know about Mary Kennedy?"

He shrugged in that so-Sam way of his. "Just what Mama says from time to time."

"She knew her?" Arlo raised her brows in surprise.

"Sugar Springs is the size of a sugar bowl," he said with a chuckle.

"Right." Everyone knew everybody.

"I think she said they played bridge or something."

"Did she mention any abuse?" The question slipped out before Arlo could stop it. She closed her eyes for a moment then opened them again to find him watching her closely. Almost too closely. No, she was letting her imagination get away from her again. "Forget I asked that. The book club has got me doing it now."

"Doing what?"

"Finding a mystery where there isn't one."

"Oh, there's a mystery around Mary Kennedy for sure," Sam said. "But if it'll ever be solved is another matter altogether."

5

"WHAT DO YOU THINK?" HELEN PULLED HER LONG, IRON-gray hair over her shoulder for Arlo to see. The deep red ends had been dyed a deep, dark purple.

Friday. Beauty parlor day, and with all the happening in Sugar Springs this week, Arlo was surprised her almost-grandmother led with this.

"It's…purple," she finally managed.

Helen's shoulders slumped. "You hate it."

"No." Arlo shook her head. "No, I don't. It's just different."

Helen scooped up a chunk of her hair and studied the ends. "It's just temporary."

"It's different is all." As traditional as Arlo was when it came to her own hair, she did like Helen's adventuresome color. She might be over eighty, but she was still as hip and stylish as she had ever been. In her own way of course.

"I told you she wouldn't like it." Fern came in next, a scarf tied neatly under her chin.

"Wait…" Arlo said as Fern undid the knot at her throat. "Did you go to the beauty parlor today?" Fern usually set her curls at home, preferring instead to bank the money and get her gossip in the new fashion—Facebook.

Fern shrugged. "Maybe."

"And what are you wearing?" Arlo tried not to sound overly shocked. She couldn't ever remember seeing Fern in anything other than a flowered housedress, except for maybe a plaid housedress, and today she was wearing—

"Overalls." Her tone clearly conveyed that she thought Arlo had lost her mind if she didn't know what overalls were.

"I can see that," Arlo stammered. "But why?"

Fern looked down at herself and turned a little from side to side. The wide legs of the overalls had been rolled up to just above the ankle. Fern's standard tan-colored running shoes were missing and, in their place, a worn pair of Converse Chuck Taylors. Her tan compression stockings were clearly visible. She had a white T-shirt on underneath and a pearl-button gingham top over it all. "I'm taking up gardening."

Arlo did her best not to giggle. She didn't want to laugh outright at Fern and hurt her feelings, but the whole idea was silly at best. "Isn't it a little late to be starting now?"

"That's what I told her."

Fern shot Helen a withering look. "It's just May."

"Where's Camille?" With Helen's change in hair color and Fern's change of dress and haircare venue, Arlo needed something to be the same. With any luck, Camille hadn't gone and dyed her hair cotton candy pink or joined the circus.

"She was right behind us," Helen said.

Fern frowned. "She got a call from her beau." She said the last word as if it tasted bad in her mouth.

"Has anyone met him yet?" Arlo asked.

Fern and Helen shook their heads.

"She's keeping him under wraps." Helen said.

"You don't think he's..." What was the word she wanted? Not on the level, bad, a charlatan?

"Too young for her?" Fern supplied. "That's exactly what I think."

"Criminal was more what I was thinking."

Fern shrugged. "He could be both."

Helen elbowed her. "Not helping."

Fern rubbed her arm. "Might be true though."

And that was the greatest concern.

"Anything new happening at the beauty shop today?" Arlo looked from one of them to the other.

Helen made a face. "Now you want the Friday gossip."

"No, I just thought—" But she couldn't finish because it was exactly as Helen said.

"You just thought with Haley's murder there would be big news at Dye Me a River."

"Well, yeah."

She waited for Helen to elaborate, but the seconds ticked by, and Camille breezed into the bookshop. "Hello, lovelies."

"Finally decide to get off the phone?" Fern grumped.

But Camille continued nonplussed. "It's a beautiful day, n'est-ce pas?"

Arlo looked to Helen. "French?"

Her guardian shrugged.

"She's in love," Fern said.

Camille beamed. "It's true that I am."

At least that was all in English.

"This is with the man you met on the internet?" Arlo asked.

"Dating site," Camille corrected, though Arlo wasn't sure exactly what the difference was.

"I'm so happy for you," Arlo managed.

"Hear, hear," Chloe chimed in.

"When do we get to meet this new man of yours?" Helen asked.

"You sure you want another one of those hanging around?" Fern asked.

"Another what?" Camille asked.

Fern opened her mouth to reply, but Arlo cut in. "Man. She's talking about a man." She hadn't been exactly sure what Fern would have said, but it was a safe bet it wasn't G-rated.

"Men have their uses, love." Camille beamed.

Helen started to say something, but Arlo shook her head. Now was not the time to talk of such things. With the sparkle in Camille's eyes, Arlo was fairly certain Camille wouldn't be up for any lectures on dating, the dangers involved, or the question of if she really wanted to get involved with someone at her age.

"He hasn't asked you for money, has he?" Fern demanded.

"Of course not, love." Then she must have really looked at Fern for the first time since she came into the shop. "What are you wearing?"

"Overalls." Fern raised her chin as if daring her to say more.

Arlo wasn't sure if Fern was really picking up a new hobby or if she bought the outfit spoiling for a fight.

"Have you been wearing them the entire time?" Camille asked, eyes still sparkling.

"Yes." Fern crossed her arms with a frown.

Arlo was pretty sure what Fern was thinking. If Camille had been paying more attention to what was happening around her instead of this new man of hers, maybe she would have noticed an hour ago. But it was simply speculation on Arlo's part.

"Well, they're quite lovely. Quite lovely indeed." The power of love was tremendous.

"As long as he's not asking you for money," Fern grumbled.

"He's not."

"Then he's retired?" Helen asked.

"I suppose," Camille said. "We haven't gotten around to talking about that."

"But he's retirement age?" Helen pressed.

"Oh, yes, love."

Arlo didn't bother to remind her guardian that retirement age could be as young as midfifties these days. She was a little more concerned with the fact that Camille and her new man hadn't discussed something so basic as income.

"Are we going to talk about the mystery or not?" Fern demanded.

Arlo thought it best not to point out that they were really there to discuss a book that they had all read at least three times. After all, when she had started the book club, they had been planning to read *To Kill a Mockingbird*. And who knew how many times the ladies had read that one.

"Of course." Camille breezed over to the reading nook like only an eighty-plus woman in a pink pantsuit and matching running shoes could.

Fern and Helen shook their heads and followed behind.

Arlo breathed a small sigh of relief. With Camille in love, she might not have to check the book club so often. With any luck, Camille's afterglow, or whatever a person would call it, would put a damper on any harebrained ideas the other two could concoct. Arlo might just be able to get a little work done today. And daydream a bit about her date that evening with Sam.

No such luck.

The bell over the door sounded, followed by, "Hello, good people."

They turned as Baxter Whitney strolled into the Books and More.

"Hi," Arlo said, making her way over to where he stood, hovering just inside the door as if afraid to come any further. "What can I do for you, Baxter?"

"Arlo Stanley," he said. He was dressed like a 1940s gangster with a flowing silk shirt, pleated trousers, and two-toned wing-tip shoes. But Baxter had always been that way. Overdressed, overimportant. Pretty much over-everything.

"I thought that was you. Is this your little shop?"

"Yes." She smiled at his description, wondering how many Arlos he knew in Sugar Springs. The idea that there was more than one was laughable.

"Nice, nice," he said, but he was looking at the papers he held in his hands rather than the store itself. The superb manners of the well-to-do.

"How's your mom?" She was aware of the rustling behind her and knew the book club had gathered around to hear the answer.

Baxter frowned. "The same. But you know Mama. She'll bounce back. She always does."

And Arlo hoped he was right.

"Speaking of which…" He held up the turquoise blue flyers he held in one hand. "She wanted me to hand these out to everyone." He gave one to Arlo, then proceeded to hand them to the book club ladies one at a time.

Come one, come all to the Thirty-Fifth Annual Lillyfield Barbecue and Funfair.

"You're still having the party this year?" Camille asked.

"There was a lot of debate over it. But Roberts won. He thinks it's important to keep things the same. For Mama's sake."

"And others there didn't want to have it?" Arlo asked.

The barbecue was important for the community. Who wouldn't want to have it? It wasn't like the entire event fell to the Whitneys. There was a town committee that gathered volunteers, students in need of community service. And there were other people involved as well. Like the high school principal who manned the dunk tank every year, allowing his students an opportunity to dunk him into the water.

His mouth twisted into an ugly shape, then morphed into a tight smile. "Well, Pam—"

"Dad-dy." Anastasia Whitney Boudreau interrupted as she swept into the shop as if she were walking the red carpet. Which was amazing, since she too was carrying a handful of the blue flyers. But her dress was too odd to be anything other than couture, and her shoes would have given any normal person a nosebleed to go along with their bunions. But that was Anastasia, and she had been this way long enough that people in Sugar Springs never gave her a second glance. Not for the way she dressed, anyway.

Thirty-five, divorced, and living at home (technically), she appeared something close to comical with her glittering, stacked bracelets and Yorkie tucked under one arm. Eccentric…wasn't that the polite term? "How many more of these are we going to have to hand out?" She pouted in a way that only the entitled jet set can.

"All of them, dearie. It is your birthday celebration after all." Baxter's expression became a bit apologetic as he turned back to Arlo. "What was I saying?"

Arlo managed a genuine-looking smile. Well, it felt genuine anyway. "I can't remember."

She had forgotten that the annual barbecue had begun as a celebration of Anastasia's birth. Mostly because since she had lived in Sugar Springs, Arlo could count on one hand the number of times she had actually seen the woman at the event, but that was neither here nor there. Judith Whitney held the affair every year as her way of giving back to the community. And of course raising money for charity.

"This year's event is to benefit St. Jude," Baxter continued.

"Always a worthy cause," Arlo replied. And a certain crowd-pleaser.

The book club ladies, still gathered behind her, echoed her sentiment.

"Hope to see you all there," Baxter said. "It'll be good to have some positive after all the unpleasantness of late." He gave a wave, then left, his daughter trailing behind him like a lost puppy.

"Some things never change," Helen said.

They broke and started back to the reading nook.

Fern chuckled. "They have no reason to."

"I disagree," Camille said as she sank back down into her favorite armchair. "I've never seen Baxter and Anastasia handing out flyers before. That's new."

"You're right," Fern said. "But it's a small change. Hardly worth mentioning."

"I wonder what he was going to say about Pam," Arlo said, then resisted the urge to slap her hand over her mouth. She didn't need to give them any more to talk about.

"I know. I would have liked to hear that," Helen agreed.

"One thing's certain," Fern said. "There's no love lost there."

....

The Cattle Drive sat off the highway between Sugar Springs and neighboring Walnut. It was a typical, casual steak house with country music playing over the loudspeakers, peanuts on every table, and the smell of woodsmoke and yeast rolls in the air. Since Sam was going to Corinth for the day, she agreed to meet him at six. She was grateful, seeing as how she didn't really know how to act, sitting side by side with him in his truck, just like old times. At least close enough to those long ago days to send her reminiscing and pondering over all the what-ifs of the last ten years.

She had no more than arrived at the hostess station when she saw him across the restaurant, waving to her.

"That's my…party," she said with a wavering smile. Why was this so awkward when it was supposed to be fun? And why was it so awkward when she hadn't even said hi to him yet?

"Go on back," the hostess replied.

Arlo gave the young girl a nod of thanks and started toward the table where Sam waited. Her heart pounded heavily in her chest as she made eye contact with him. This was going to be an enjoyable night, she promised herself. Two old friends catching up on the last few years. This had nothing to do with prom or Mads or anything that happened back in high school. What happens in high school stays in high school, right?

Her smile felt stiff on her lips as she neared him.

"Get down." He clasped her arm and pulled her level to the top of the table.

"What's wrong?" Her mouth went dry to match her pounding heart and shallow breathing. If she wasn't careful, she would have a full-blown panic attack and all because she was on a date with her ex–high school sweetheart. Her *second* ex–high school sweetheart. Mads had always been the first.

"Camille," he whispered, pointing to a table not far from where they were.

Arlo managed to ease into the chair opposite him, her breathing slowly returning to normal even as she kept her head as low as she could. But that made looking for someone impossible. She couldn't see over the salt shakers, much less anyone's head. "I can't see."

"That may be a good thing," he quipped in return.

"Camille is here?" she asked.

"With a man."

"She met him on the internet," Arlo explained.

"*That's* the guy from the dating site?"

"I'm pretty sure." She tried peeking through the sea of bodies, tables, and various condiment dispensers to get a look at her elderly friend, but to no avail. "I can't see him. But she's only mentioned one man."

"Did she say anything about him?"

"Only that he was sweet and thoughtful, and that she was in love. Why?"

Still keeping his head low, Sam pulled out his phone, prepared to type at a moment's notice. "Do you remember his name?"

"Joe."

"Joe what?"

"I don't know. Just Joe."

Sam sighed and put his phone on the table.

"Can I bring you something to drink?" The waitress bent low when she asked the question.

"Beer," Sam said. "Arlo?"

"Same."

"Got it." The waitress straightened as if this was the proper way to order drinks and made her way to the bar.

"I can't see down here," Arlo protested. "And I'm starting to get a cramp."

Sam leaned forward and placed one hand on the back of her neck. "Trust me. You do not want to see this."

"Now I want to see it even more than before." She shook off his hand, and keeping as low as possible while still able to see over the crowded restaurant, Arlo scanned the area.

"Oh. My. *Stars*!"

"Shhh…"

She ducked her head once again and stared at Sam across the table.

"We've been made," he said through his smile as he

waved to someone across the room, Camille and her Joe, Arlo was certain.

Arlo pasted on her own smile and turned back to the table where Camille sat.

She hadn't had time to mull over many of the possibilities before she had actually looked at Camille and her dinner partner. She wasn't sure what she had expected. A much younger man, a man of a different race, even a woman were all possibilities that ran through her head, but this man…

"Those are prison tats," Sam said, still talking through his smile.

"Why are you talking like that? Camille doesn't lip-read." At least she hadn't been able to the last time they had come to the steak house following Daisy James-Harrison, Wally's widow. Then again, it had been a month or so since Daisy left town, and Camille had been on the internet a great deal. Who knew what all she had picked up?

Arlo waved at Camille and the creature seated opposite her. He was a large hulk of a man with a shaved head and numerous visible tattoos.

Camille smiled and waved back. She said something to the man. Joe, Arlo reminded herself, and he turned toward their table as well. Arlo and Sam waved again.

She could say one thing about the man. He had a nice smile. His teeth were white and even, and didn't seem to go with this tough guy persona. Perhaps they were dentures.

"He's not what I expected," Sam said.

Give the man an award for understatement of the year.

"How do you know those tattoos came from prison?"

"Black ink, for starters."

Arlo turned back to Sam. "Don't all tattoos have black ink?"

"Well, no," Sam said. "Most do, of course. But since there aren't many places to get something to use for tat ink in a prison, they usually use ink from a pen, soot, or pencil lead. All black, so there's no hint of color."

Arlo stilled a shudder. "As Camille would say, that sounds simply ghastly."

Sam nodded. "It kind of is, I suppose. Now, see that spiderweb on his elbow?"

"No," Arlo exclaimed, then lowered her voice to a more inside-voice level. "I was too busy looking at the spiderweb on top of his head."

"Yeah." Sam cleared his throat. "Spiderwebs signify being trapped. One on the elbow usually means time spent in prison."

"So, you're telling me that he's an ex-con?"

"Without a doubt."

"What about the spiderweb on his head?" Arlo asked.

Sam shrugged. "Trapped."

Or imprisoned.

"Can't it be that he just likes spiders?"

Sam pressed his lips together but didn't answer.

Arlo started to rise, but he placed a hand on her arm to stop her. "Slow down there, partner. Marching over there like you're her mother isn't going to help anything."

"I don't think she should be dating him."

"Sit, mother hen." Sam said with a small chuckle.

Arlo plopped back into her chair. "It's just—"

"I know." Sam stopped as the waitress brought their beers. "Ready to order?" she asked, not making one comment about the way they had been sitting earlier.

Sam looked to Arlo; she waved a hand in his direction. "Whatever you think." She wasn't sure she had much of an appetite now.

Sam ordered them steaks with sides and salads. Arlo barely registered that he had remembered she liked blue cheese dressing over ranch and didn't eat butter on her baked potato. The thought would have warmed her, had it not been for her friend and that friend's new ex-con boyfriend sitting right across the restaurant from them.

"Should I go introduce myself? I should go introduce myself." She started to stand once again, and once again, Sam stopped her.

"Let them alone."

Arlo looked back. Camille and Prison Tat Joe were gazing deeply into one another's eyes. From here, the sentiment looked genuine, but like most steak houses, the Cattle Drive was dim and shadowy, like someone forgot to pay the electric bill.

"Are you—"

"I'm sure."

"But if he's an ex-con."

"Anyone can go to prison, Arlo."

She knew that, and she wasn't trying to be prejudiced against the man. Though she was. But in the past few months, Camille had become more than one of her almost-grandmother's friends; she had become like a second grandmother to Arlo, and she would hate to see her hurt.

Arlo released a deep breath, but her shoulders remained tight, her stomach clenched. "You're right, of course." But there was something else bothering her about the man as well. Though in her current agitated state, she couldn't remember what it was.

"Relax," Sam said.

She tried again, with a little more success.

"Find out his last name," Sam said. "I'll run a background check on him, see what comes up. Then, once we know what we're dealing with, we can go to Camille and have a talk."

"An intervention." A dating intervention. That was exactly what they needed. She had to do something to protect these crazy old women from themselves.

"A talk," Sam firmly repeated.

"A talk," she echoed.

The rest of the evening went by in a flash. Arlo seemed unable to look away from the elderly pair across from them but did her best to listen to Sam talk about his business in Corinth that day and his mother's recovery.

But in the end, she knew it was a poor attempt at best.

"I'm sorry," she said as he walked her out to her car. The tiny Rabbit convertible sat on the opposite side of the parking lot from his large man's man truck. She was pretty sure her car would fit into the bed of his pickup.

"For what?"

"I wasn't very good company tonight. Seeing Camille and Joe like that." She shook her head. "It just threw me."

"It's okay. But you owe me."

She stopped by her door and turned to face him in the dimly lit parking lot. "I owe you what?"

He smiled. That sweet Sam smile she had known since she was sixteen. "Another dinner."

"Deal," she said. Maybe that one wouldn't have so many distractions, and she could find out really and truly why Sam had asked her out. They hadn't once talked about the incident from ten years before.

"I'm sorry I hurt you," he said.

"What?"

"Ten years ago. I was a fool. Young and stupid."

"We all do stupid things when we're young." She finished with a forgiving smile. "All of us."

"I suppose." Sam nodded.

And she waited. Was he going to kiss her good night? Maybe on the cheek even?

Instead, he smiled and turned away. Three steps later, he spun and walked backward toward his truck. "I'll follow you home," he said.

"No need." She waved away his concern.

"Drive safe." He opened the door of his truck. And that, as they say, was that.

Arlo sighed, more confused than ever. She got into her car and put the key in the ignition, suddenly remembering what it was that had been bothering her during dinner. Joe. She thought she had seen him before. At Lillyfield. The day Haley was murdered.

6

Saturday morning dawned in true Mississippi-in-the-early-summer glory. Temperature eighty-five degrees, and humidity already at 75 percent. A haze hung over the town, an omen of a steaming hot day full of sun and sweat.

For Arlo it was the end of her work week but also the busiest day. Main Street had more foot traffic on the weekend than during the week, and since they were closed on Sunday, that left one day for shopping.

Normally this was her favorite day. She loved the bustle of Saturdays, but this week had been something of a trial with the murder and Courtney being out. And then last night with Sam. He was upstairs in his office. She had heard him shuffling around a couple of times when she was up on the second level. Not that she had been listening or anything. But he hadn't been in to even get a coffee. And that made her wonder if he was avoiding her after their date. After what he said. He was sorry that he had hurt her. Just as she was sorry she had hurt Mads. But was it a crime to want to be loved? No, she decided. She went about it the wrong way. Throwing Mads over for Sam, then having Sam throw her over for college out of state was karma at its finest. And she wished he had never brought it up. *Let sleeping dogs lie*, wasn't that what Helen was always saying? Or maybe it was someone else. No matter. She had made him uncomfortable, and now he was avoiding her. Great. Just great.

Chloe was behind the coffee bar making drinks for the line of teens seated on the stools, and it seemed as if every reading area had at least one book enthusiast planted in it. Even Faulkner was getting into the mood, shouting out specials that didn't really exist. Classics for $0.99, Shakespeare for $2.99, and new releases at a 100 percent discount. Thankfully, the town had grown used to the bird's antics, and no one took his advertisements seriously.

The bell over the door rang, and another group of young moms and their toddlers entered the Books and More. Maybe she should start a story time on Saturday morning. It might be good for the young readers. She would have to give that more thought. It sure couldn't turn out any weirder than her Friday night book club.

"Arlo." Helen waved her over to the couch in the front reading area, where she and Fern had gathered for their Saturday morning meeting.

"What's up?" she asked, wondering what strange question she would get this time. She hadn't been listening much this morning and had no idea if the ladies were talking about *Missing Girl* or the missing piano teacher.

"Camille's not here."

"I can see that," she said, waiting patiently for Helen to get to the point.

"We've tried to call her all morning, but there's no answer," Fern said.

"Goes straight to voicemail," Helen continued.

"Okay."

"Well, she went out that with man she met last night, and no one has heard from her since then. You don't think something bad happened..." Fern trailed off.

Arlo's stomach fell. After seeing this Joe person last night and watching Camille interact with him, that was exactly what she was thinking. And to think that he might have been at Lillyfield when Haley was killed. She mentally pulled herself together. "I'm sure she's okay," she said with convincing certainty, even when *certain* might be the last word she would use to describe herself. "You say you've tried calling her."

"Several times." Helen nodded.

"And neither one of you has met this man?"

They shook their heads.

"We messed up, didn't we?" Fern smacked Helen on the arm. "I told you we shouldn't have let her go out with this fella."

"I told you," Helen countered.

"We both did and let her anyway. Now she's probably dead. Or worse."

Arlo wasn't sure what exactly was worse than dead, but now was not the time to ask. "I'm sure she's okay." But the image of Joe and his tattoos kept floating through her mind. She pushed the thought away. So he was a little scary looking, and he had obviously spent a little time behind bars. And he might or might not have been at Lillyfield when a young girl was killed. That didn't mean he was a danger to Camille or anyone for that matter. This was the twenty-first century. A time when people weren't judged by their appearance alone.

But she knew that wasn't true.

Can't judge a book by its cover, she reminded herself. But it was so easy to fall into that habit.

"Do either of you know his name?" she asked.

"Joe," they said in unison.

"His *last* name."

"Foster maybe. Joe Foster." Fern turned to Helen for confirmation.

Helen shrugged. "Did she even say?"

Fern nodded. "We're terrible friends." She thought about it for another moment, then turned back to Arlo. "Foster," she said. "Pretty sure."

"Is that your final answer?" Arlo quipped.

"Arlo Jane!" Helen exclaimed. "Be serious about this. Our friend is missing."

"Sorry." But she needed something to lighten the mood. Helen and Fern were bad enough, and then when she added in her own knowledge of Joe Maybe Foster...

"What should we do?" Fern asked.

Arlo thought a moment. "Does she have *Find My iPhone* enabled?"

"I don't even know if she has an iPhone," Helen wailed.

"She does," Arlo assured her.

"If she's been abducted, I'm sure this Joe person has already removed any tracker in her phone." Fern was in full spy mode.

"Why don't you just go over to her house and check on her?"

The two ladies stopped, turned to her as if they couldn't

believe their ears, then nodded. "Okay," Helen said. "Let's go." She stood. "Arlo, are you coming?"

"We'll have to take your car, Arlo," Fern said. "Me and Helen drove together."

Helen drove a tiny Smart Car, the only one in Sugar Springs. Cute and economical, but only room for the driver plus one.

"We can take my car. Sure thing." And she would have to stop and get gas. Why did every part of her life seem to be so complicated? Arlo checked her watch. It was not even noon. "I thought you guys were meeting for lunch."

"Well, we thought we'd get an earlier start today."

"And did you tell Camille?"

"Of course."

There went that theory.

"Why don't you give her a few more minutes?" Arlo suggested. "Maybe she just overslept."

"This is Camille we're talking about here."

Fern was right. The thought of Clockwork Camille oversleeping was akin to winter in hell.

"Twenty minutes," Arlo said.

"Ten," Helen said emphatically.

"Fifteen," Arlo countered. She needed at least five more to get up her courage to walk up the stairs to the third floor and confront Sam.

"Fine." Helen sighed. "But not a minute more."

Arlo lost a few precious moments showing the toddlers and their mothers the newest book she had for their age group, a colorful tale about animal ballerinas; then, unable to stall any longer, she made her way to the staircase that led directly to the third floor.

The doorway had been blocked with a display until Sam and his PI business had moved into the building. Now they kept it shut but unencumbered so Sam could come down whenever he felt the urge.

Now that she thought about it, Helen had been the one to suggest the change, and Arlo wondered if she had some sort of ulterior motive for the idea. Knowing Helen, no doubt.

She knocked on the door at the top of the stairs and waited for Sam to answer before entering. There was another stairway and door that led up to the third floor directly from the street, the entrance that clients used. Not that she had seen that many people come in and out of Sam's office. Not that she had been looking. But he could be in a meeting.

"Hey, Arlo." He was seated behind that overlarge L-shaped desk he had made out of two desks pushed together at right angles. His three laptops were open in a neat little row, and Arlo realized she had never asked him why he thought it necessary to have three at the same time. But that wasn't why she was here today.

He had made a lot of changes to the space, though a great deal he had left the same. There were no rugs on the planked floor and only a couple of large abstract paintings hung on the exposed brick of the walls. He had set up a large-screen TV in one corner with a futon nearby. In case he needed a nap, she supposed. Weren't PIs always napping in their offices? Or maybe she watched too many detective shows.

"Are you still willing to do a background check on Camille's new man?"

"Of course." The smile froze on his face. "Why? Did something happen?"

"No," Arlo said. "Not really."

"Something's bothering you. I can tell."

"You saw him last night." She let out an anxious chuckle. "I keep telling myself not to judge a book and all that. But then she didn't show up for book club today, and the ladies are worried. She isn't answering her phone." She didn't know why she wasn't telling him about the possible Joe sighting at Lillyfield. Maybe because it might not have been him. But there weren't a lot of people in tiny Sugar Springs that were tatted up like Joe Foster.

"Holy crap!" Sam was on his feet in a second. "I forgot all about book club."

"You really don't have to come, you know."

He grinned that Sam smile that swept her heart away all those years ago. Even today, it sent a little pang through her midsection. "I like it."

"You're sweet." The moment she said the words she wished she could call them back.

He stopped, still smiling, but not saying a word. The moment suspended and grew thick, uncomfortable.

"Foster," she said.

"I beg your pardon?"

"Joe's last name is Foster."

Sam nodded and jotted it down on his blotter pad. Arlo wondered what it looked like at the end of the month. Did Sam still like to doodle when he talked on the phone? Why did she even care?

She didn't at all.

"Looks like someone is settling in." She pointed to Auggie, who had curled up on the chair next to the window. The window where Wally had—

She pushed the thought away and focused on the ginger-striped feline. She had never seen him so content. He had a perfect patch of sunshine and appeared to be soaking up every ray.

"I may have to get my own cat when Chloe decides to come get him."

"I'm surprised she hasn't already."

"She said she didn't want to move him too soon since he was shuffled around so much when she was in jail."

Arlo knew what Chloe said. She also knew that since Sam had Auggie, her son Jayden got to bring his dog over when he spent the night on the weekends. Jayden was nine, and having his pup around was a really big deal. And since Chloe had moved out on her own and left Jayden living in her parents' house, having Jayden happy was a big deal for her.

"Yeah," Arlo said.

"Are you coming?" Helen's voice floated up the stairwell to them. "It's been sixteen minutes."

"Hey, you don't think this Joe person had anything to do with Haley, do you?"

"Why would I think that?" Sam asked.

Arlo shook her head. "I don't know. He's new to town and…I'm not being fair, but he is one scary dude."

"Scary doesn't actually mean dangerous."

But they both knew that men like Joe Foster were the first ones dragged in when a crime had occurred. She hated herself for the generalization, but there it was. Society didn't always look favorably on the different. Especially when that different included tattoos and a prison record.

"You'll check him out though, right?" she asked.

"Of course."

"Seventeen minutes," Fern called.

"I gotta go," she said. She had wanted to ask him again about last night, but time hadn't allowed. Or maybe that was a good thing.

"I'll let you know if I come up with anything."

"Thanks." Arlo smiled and made her way back down the stairs to the main floor.

"What were you two doing up there?" Fern asked.

"Nothing." She couldn't very well tell them that she had seen Joe Foster and Camille out the night before. They would worry about their friend too much. Especially if she told them about his appearance.

"I'm staying here to help Chloe," Fern said. "You and Helen go on. But text me when you find her."

"I'll call you," Helen corrected. She wasn't the most tech-savvy geriatric in Sugar Springs.

"Text is easier," Fern argued.

"I'll text," Arlo said and led Helen outside and into the overwarm late morning sun.

They climbed into Helen's car and started toward Camille's house.

"I didn't tell Fern this," Helen started. "But I am really worried about Camille."

"Fern's really worried too," Arlo reminded her.

"Yeah, but I googled him, and I couldn't find anything. Nothing at all."

Arlo blinked. "Wait. You googled him? You?"

"Don't act so surprised." Helen shot her an exasperated look. "I know how to use a computer; I just choose not to."

"What computer did you use?"

"The one in my office at the inn."

Arlo stifled a snort. The computer was so old, it was one step from an electronic paperweight. "No wonder you couldn't find anything. Does that thing even have internet?"

"Don't get cheeky."

"I thought you didn't know his last name."

Helen gave a negligent shrug. "She told me the other night. I just didn't remember when you asked."

Which was not like Helen at all. The woman had a memory like a steel trap.

"And that really made me wonder," she continued. "What if he's not a real person at all?"

Arlo shook her head. "He's real. I mean, of course he's real. Do you think Camille just made him up?"

"Maybe she's…slipping."

Arlo let out a choked laugh. "Camille? No. She's as mentally fit as ever." Helen, on the other hand, she wasn't so sure about.

"Then he must have roofied her, and who knows what he's done with her by now."

"Camille has not been roofied. How do you even know such things?"

Helen shot her a look. "I have cable."

"Fern told you."

Helen sniffed. "Maybe."

"She's fine," Arlo said again.

"What if she was roofied? She could have been kidnapped or maybe sold into sex slavery."

If Arlo hadn't been so worried, she would have laughed.

"So much could have happened." Helen shifted in her seat, and Arlo wondered how comfortable she was in the tiny car. Arlo was tall enough, but Helen was even taller, more statuesque. Like a bedazzled Jane Russell. Curvy, robust, and with really great hair. Especially for eighty-something.

"I'm sure Camille is fine." She used her most reassuring voice, but it did nothing to soothe her own nerves.

A few minutes later, they pulled into the subdivision where Camille lived. She had paid off her house before leaving teaching—or so Arlo had been told—and had never seen the need to sell and move to something smaller. *Condos were for old people*, she would say with a sweet smile. Somehow that Aussie accent took all judgment out of the words.

A wave of worry washed over Arlo.

Please let her be okay.

"Her car's not here," Arlo said as they pulled to a stop in front of Camille's pale-blue two story. There were cream shutters and a raspberry-colored front door that somehow made the whole setup look like candy.

"She parks in the garage," Helen said. She cut the engine, and they got out.

Arlo swallowed hard, took a deep breath, and tried to get her nerves under control. If something had happened to Camille, she would never forgive herself. She had seen Camille at the restaurant the night before. She had noted her potentially dangerous situation, and she had done nothing. She was a terrible person.

Helen peeked into the windows of the garage. "Her car's here."

"Thank heavens," Arlo said. It could be a good sign. She hoped it was a good sign. "Ring the bell."

Helen stepped around the pots of pink geraniums and

pressed the doorbell. They waited. She pressed it again. They waited longer. No answer. Helen pressed it a third time. They waited an eternity.

"Let me." Arlo stepped forward and pressed the button, not letting up until Helen opened the storm door and started pounding on the deep-pink painted wood.

"I think I hear something."

They stopped their summons and listened.

"Unless you have Girl Scout cookies, go away."

"Camille?" Arlo asked.

She opened the door, and Arlo nearly melted with relief.

"Camille!" Helen exclaimed. "What are you doing?"

Camille blinked innocently at them. Her normally perfectly coiffed hair stood on end. And seeing as how it was Saturday after Beauty Parlor Friday, that was something to behold. "I was sleeping." She yawned and covered her mouth with the back on one hand.

"It's nearly twelve thirty," Arlo said.

Camille squinted at her watch. "Is it?"

"You missed book club," Helen's tone bordered on accusatory.

"Oh, mercy, I did!" She looked up at them, her expression clearing from sleepy cobwebs to alert and remorseful. "Oh, I'm sorry. Let me get my things. Come in, come in." She stood back to allow them to enter.

Arlo shook her head. "I have to get back to the store."

"Of course you do, love."

"We just wanted to make sure that you were okay." Helen didn't add anything about Camille's date the night before. Arlo thought it best to follow suit.

"Why didn't you just call me?"

"We did," Arlo explained. "Your phone went straight to voicemail."

"Oh, shoot." Camille frowned. "I called myself plugging it up last night on the charger. It was almost dead, and we'd had some wine..." She smiled in remembrance.

"Get yourself ready and over to the bookstore," Helen grumbled. Then she reached in gave Camille a tight squeeze. "I'm just glad you're okay."

....

Arlo could feel the secret stretching between her and Camille. Even from all the way across the store, it was like an invisible line linking them together. She felt it. She was pretty sure Camille felt it, but she prayed that no one else was aware.

The ladies held their book club meeting while Arlo half-heartedly listened to their chatter and shelved the new releases on the front book display. Should she say anything to Camille about Joe? She shouldn't. Definitely not. She didn't want to be that person, the one who meddled in all her friends' affairs. Camille was a grown woman. She knew what she was doing. Who she was dating. Arlo had no stake in it.

She used the box knife to slice open another carton, careful not to cut anything she didn't want to cut. Like the books or herself. She needed to get her mind back on the matter in front of her, but her thoughts kept drifting toward Camille and Joe.

What if something happened to her? What if Arlo said nothing about possibly seeing Joe at Lillyfield, and then he hurt Camille? How would Arlo feel about it then?

Awful, that's how. She needed to talk to Camille. Now. Today. But away from the book club.

"I know what you're thinking, and you're wrong."

Arlo had been so lost in her own thoughts and the chore at hand, she hadn't noticed that Camille had joined her.

"You know what I'm thinking?"

Camille nodded. "Joe looks a bit...unusual." Arlo would have gone with scary. "But he's a sweetheart."

"It's just a bit of a shock." Arlo let out an uncomfortable chuckle.

Camille just gave her a serene smile. "It was for me too, love. But that's the way it goes sometimes."

"I suppose. Just...have you looked into his man? Do you know where he comes from? What he did for a living? Does he work now?" She kept her voice low so the others couldn't overhear, but she could feel her tone rising with each question.

Camille patted her hand, that serene smile still firmly in place. "You're so sweet to be concerned, but Joe is a teddy bear."

Arlo wished she had Camille's confidence in the matter. "So when does everyone get to meet him?"

Camille looked back to Helen and Fern, who were side by side on the couch, their copies of *Missing Girl* open in their laps as they compared marked passages within the book. "Soon," she said. "Just not yet." She turned to walk away.

"What if I told you I think I saw him at the mansion the day Haley was killed? Would that make a difference?"

Camille stopped. "Thought you saw him or know for certain you saw him? Those are two very different things." She started back toward the reading nook. This time Arlo let her go.

7

Sunday mornings were Arlo's mornings to sleep in. And she enjoyed the luxury. On the list of whether she should get a pet or not, not being able to sleep late on Sunday went on the con side of a getting a puppy. She wouldn't be able to sleep in if she had to get up and let the dog out. Of course, a cat would be easier, but she could just as easily get one like Auggie as she could get one she could truly enjoy.

She stretched once more, then picked up her phone to check the time. She already had a text from Chloe.

The Diner at 10?

Arlo typed back.

Meet you there.

It was a Sunday morning tradition for the two of them to eat breakfast at The Diner. Though usually it was after church. Arlo slept in, and Chloe went to the nondenominational church just off the highway. But if they were meeting at ten, that meant Chloe had skipped out on today's sermon.

Arlo rose from the bed, took a quick shower, and pulled on a pair of jean shorts. Her waist-length hair went into a ponytail that she pushed through the back of her Mississippi State baseball cap. One comfy T-shirt and a pair of running shoes later, she was out the door and headed to The Diner.

The place had a real name, though it had been forgotten long ago, not reinforced with even a fading sign. Now the place was simply The Diner.

"No church today?" she asked after giving Ashley Porter, the teenage daughter of the café's owners their order. The biggest question was who was cooking this Sunday morning. Ashley's mother and father took turns so the other could attend church. Today was Tyrone's turn to be at the restaurant and that meant melt-in-your-mouth omelets. Truly everything on the menu was good, down-home cooking, but when Ashley's mother Neddie was behind the grill, Chloe and Arlo always ordered her biscuits and gravy. When Tyrone was cooking, it was eggs all the way.

Chloe gave a sigh that Arlo couldn't interpret.

"What's wrong?"

"Nothing. I…I just want to be able to go from here directly over to the house to get Jayden. You know, not waste any time."

Chloe had just graduated from high school when she found out she was pregnant with her son. Wally, the boy's father, had skipped town, and Chloe remained living with her parents. But there came a time when she wanted to be out on her own. Yet doing that would mean shaking up

Jayden's life and taking him away from the comforts Chloe's family could afford. So she had allowed Jayden to remain living with his grandparents. It was a decision that Arlo knew she contemplated daily. Chloe couldn't move back in, but she surely couldn't ask Jayden to come live with her in her tiny cottage that had once been the servant's quarters for Lillyfield mansion.

"You going to take him to the park today?"

Chloe shot her an apologetic smile. "You up for that?"

"Me?"

Chloe didn't answer as Ashley arrived back at their table with Arlo's coffee and Chloe's hot water for tea.

"How's Courtney doing?" Arlo asked. Ashley was Courtney's best friend. The pair were rarely seen apart. They hung out together, cheered on the Blue Devils varsity squad together, even came into the bookstore together. In fact, Ashley's weekend shifts at The Diner and Courtney's afternoons at the coffee bar were some of the few times that the Sugar Springs residents didn't see the girls together.

Ashley finished pouring Chloe's water for tea and propped one hand on her hip. "I dunno. Just sad, I suppose."

"That's to be expected," Arlo said gently. She had never lost a sibling. She could only imagine how difficult that would be.

"Just give her time," Chloe added.

"I just—" She stopped as her deep brown eyes filled with tears. "Why would anyone do something like that to Haley?"

There's a lot of evil people in the world.

But she managed to keep that thought to herself. It wouldn't help Ashley one bit.

"I don't know, sweetie," Chloe replied. "I wish I had an answer for that."

"Me too." Ashley let out a mirthless laugh as she wiped the tears from her eyes. "Courtney won't talk to me. How I can help if I don't know what she needs?"

"Grief is a funny thing," Chloe said. And she would know, having just lost the love of her life a couple of months before. "Just give her time and be there when she's ready. That's all you can do."

Ashley shot Chloe a grateful smile. "Thanks. For the advice. And for listening."

Chloe returned the smile with one of her own. "Anytime."

Arlo watched Ashley walk away to return the hot water urn to the small waitress station.

"Are you up for it?" Chloe asked.

Arlo dragged her attention away from Ashley and settled it on her friend. "Up for what?"

"The park."

"Sure," she chirped, a little too brightly.

"You don't want to go."

"It's not that. I just have piles of laundry to do and a ton of house cleaning." Not to mention mulling over and over about what to do about Sam and whether or not she should tell anyone about seeing Camille out with her new beau. And how scary that beau really was. Looked. She didn't know for a fact that he was bad news. Only that he appeared to be.

Can't judge a book.

But after all that, she reminded herself that Camille believed in Joe, and she should too. Arlo just hoped that he was introduced to the book club soon. Maybe she wouldn't feel like she was sitting on a ticking time bomb if she knew the man firsthand.

"I need you." Chloe reached across the table and squeezed Arlo's hand. "He'll want to play ball, and you know how hopeless I am at that."

She certainly did. "So, you think playing with me is a good substitute for playing with you?"

"As long as I'm there…" She trailed off.

Poor Jayden. Heir to one of the largest sport equipment chains in the area and born to two very unathletic people.

"Why don't you ask Mads? Or Sam?"

"You could ask them for me." Chloe flashed her a saccharine sweet smile.

"Me?"

"They won't turn you down."

"What's that supposed to mean?"

But Chloe didn't answer as Ashley arrived at their table with their steaming plates.

"I'm gonna need—"

"Ketchup and Louisiana." Ashley pulled them from the front pocket of her shorty apron.

"You are a good girl, Ashley. I don't care what your father says about you," Arlo quipped.

Ashley's mouth fell open.

"She's kidding," Chloe hastily interjected.

"Just trying to make you smile," Arlo explained.

Ashley's eyes once again sparkled with the thick sheen of tears. "Thanks. I wish all my customers were as nice as you two."

Chloe sprinkled pepper on her omelet and hash browns

while Arlo doctored hers with all the ketchup and hot sauce she could fit on top.

"Who's being mean to you?" Arlo said.

"Yeah," Chloe added. "We'll beat 'em up for ya."

Ashley laughed. This time the sound was genuine. "I'd like to see that. It's that big woman who works out at Lillyfield. Kim…no, Pam something or another."

"I don't think I know who that is." Chloe took a bite and waited for Ashley to elaborate.

"She's new. Comes in on Mondays. I suppose that's her day off or something. Anyway, she's just…angry. I guess that's the right word. Always frowning."

"I met her when I was out there trying to pick up a book donation," Arlo piped in. She didn't mention that it also just happened to be the day Haley was killed. "She's been taking care of Mrs. Whitney since her stroke."

Ashley nodded. "I heard her tell Joey, you know, from the dry cleaners, that she was a nutritionist."

"Yeah." Chloe nodded. "That's right. She was hired right before Judith's stroke. I remember because I thought it was ironic that Judith had hired someone to help her make better, healthier choices, then she had a stroke."

"Too little too late," Arlo murmured. Wasn't that how it always went? People wanted to change, but sometimes not until it was too late to do anything about it.

Ashley frowned. "She doesn't eat like a nutritionist."

"Oh, yeah?" Arlo and Chloe shared a look.

"Gets biscuits and gravy every time she's in. Whether Mama is cooking or not."

"I heard that," Tyrone called from behind the counter. His voice was stern, but he wore a teasing grin.

Ashley shot them an apologetic smile. "Busted. I better get back to work." She glanced down at their mugs. "I'll bring you some more coffee and hot water."

"And a new tea bag," Chloe asked with a beseeching smile.

"Of course," Ashley said before spinning away.

"Now what do you mean by Mads and Sam won't turn me down?" Arlo asked.

Chloe shrugged and spent way too much time trying to get the perfect amount of egg, cheese, and mushroom onto her fork. "You weren't supposed to remember that I had said that."

"Not a chance."

"Fine," Chloe said and set down her fork. Arlo continued to eat. "I've seen how they both look at you."

Her stomach dropped, and she wasn't sure how she was going to swallow the bite she had in her mouth. "How's that?" she managed to say around the food.

"Like you're dessert."

She almost choked but managed to recover and swallow the bite in the same second. "Dessert?"

"Sam looks at you like you're the dessert he can't wait to eat, and Mads looks at you like a diabetic."

"Now I'm really not following you."

"Mads looks at you like something he wants but knows he can't have."

"Maybe you should make an appointment with Dr. Grover."

"I do not need to see the optometrist."

"I'm not so sure about that."

The conversation lulled as Ashley refilled their cups then moved to the next table.

"When have you seen these looks?" Arlo demanded.

"All the time."

"Why haven't I noticed them?"

"'There are none so blind…'" Chloe quoted.

"If I can't see them, how come you can?"

Chloe stopped, pressed her lips together, even twirled one of her springy curls around her index finger. "I noticed because…well, because I see them look at you, and I wish someone would look at me the same way."

Arlo didn't know how to respond. Instead she shoveled a large bite of omelet into her mouth and chewed as if her life depended on it. Why had she never noticed those looks, and why was Chloe telling her about them now?

8

"YOU DON'T SAY," HELEN SAID AS SHE AND ARLO BROWSED the cake baking aisle at the Piggly Wiggly the following day.

After a Sunday afternoon in the park with Jayden and Chloe, Arlo had finally managed to push Chloe's words from her mind. Sam and Mads—two ships that had already sailed. But that didn't mean they couldn't remain friends. They were adults after all.

Which was why she was helping Helen pick up the ingredients for Mads's birthday cake. Helen baked him a cake every year and had for as long as he had been back in Sugar Springs. She said it was to ensure that the police always viewed the Inn with favorable eyes, but Arlo suspected it had more to do with her and Mads than Helen was letting on.

"I think it'll be good for both of them," Arlo said. "Though I haven't had long enough with Chloe that we could talk about it." Arlo had barely arrived at the Books and More this morning when Chloe had hit her with the surprise that she was moving Jayden into her cottage at Lillyfield. It was a long time coming, but Arlo had known that it would happen eventually. Maybe not in the small little cottage, but she had known that they couldn't stay apart for long. A mom and a son needed to be together. But she hadn't had a moment to ask when and how they were going to arrange it or even what Chloe's mom and dad had to say about the matter before Helen had breezed in and taken her away to search for sprinkles for the cake.

"I think strawberry," Helen said. "Hasn't that always been Mads's favorite?"

Arlo shook her head, silently thankful that she had something else to think about, even if it was cake flavors. "Sam likes strawberry. Mads likes banana rum."

Helen's eyes lit up. "Banana rum. We could decorate it with pecans."

Arlo knew in an instant that she had lost her. Helen was a fine baker, and Mads did like his cake. It was a good combo, and Arlo wouldn't complain. She just hoped that Helen wouldn't think that baking Mads a cake for his birthday would somehow reconcile the two of them. As far as Arlo could see, it just wasn't happening. Heck, she couldn't even get past trying to discuss things with Sam.

They all three tiptoed around each other, prom night ten years ago hanging heavy between them, but none of them wanted to say anything. Arlo supposed one day they would have a reckoning; she just wasn't sure where and when that would be.

"Fern!" Helen called.

Arlo turned as Fern whirled around and placed one finger over her lips to shush them. She flattened herself toward the side of the aisle, pushing boxes of pudding mix down in the process.

"What are you doing?" Helen asked. She handed Arlo a bag of flour and a package of powdered sugar, then proceeded toward the pecans.

"She's here." Fern pushed the words softly through clenched teeth as she inclined her head toward the center aisle.

Arlo shuffled the items in her arms and waited for… whatever it was Fern thought was about to happen.

Helen sucked in a breath and opened her mouth, no doubt preparing to ask who *she* was, but before she could get out even one word, a woman pushing a cart walked past them down the center aisle.

She was tall, rivaling Helen in height and stature. She was broad and solid and, unlike Helen, not as elegant by far.

"Pam," Fern hissed.

"What's so interesting about Pam?" Helen demanded in a normal tone.

Fern cringed, then pressed one finger over her lips once more. "She's buying groceries."

Helen nodded indulgently while Arlo shifted the groceries in her arms. One hand was beginning to go to sleep.

"Did you see what was in her basket?" Fern asked.

Helen and Arlo shook their heads.

Fern motioned for them to follow, then ducked her head low before swinging out into the center aisle of the store. She almost duckwalked to the next aisle. Or maybe it was her version of a true duckwalk. After all, it would be hard to get down that low at Fern's age. But when Arlo factored in Fern's faded overalls and worn Chucks, she had to work to keep her laughter to herself.

Fern threw herself down the next aisle.

Helen and Arlo followed, but once they got there, Fern was casually studying cans of peaches. "See her over there?" Fern asked. She didn't take her eyes from the can she held in her hand. "That's her. Across the way. Looking at the paper towels."

Arlo and Helen turned to look across the aisle at the woman, the same woman they had seen at Lillyfield the day of the murder. Pam.

"Don't look!"

Helen and Arlo turned back around.

"You see what was in her basket?"

Helen harrumphed. "How can I when you keep telling me not to look?"

Fern shook her head. "You don't need to look. I'll tell you what's in there. Chips, candy, granola bars—which are not healthy at all, you know—and a cake from the bakery. And now she's headed toward the ice cream."

"That's all very interesting, Fern," Arlo said. "Elly, I need to get back to the store."

But Helen had been sucked in. "She's a nutritionist, and she's buying ice cream?"

"And not the healthy kind."

Arlo wanted to ask if there any truly healthy ice creams but managed to bite back the question. It would only prolong this trip to the store.

"You know what this means?" Fern asked. She raised her eyebrows at Helen, most likely realizing that Arlo was a lost cause.

"It means she likes junk food. It's a problem a lot of us have," Arlo said. "Elly…"

Her onetime guardian, almost-grandmother, was lost to her. "We need to find out what all she has in her basket."

Fern grinned in a mischievous, almost devious way. "I already have." She took a small notebook from the chest pocket of her bib overalls. She opened it and took the pencil from behind her ear. Today she was wearing a big straw hat in addition to her new getup.

"Just like I told you: chips, cake, granola bars," she said the last as if they were somehow the evilest of all.

"What does this mean?" Helen asked.

Fern pressed her lips together. "It means she's lying about being a nutritionist. What sort of nutritionist buys that kind of food at the grocery store?"

"The sort that lies," Helen said with a decisive dip of her chin.

"The food is not for Judith," Arlo said. "Obviously. And the woman is allowed to eat whatever she wants on her own time." But even as she said the words, they sounded strange. She was allowed to eat whatever she wanted to eat; it was America after all, but…

"And if she lied about that… " Helen mused.

"Ladies," Arlo started, not sure what she would say next, but she needed to get their attention at least. To no avail.

Fern glanced down the aisle to where Pam the so-called nutritionist was still shopping, this time studying the ice cream as anticipated. "If she lied about that," Fern repeated, "what else has she lied about?"

....

"I wonder if Sam could run a background check on her," Fern said once they were all back at the Books and More.

Chloe had gone to the school to work out the paperwork

for Jayden's move, updating all the emergency contacts and such, which left Arlo to rein in the book club alone.

"Of course Sam *can* run a background check on her," Arlo said. "But you *won't* ask him to."

"I won't?" Fern asked.

"Then I will," Helen put in.

"Neither of you will. That woman has the right to buy whatever groceries she wants to at a store. This is America, not Communist China."

"I'm pretty sure that the Chinese can buy what they want to at the grocery store," Helen said.

"My point exactly," Arlo returned. "Besides"—she nodded toward the coffee bar where a customer waited—"it's time for you to work your magic, Miss Fern."

Fern whipped off her floppy straw hat and fluffed her blue-tinted curls. Miraculously they sprung back into place. But that was the power of Teresa at Dye Me a River.

"Don't tell me Camille is out with her new man again." Arlo stumbled over the word *man*, not that he wasn't a man, but other descriptions popped to mind. None of them should be said aloud.

She mentally chastised herself for being so unfair and waited for Helen to reply.

Her guardian sadly shook her head. "I just wonder when we're going to get to meet him. Before the wedding, I hope."

"There's not going to be any wedding," Fern called from the coffee bar. Her tone was akin to a drill sergeant barking orders; then she turned back to the customer with a sweet smile and pushed his coffee across the counter to him. "There you are." Her voice had turned saccharine sweet.

Arlo started toward the book cart she had left when

Helen had come by demanding she go buy cake supplies with her. Arlo needed something to do with her hands. And something to keep her mind occupied.

"I still hope we get to meet him soon," Helen said. She made her way over to the reading nook, where Faulkner squawked from inside his cage.

"Pretty bird," he chirped. "Pretty bird."

"Yes, you are," Helen crooned in her baby talk voice.

"Let me outta here," Faulkner demanded.

Arlo shook her head and turned back to the self-help section. Too bad there weren't any books on how to deal with your geriatric book club when it got out of control. Maybe she should write one. First, she had to figure out what to do.

Fern wiped down the coffee counter as Helen let Faulkner out of his cage.

"Are you sure Auggie is upstairs?" Arlo asked.

"I don't see him down here," Helen said.

Faulkner climbed his way to the top of his cage using both feet and his beak for balance and stretched his wings as far as they would go. He flapped them a couple of times, then shook his head and turned to Helen. "Gimme a kiss, sugar."

"Sugar?" Arlo looked to her guardian. Helen leaned in with lips pursed to give the bird a kiss.

Arlo went back to shelving books.

"Do you think she doesn't want us to meet him?" Helen asked. She ran a finger down Faulkner's head, then back up, ruffling his feathers. He chirped happily, then made a sound like a purring cat.

"Why wouldn't she want us to meet him?" Fern asked. She plopped her hat back on her head and returned to the reading nook.

"I don't know," Helen said. She gave her sturdy shoulders a small shrug. "It just seems like she doesn't want us to."

"Maybe Camille is one of those people who likes to compartmentalize her life. You know, keep the book club separate from personal life and—"

Helen interrupted with a laugh. "Camille? Not Camille."

"Something is up," Fern said.

"Kind of like something was up with Pam and her groceries," Arlo put in.

"There *was* something up with that woman and her groceries." Fern's tone brooked no argument. And Arlo's comment definitely steered the conversation back to Pam and her grocery purchases.

Way to go.

"But it's more than that," Fern continued. "She was there when Haley died."

"And questioned by the police." Arlo turned back to the self-help section. At least she got them to stop talking about Camille and Joe, she thought as they started to discuss where she could have been when Haley fell. They were stuck on Pam while Arlo couldn't get her mind off Joe.

He just didn't seem to be type Camille would go for, but there they were. *Maybe he's got a good heart.* She really hoped he had a good heart.

. . . .

Sometime after lunch, the bell over the door rang.

"Where do you want these?" Mads called out, his eyes barely visible over the stack of cardboard boxes he carried.

"I don't know," Arlo said, not expecting a shipment. And even then, why would Mads be bringing it? "What is it?"

"Books from Lillyfield," Jason explained, coming in behind him with a similar stack of boxes.

"Over here." Arlo pointed to a place out of the way where she could go through them and still be available if anyone needed her help in the store.

Mads and Jason set the boxes down; then Jason jerked a thumb over one shoulder. "There are two more in the cruiser."

"I'll let you get them," Mads said.

"Gee, thanks," Jason grumbled, but trudged toward the door.

"I take it your investigation at Lillyfield is complete." At the word *investigation*, the book club immediately came to attention. If it would have made any difference, Arlo would have slapped her own hand over her mouth to keep the words from escaping.

"Do you know who killed Haley?" All the ladies were on their feet and coming toward them, but it was Helen who spoke.

"Now, ladies." Mads held up both hands as if in surrender. Like that was going to happen. "This is an official, ongoing police investigation."

"But you're letting Arlo have the books, and you wouldn't let her have them before," Fern pointed out.

Just then Jason came back into the shop carrying the remaining two boxes. He sat them with the others and stood next to his chief.

Mads turned back to Arlo. "We've checked through the books thoroughly, and there's nothing in them to assist in our investigation."

"Thank you, Chief." She resisted the urge to salute him.

And he knew it. Mads shot her a wry look in response to her cheek.

"Speaking of the investigation," Fern said. "How close are you to making an arrest in young Haley's murder case?"

Mads looked over to Jason for the answer.

The chief officer stuttered a bit, then finally found the words. "We're closing in. Yeah. Getting close now. Got a few more leads to follow up. Fingerprints. DNA. You know the stuff."

"So tomorrow?" Helen pressed. "Next week?"

Jason cleared his throat. "Soon," was all he said.

Fern geared up to ask another question, but Mads beat her to the punch. "I'll leave you to it then." He turned on his heel, but stopped at the door. "By the way," he said. "I don't know if you've heard, but Haley Adams's funeral is tomorrow."

She shook her head. Word hadn't made it that far. "What time?"

"Ten, I think," he said; then with a small wave, he and Jason left the shop.

Armed with the news that Mads had just given them, the ladies drifted back toward the reading nook discussing tomorrow's funeral.

Arlo looked at the stack of boxes that would have to be gone through. At least it would keep her mind busy for a while, but she knew it wouldn't be enough to completely distract her from investigations, fifty-year-old cold cases, and a friend who might be dating a murderer.

9

TUESDAY TURNED OUT TO BE THE PERFECT DAY FOR A funeral, if there was such a thing. The sun was shining, the sky was blue, but the tears remained bitter and salty.

Mads had finally released the body of Haley Adams so the family could bury the poor girl. Arlo was glad. She'd never had such a loss but knew that the Adams surely needed closure if they were to move on. Killer found or not.

Arlo and Chloe sat in the back row of the folding chairs covered by the tent top as Rufus Campbell, the pastor of the Free Will Baptist Church, talked about life cut short and the tragedies that those left behind had to deal with. The women of the book club flanked them. And still others milled behind, standing on the real grass instead of the turf that had been brought out for the occasion. Most of the crowd were high school students, friends with Haley or her sister, Courtney. Haley might've already graduated, but she still had a lot of buddies in town. Arlo figured the school had given the students a pass for the day to miss their classes and come to the funeral. Arlo was certain that some had come out just to skip school, but all the faces she saw wore sad expressions. But none sadder than that of Dylan Wright, Haley's longtime boyfriend.

He stood next to Courtney, Haley's sister, their hands clasped together as the pastor spoke. They stood among a group of older kids, no doubt Haley's friends from Ole Miss. The number of young people at the funeral just went to show how many lives Haley had touched and how far-reaching the grief.

Arlo and Chloe made the decision to close the store for the funeral, out of respect and so they could all attend. Now that she was there, Arlo was so glad that she had made that decision.

As far as Arlo could see, there wasn't a dry eye in the house. A few of the young people said things about Haley, but Arlo noticed that Courtney kept her seat. She didn't know if the young girl didn't like public speaking or if she was too choked up to do much more than cry.

The pallbearers presented the family with their bouton-nieres as a keepsake, and Brother Campbell said his final prayer. Announcement was made that there were cookies and punch in the fellowship hall of the church, which sat just to the north of the cemetery, but only the boys made a beeline for the refreshments. Everyone else milled around, offering their condolences to the family, placing a random rose on the grave, or even just taking the occasion to visit with those they hadn't seen in a while.

Chloe gave Arlo's arm a small tug. "I'm going over to talk to Haley and Courtney's parents."

Arlo nodded in return. "Give them my condolences as well."

Her best friend slipped away, and Arlo was left alone with the Friday night book club ladies. Thankfully now was not the time to talk to Camille about Joe, but the woman kept shooting Arlo furtive glances as if the two of them shared a secret. And she supposed they did. A big one.

"I just don't understand it," Fern said.

Camille shrugged delicately. "What's not to understand? You've been going around in overalls. Those are quite androgynous."

Helen lifted one brow. "Androgynous?"

Camille sniffed. "It's a word."

Helen shook her head. "I know it's a word. But do you really think overalls are androgynous?" Arlo just couldn't imagine they were having this conversation at this time.

"I just don't understand why girls don't want to look like girls and boys don't want to look like boys."

She shot a pointed look at the teens who remained circled around Courtney.

It was true; Arlo had never noticed it before. Or maybe it was because all of the jock/football player types had headed in for the food that was offered. When they were in the mix, it wasn't so obvious. However, now that they were gone, all that remained outside were the artistic kids that went to Sugar Springs High School. Boys and girls alike wore cardigans, various colored jeans—though none wore blue—and those flat skater shoes that seem to be so popular these days. Some of the boys had long hair, longer than some of the girls. Some of the girls had short hair, shorter than some of the boys. And almost every one of them had some sort of color mixed in somewhere.

"And not one of them wore a dress," Fern complained.

"Again…overalls," Camille said.

"Not at a funeral." Fern swept an arm down her outfit. She was back in one of her staple housedresses, navy blue with tiny little tan flowers, which matched perfectly to her tan compression stockings and tan running shoes. A floppy hat, as she had been wearing lately, was replaced with the small straw bowler type that boasted a big red poppy on one side.

Camille gave a nod of approval.

"I just don't understand their hair," Fern said, once again eyeing the group of teenagers. "There are just so many colors involved."

Camille laughed. "Your hair is blue."

Helen caught Arlo's expression and looked down at her own purple-tipped braid.

Arlo smiled and gave a small shrug.

"What we should really be concerned about is why Judith Whitney didn't come." Camille pressed her lips together, a sure sign of her disapproval.

"I don't think Judith could've made it," Helen said. "Even if she had wanted to, I can't imagine that her doctor would let her out of the house having only had a stroke a few weeks ago."

Fern shrugged. "I suppose it depends on how bad the stroke really was."

"Bad," Arlo said. "If what I'm hearing is true." And she was fairly certain that most of it was. Small towns tended to exaggerate but usually got the main details correct. And those were that Judith could neither walk nor speak. She couldn't sit up on her own or feed herself. She was completely immobile. Even if only half of that was true, Arlo couldn't imagine Judith coming to a funeral.

"Isn't that her butler?" Helen asked. She nodded toward a group of people standing close and talking amongst themselves. It was Roberts, the man with the snooty attitude who had been at the mansion the day Haley had died.

"You've been watching too much *Downton Abbey*," Arlo accused lightly. "He's not a butler, remember? He wanted to be called *house manager*."

Helen shrugged. "And there's no such thing as too much *Downton Abbey*."

"Who is that he's with?" Fern asked. She squinted and lifted the glasses that hung from a beaded chain around her neck.

Arlo glanced back over to where the butler/house manager stood with his group of co-workers. Pam stood at his side, and as far as she could tell, everyone around him worked at Lillyfield.

"That's Pam. The nurse or nutritionist or whatever they're calling her," Helen said.

"No. That other man." Camille all but pointed at the shorter man standing next to the others from Lillyfield. "He looks sort of familiar."

He did, and Arlo had to do a double take. He had a gleaming bald head that shone in the sunlight like polished marble, and he had tattoos. A lot of tattoos—over his head and neck, across the backs of his hands—though these were more colorful than the ones she had seen on Camille's Joe.

Was he the man she had seen at the mansion? The man exiting the elevator with Roberts? If he was, then that would put Joe in the clear. But she hadn't gotten a good enough look at the man to tell.

"That's Dutch," Helen said.

"You've met him?" Fern demanded. "How do you know him?"

Helen shrugged. "Chefs have to stick together."

"How come you've never mentioned this?" Fern paused, eyes narrowed. "His mama named him Dutch?"

"I'm sure it's a nickname," Arlo said. Then again...her parents and named her after a folksinger.

"He looks..." Fern started but trailed off.

Arlo was glad. He looked too much like Joe, though Fern had no idea, and Arlo wasn't sure how Camille would take the criticism. Then again, she might not have even made the connection.

"I heard he spent time in prison," Fern said.

Great.

"I didn't think you knew who he was," Helen pointed out.

"I know him by name, not by sight." Fern flipped a hand toward him and the other Lillyfield employees.

"If he spent time in prison," Fern started.

"He could be the killer." Helen finished for her.

Double great.

"Just because he's been in prison does not mean he's a killer." Arlo needed to remember those words herself. As far as she knew, Dutch, the cook from Lillyfield, had been an upstanding part of the Sugar Springs community for many years now. Well, he hadn't caused any trouble, anyway. Like the rest of the household, he mainly kept to himself.

"But they say the killer always returns to the scene of the crime," Camille said.

"This isn't the scene," Arlo pointed out, sweeping an arm toward the cemetery.

"But it's sort of like that," Fern protested.

"I think she's right," Helen said. "It's in all the shows. Someone dies, and the killer comes to the funeral, all sneaky like."

"But he's not sneaking," Arlo said. She wished she had Chloe for backup, but she was still talking with Courtney's family. "He's standing there, side by side with Pam and the not-butler." And he was looking into the grave as if he had lost his best friend.

"I don't know," Fern said in an almost singsong voice. "It seems pretty suspicious to me."

"You were just suspicious of the teenagers' hair," Arlo pointed out. But the ladies were too far gone to pay her much mind.

"As far as I'm concerned, he's our number one suspect," Fern said.

"Do you think we should tell Mads?" Helen asked.

Arlo sighed. Her guardian was usually the voice of reason, but lately she seemed to have lost her stable footing. "No, we should not tell Mads. Just because you think someone might be a killer doesn't mean you should go tell the police." She couldn't believe she even had to say the words.

Thankfully Camille nodded. "I agree with Arlo. I don't think he did it."

"But he looks so—" Fern flicked a hand in his direction, unable to come up with the words to adequately describe him. Not that they needed it.

"Looks can be deceiving," Camille said.

"She's right," Arlo said.

"And just because he attended the funeral doesn't mean

he has any sort of connection to the murder. They did work together," Camille added.

"And Haley was a real sweet girl," Helen added.

"He seems awfully attached to her." Fern didn't take her eyes off the man as she spoke. He did seem overly upset by the entire matter.

As they watched, the big, bald cook with his many colorful tattoos pulled a handkerchief from his coat pocket and dabbed his eyes. Of all of them, except for maybe the pastor, he was dressed the most appropriately for the funeral. The man had donned a black suit, white shirt, and gray tie that reflected the somber day.

"Maybe they were friends." But even to her own ears it sounded strange.

Why would the two of them have been friends? It didn't appear that they had anything at all in common; the man was old enough to be her father. Or maybe the question was why wouldn't they have been friends? They worked in the same household. Haley's father was a good man, but perhaps Dutch offered less biased advice to the young med student.

The questions and reasons jumbled around in Arlo's head until they were as tangled as a ball of yarn after a cat attack.

Did Dutch have anything to do with Haley's murder? That was the real question.

. . . .

"When is the big move?" Fern asked a little later that same afternoon.

Arlo returned to the bookstore immediately after the funeral, still wearing her slim black pencil skirt and sleek kitten heels. That morning she had donned a white button-down with crisp darts in the front. The ensemble broke her three major rules for work—uncomfortable shoes, skirt, and white. White anything in a bookstore that handled used books as well as new was a big no-no. As far as she was concerned anyhow. Nothing stayed white there long. Uncomfortable shoes went without saying, though more often than not she found herself in love with a pair that was inappropriate for work, and she bought them and wore them regardless. A shortish skirt was a disaster waiting to happen with all the ladders in the place.

But she hadn't taken the time to go home and change. Chloe had stayed with Haley's family a little longer, with Fern promising to look after the coffee bar. Arlo wasn't sure how much traffic she would get after such a solemn occasion, but she couldn't sell any books—or coffee—if she wasn't open.

"Jayden, you mean?" Arlo asked. That was the only move she could remember as looming on the horizon, Jayden moving into the little cottage with Chloe.

"That's the one," Fern said. Of the Friday night book club, Fern was the only one to return to the Books and More with Arlo. But since no one was stopping in for a drink, she was—under the guise of "helping out"—currently rummaging through one of the donation boxes Arlo had gotten from the mansion.

"The one what?" The male voice spoke from behind her.

Arlo whirled around one hand on her chest. "Seriously, Sam. If you don't stop sneaking up on me, I'm gonna put a bell on you."

He chuckled, that warm sound that sent tingles through her. Or maybe it was just nostalgia? "I make plenty of noise."

"Uh-huh." But Arlo knew her message got across. He was way too good at sneaking up on her.

"And I repeat," he said. "The one what?"

For the life of her, Arlo couldn't remember what they had been talking about before Sam came in.

"When Jayden is moving in with Chloe," Fern prompted.

"Oh." Arlo hoped her cheeks weren't as red as they felt they had to be, considering the heat filling her face. "Saturday evening after we close. You want to loan us your truck?"

"I'm sure I can help." There went that Sam smile. "Are you sure you can get it all done if you're starting so late?"

"We have to," Arlo said. "We can't both take off on a Saturday. And I don't want to leave her to do it alone."

"We should hire someone else," Fern said. "In addition to Courtney."

Arlo smiled at her use of the word *we*. "I thought I'd hired you."

Fern chuckled. "Will work for coffee."

"I have a nephew who's looking for a job," Sam said. "He's coming home from school." He stopped and shook his head. "Some people just aren't cut out for college, I guess. He's really smart but…he's a hard worker. If you decide you need someone."

Arlo nodded. "We might could use a little muscle around here. Have him come in and fill out an application."

Sam smiled. "I will."

"What do we get to do in the meantime?" Fern asked. She had taken one of the books from the box and was turning it this way and that as she studied it.

Again with the *we*.

"Make do like always," Arlo said. "Where is everybody?"

"Camille is out with her guy again." Fern frowned and set the book to one side.

"Helen?" Arlo prompted.

"She had to go back to the store. She needed some more pecans for Mads's cake. Though secretly I think she's just trying to butter him up to get him to reopen the Mary Kennedy case," Fern said.

Arlo shrugged. "Maybe." It did sound like something Helen would do.

"That's right," Sam said, his tone musing. "His birthday is coming up."

"I'm surprised you remember that," Arlo said.

"I remember a lot of things," Sam said. His gaze snagged hers, and a moment passed between them. A moment of secrets. Neither one was willing to talk about what happened between them all those years before, just as neither was going to bring up what they knew about Camille's guy. At least not yet anyway. Sam hadn't come to her with any news about Joe Foster. She could only believe that he didn't have anything new to share. Or was there something more in that look…?

"What was that?" Fern asked. "What was that look?"

Sam stopped. "What look?" He gave a small chuckle to reinforce his words.

Arlo did her best to turn her legs from noodles back into real legs. "I was just thinking about Jason," Arlo said. "How he's handling the investigation into Haley's death."

"You mean Haley's murder," Fern said emphatically.

She just had to bring it up. "Fern." She didn't need to say

much else. And she probably wouldn't since it would do no good. But Arlo really wanted the girls to stay out of police business. It had been a whole different matter when Chloe had been pinpointed for murder one.

"I know, I know," Fern waved one hand and then settled down into her chair. She had pulled the box of donations over to the reading nook so she could sit while she pilfered through it.

"Send your nephew in," Arlo said to Sam. "We can't have him trained by Saturday, but if we like him, we can get him started as early as next week."

"He comes home on Friday. My sister's already gone up to help him move his stuff."

"Where was he?" Arlo asked.

"Auburn," Sam answered.

"Tough school," Fern said without looking up from the pages of the book in her lap.

"I think he just bit off more than he could chew. His dad wanted him to be a veterinarian, Lord, knows why. He's more…artistic than that. I think you'll like him. And he loves to read."

"Sounds like my kind of guy." Arlo smiled and caught Sam's gaze once again. There was a time when he was her kind of guy. What she couldn't figure out if he still was. Or if he ever would be again.

"Arlo." Fern slowly rose, the box of books still nestled between her feet. "Arlo. Arlo. Arlo!" Her voice raised in excitement or surprise, Arlo couldn't tell which. "I have it! Right here! Right in my very hands! Weston Whitney's diary!"

10

"YOU FOUND ONE OF THE JOURNALS?" HELEN ASKED AS she entered the bookstore less than half an hour later. Camille was hot on her heels.

"Three of them," Fern held them up triumphantly.

"And they were in the donation boxes?" Camille asked. She plopped down next to Fern on the couch and reached for one of the tomes Fern held.

"Like they were meant for us to find," Fern confirmed.

Arlo was vacillating between keeping the books—after all they had been donated to her store—and returning them to the mansion. So far, she was leaning toward returning them to Judith Whitney, but what harm was there in letting the book club read them before she did that? It would give them something to do that truly would make them feel like they were participating in discovering the truth about Mary Kennedy, and it kept them away from Lillyfield and the real murder investigation.

Not to mention the peace it brought as the ladies buried themselves between the pages, barely looking up to acknowledge Chloe as she brought them a tray of coffee and placed it on the coffee table between them.

"I've got it!" Fern snapped her book shut and jumped to her feet.

"Got what?" Helen and Camille demanded.

So much for the peace. It had lasted a good half hour or so.

"Wilson's Jewelry," Fern replied as if that answered it all.

Helen rolled one hand in the air, urging Fern to continue.

"Listen to this." Fern opened her journal and began to read. "*It's quite a shame really, but I see no way around it. Mary has to be stopped one way or the other, and this seems the best by far. I'll report the necklace stolen. Even if she finds it and tries to return it to the police, she'll look as guilty as sin. And the problem will be solved.*"

"That sounds like Weston planted the necklace on Mary hoping to have her arrested for its theft." Helen said, and Camille agreed with a nod.

"Yet the necklace was never found," Camille added.

"Henry Wilson would have sold Weston the necklace," Fern continued. "He sold them all their jewelry. Even the one that Mary Kennedy was accused of stealing."

"It's possible," Camille said.

Wilsons' was the only jewelry store in Sugar Springs at that time.

"If it's as valuable as rumored, Weston would have had to order it special. Maybe Henry remembers more about that time. Maybe he has clues that no one had ever asked him about."

It was as far-fetched of an idea as finding the man who sold Mary the car she had been driving, but Helen and

Camille were on their feet before Arlo could say so. Maybe that was a good thing, or they would chase down the car salesman next.

"Let's go." Helen grabbed her purse.

Camille looped her own handbag over one arm, and the three of them started for the door.

They stopped before they got there.

"Are you coming?" Fern asked.

Arlo shook her head. "I've got plenty to do here." It was the truth. Plus, she didn't want to go marching down Main Street to question an innocent man about a necklace he sold a man fifty years ago. Surely the ladies couldn't get into trouble talking to Henry Wilson...

Camille shrugged. "Suit yourself."

After the ladies had left the store, Arlo felt as if a great weight had been lifted from her shoulders. She wasn't sure when it had happened, but somehow she had become protector of Sugar Springs. Or maybe it was protector of three little old ladies who had more gumption than sense. Either way, the responsibility was crushing.

"Hey, Arlo." Sam approached from the third-floor doorway. "Can I talk to you about something?" His voice sounded serious, as in deadly serious, and serious was not a normal setting for Sam.

"Of course." Arlo nodded, that pressure hovering now around her neck. She rolled her shoulders and headed toward the staircase that led to his office.

The phone started to ring.

Arlo shot Sam an apologetic look, then held up one finger as if to say, *Gimme a sec, please.* She backtracked to the end of the coffee bar where the cordless base was stationed.

"Books and More. Can I help you?"

"Get down here now!" Helen screeched. Helen. Who had left less than five minutes ago.

Anxiety seared through Arlo. She waved Sam away and started for the front door. Something was wrong. Terribly wrong.

"To the jewelry store?"

"The police station. You are not going to believe this." Then Helen was gone.

"Something's happened," Arlo said breathlessly. "Chloe!"

Chloe stepped out from the stockroom carrying a sleeve of to-go cups. "What's wrong?"

"I gotta go," Arlo said. "I'll explain later."

"Be careful," Chloe called behind her.

Arlo sent her friend a thankful look, then headed outside, only vaguely aware that Sam followed her.

She rushed toward the police station, which sat off the main road between the bookstore and the jewelry store, just down the street. The ladies would have had to walk right past it to go talk to Henry Wilson while he was at work. She supposed Henry was at work. He was a hundred if he was a day, but his family couldn't stop him from putting on a suit and coming to work every day. Of course, he sat in a chair behind the counter and slept mostly, but it was his store and who was going to say anything?

A bit of relief flowed through Arlo when she spotted the ladies up ahead. They were all on their feet, but they were pressed against the side of the building behind them. From where they were, Arlo suspected they could see the station, but from their positions they didn't want someone to see them.

Helen looked over and saw Arlo. She waved for her to hurry, then turned her attention to the street before her.

Arlo hurried even though the ladies appeared to be fine. From where Arlo was, she couldn't see any blood, so that was a good sign.

"What is it?" she asked when she was close enough that she didn't have to yell.

"Courtney," Helen said.

"And Dylan," Fern added.

"Dylan Wright?" Arlo asked. "Haley's boyfriend?"

"One and the same." Camille nodded.

She stumbled a bit, and Sam caught up with her. They exchanged a look.

"Hurry," Helen called. "You're going to miss it."

"Miss what?" Arlo asked.

"I don't know, but hurry."

Arlo was breathless when she reached the edge of the dry cleaners. It faced Main but sat in front of the police station, which was situated down Fourth.

"Look! Look! Look!" Helen pointed to a spot down the street. On the far side of the police station, Dylan and Courtney stood embroiled in what looked like a serious conversation.

Dylan appeared to be trying to go into the police station, and Courtney was doing her best to stop him. He would shake off her grasp and take two steps away before she grabbed him again and pulled him in the opposite direction. He would shake her off once more, and the entire sequence would repeat.

"What are they doing?" Camille asked.

"It looks like he's trying to go in, and Courtney doesn't want him to."

"I can see that," Camille grumbled.

"Then why did you ask?" Fern demanded.

"I suppose I mean why," Camille returned. "Why are they doing this?"

Fern shrugged. "Your guess is as good as mine."

"Let's go find out." Helen pushed off the brick and started toward the couple. They were so locked into their own world that they didn't see Helen or the other ladies heading their way.

Arlo looked to Sam, who shrugged.

With a sigh, she started after them, Sam once again trailing behind.

Dylan finally broke free and darted into the police station. Courtney stood outside for a moment, sobs wracking her thin shoulders before she turned and ran in the opposite direction.

"Courtney," Helen called, but the girl didn't turn around. She either didn't hear or didn't want to talk.

"Should I go after her?" Sam asked.

"I think so, yes," Arlo said.

Sam nodded and started after Courtney while Arlo begrudgingly followed the ladies, who had quietly ducked into the police station.

It wasn't hard to find Dylan. He was standing in front of Frances's desk, his arms out in front of him like a B-movie zombie, hands slack at the wrists. His nose looked red and his eyes puffy as if he had been crying.

Frances and Mads both stood behind her desk watching Dylan as if he were a magician about to pull off the trick of the century.

"I did it," he said just as Arlo, Helen, Fern, and Camille stopped behind him. "Lock me up. I killed Haley."

11

THERE WAS A MOMENT OF SILENCE, BARELY A BREATH, before everything erupted around them. Camille, Fern, and Helen all started talking at once.

You cannot be serious!

Dylan Andrew, I know your father! What's he going to say about this?

Mads Keller, please tell me you are not going to arrest this child!

And on and on again.

Sam came in behind her. Arlo could only watch in disbelief as Mads circled around the desk and grabbed Dylan by the elbow.

"Don't you want to put cuffs on me?" he murmured as Mads led him toward the holding cells at the back of the station.

"Are you going to make a break for it?" Mads asked. Arlo could barely hear him over the protests of the book club.

Dylan's response was lost as they disappeared from view.

"Ladies," Sam started, but no one was listening. "Ladies... *Ladies!*"

The book club's chatter died away, and all attention was turned to the private eye.

"Weren't you on your way to the jewelry store?" he asked.

Fern sniffed. "Yes," she admitted.

"Perhaps we should just head back to the bookstore," Arlo suggested.

The chatter immediately rose to a deafening level.

We can't leave now.

That poor child is in jail.

You know Dylan. He could never do such a thing. He loved Haley. He would never hurt her.

And on and on once more.

"Mads and Frances have a great deal of work to do now," Sam reminded them. "I think we should give them time to get that work done. I'm sure there will be an opportunity for questions later." Sam shot Frances a questioning look.

The receptionist/dispatch/softball player shrugged, then nodded.

Then to Arlo's relief and dismay, the book club filed relatively quietly from the police station.

There were still a few grumbles about that poor boy, but for the most part it was a smooth transition.

And Arlo wasn't about to admit that she was jealous that Sam could get them to do practically anything while her instructions fell on deaf ears. The point was Mads was left in peace while he tried to get to the bottom of Dylan's confession.

Conversation was sparse and sporadic as they made their way back to the Books and More.

Chloe met them at the door. "What happened?"

Everyone started talking at once, until Sam spoke up and the women fell silent once more.

"Dylan Wright turned himself into the police."

"What?" Chloe's disbelief was palpable. "Why would he do something like that?"

"One would presume it was because he was guilty," Arlo started.

A round of protests went up from the book club.

"I know, I know," Arlo said in hopes of quieting their words.

"Dylan cannot be guilty." Chloe shook her head. "Can. Not. Be."

"He confessed." Sam pressed his lips together.

"I don't care," Chloe said. "I don't believe it."

A murmur of agreement went up from the book club, and Arlo had to join in. Dylan would have been the last person she would have suspected, and she didn't believe his confession for a minute. Add in Courtney's strange behavior before he entered the police station, and it seemed they had another mystery on their hands.

"I don't either," Sam said.

Which was saying something. Sam didn't know Dylan the way the rest of them did. Sam had been gone for years, only coming back sporadically to visit with his mother. He hadn't watched Dylan grow up, play little league or high school football for the Sugar Springs Blue Devils. He hadn't watched him fall in love with Haley Adams and then go away to school to be a doctor just like his father. And yet Sam could still see the problems with the confession.

"What can we do?" Camille asked.

"Nothing." Sam sighed.

Fern scoffed. "There has to be something."

Sam nodded. "Okay, how about we trust Mads to do his job? If we can see that Dylan is innocent, then he should be able to as well. Give Mads space to work and pray for the best."

Helen nodded and looked around at the rest of the book club members. She kept on until they were all nodding. "Yes," she said. "That is something we can do."

But Arlo had a feeling it wasn't going to stop there.

....

Arlo stared at the computer spreadsheet and tried to get it to make sense, but she couldn't concentrate on the numbers. They all seemed to blur together until they looked like hieroglyphics swimming around the screen. Her concentration was shot. No big wonder, what with all they had going on. Haley dead, Dylan in jail, Courtney on leave for who knew how long. It was frustrating at best, this feeling of helplessness.

She turned off her computer and sat back in her seat. Accounting was her least favorite part of owning her own business. Once they got up and really running, she was hiring a bookkeeper for the job. There was a firm at the end of the block that would suit her just fine. She just had to be able to afford it first. Until then, it was all up to her. But not today.

She sighed, pushed back from her desk. This was getting her nowhere fast. She exited her office and headed for the door that led to Sam's. All eyes turned to her. Well, those belonging to Fern, Helen, and Chloe did. Sometime during the afternoon, Camille had gone off, most likely to be with Joe.

"I thought you were working on the books." Helen said. She had one of Weston Whitney's journals in her lap and her copy of *Missing Girl* within arm's reach. Arlo figured she was comparing the two, for whatever it was worth.

"I'm finished now."

"That was quick," Fern said. She shot Arlo a pointed look. She also held one of the Whitney journals, though her copy had already grown a few sticky notes and slips to mark passages. Lord only knew what she was finding in there. Arlo was afraid to ask.

"Real quick," Helen agreed.

Arlo knew what they wanted. They wanted her to confess to being distracted. But she wasn't about to. She wouldn't confess to being distracted by the case or by Sam.

Arlo turned to Chloe. "I'll be upstairs if you need me."

She ignored the gasps of mock surprise as she headed for the third-floor doorway.

Let them think what they want.

She was a grown woman, and she could go upstairs and talk to her tenant if she wanted to. And it had nothing to do with prom night or high school or Mads or anything. This was about Camille. And keeping her friend safe.

Arlo rapped on the door frame. "Knock, knock."

Sam whirled around from his place in his L-shaped desk. Surprise clearly registered on his face. "Hey!" He seemed pleased. That was a good sign, right? Didn't matter. She wasn't here for signs.

"You wanted to talk to me?" she asked.

He seemed a bit stumped. "Me? No. It was nothing." But it hadn't sounded like nothing. Or maybe she was reading too much into it. "What's on your mind?"

"I was just thinking about Camille." She inched her way into the room. "Have you found out anything more about Joe Foster?"

"Sadly, no. It's like he just suddenly appeared."

Arlo crossed her arms and thought about that a moment. "Like he didn't exist before six months ago."

"Exactly." Sam closed the middle notebook on his desk and turned to the one on his left. He typed in a few things, then motioned Arlo to come over. "I have this." He showed her a receipt for an apartment in Corinth. "I checked with the manager there," Sam said. "He told me that Joe moved down from Memphis. He had all the paperwork and stuff he needed with his name on it—a light bill, that sort of thing. But this is the first time I can find Joe Foster."

"Is Joe Foster an alias?"

"Good question," Sam said.

"And the answer is…?"

"Most likely."

"Why would he need an alias?"

He leaned back in his chair and turned to face her once more. "Could be a lot of reasons."

"But no one would have an alias unless they were trying to hide something." When authors chose a pen name, a lot of times they were trying to hide their true identity. Especially when erotica became such a big genre. No one wanted to know that the middle school English teacher was writing such hot and sexy scenes after going home from teaching their children. But she didn't think Joe was an author—of erotica or anything else. She was all for not judging the book, but some things were simply obvious.

"The real question is what's he trying to hide."

"Arlo!" Helen must've been standing at the foot of the stairs as she called up to her.

Arlo sighed. "I'm being summoned."

"It appears that way."

Even up two flights of stairs, she could hear Faulkner in the background. "Arlo! Arlo! The butler did it. He did it."

"Arlo!" Helen called again. "Come down here, please."

"I gotta go," Arlo said. "But if you find out anything—"

"You'll be the first to know."

Arlo gave Sam a small wave, which he returned as she headed back down the stairs. "What is so important?" she asked. Helen was waiting by the door while Fern gathered her things.

"We have to do something," Helen said. She pulled herself up to her full, impressive height and waited for Arlo to challenge her.

"I know Camille isn't here, but my suggestion would be talk about the book." *Any book for that matter.*

Fern stopped shoving books into her canvas bag and shot Arlo a nasty look.

"We were thinking more along the lines of going down to the police station and talking to Mads about Dylan." Helen folded her arms in front of her and waited for Arlo to protest.

She hated to be that predictable but… "Absolutely not!" She did her best to make her voice as calm as possible and even keep it at an acceptable volume for indoors. She failed miserably. "It's been two hours since Dylan confessed."

"My point exactly. Two hours! Who knows what that poor child has gone through while we've been languishing here talking about made-up mysteries and eating scones?" Helen admonished.

"Elly—" Arlo stopped, unable to find the right words to keep Helen and Fern from marching down to the police station and disrupting everyone's job there.

"We could ask him about Mary Kennedy while we're there." Fern gave a decisive nod. "I think I might have found something in one of the diaries."

"Or you could wait until tomorrow. Give him time to do his job properly before crashing his day."

"Tomorrow is Mads's birthday," Fern reminded them.

"That's it." Helen snapped her fingers. "I'll go home and get his cake. Then we can give it to him today."

"And ask about both murders while we're there," Fern said.

"But his birthday isn't until tomorrow," Arlo protested.

Helen stood and shook her head. "I don't know any man who would complain about getting his birthday cake early."

And for that, Arlo had no comeback.

"Call Camille," Helen told Fern. "We're going to need her back for this too."

. . . .

So that's how Arlo found herself singing "Happy Birthday" to Mads less than half an hour later and one day early.

"You look like a monkey. And you smell like one too," the ladies sang.

Arlo stopped singing halfway through the song. She couldn't confess a love for him—*happy birthday, we love you*—and she wasn't about to say he looked like a monkey. It didn't matter. No one noticed that she had stopped.

"Thank you," Mads said. "My birthday's not until tomorrow. But I do appreciate it."

"Better early than late," Helen said. "Am I right?"

Mads chuckled. "I suppose so."

"Do you have the plates?" Arlo asked.

She knew full well that Fern had the plates and napkins, and Camille had the plastic forks. Even worse, Helen had found some of those pointy birthday hats and insisted they all wear them. Or maybe the worst part was that they were pink and lavender with rainbows and big-eyed horses. And she had even bought party noisemakers to match. But Arlo hadn't protested. Her main objective was to move this party along as quickly as possible.

"Let's cut the cake," Helen said.

They cleaned off a spot on Frances's desk and stacked napkins, plates, and forks alongside the banana rum cake.

"It looks delicious." Mads said. "Is it banana rum?"

"Of course it is. Isn't that your favorite?" Helen said.

"I can't believe you remembered that," Mads said. "It's been a long time since I had your banana rum cake."

Arlo wasn't about to throw her guardian under the bus, but the thought did cross her mind. Arlo herself was the one who remembered Mads's favorite type of cake. But it really didn't matter. And she surely didn't want to draw any more attention to herself than absolutely necessary. Standing in the police station eating cake off Power Rangers plates while wearing a hat with a pink pony on it was bad enough.

"There's something I've been wanting to ask you," Fern started once everyone had a piece. There weren't enough chairs in the lobby, so they were all standing around Frances's desk, each holding a cake plate in one hand and a fork in the other.

Arlo had to admit the cake was delicious. She didn't mind the inconvenience of standing and eating it. Calories don't count when you eat them standing up.

"We need to take Chloe back a piece of this if you don't care, Mads." Arlo said.

"Not at all," Mads grinned. "If I have cake at my house, I'll just eat it. I don't think I can stand the pounds."

Far as Arlo was concerned, he looked the same as he did when he left the NFL. She couldn't say high school. He had beefed up a lot playing pro football. But he was still as trim as ever. Or maybe it was the lack of cake that kept him that way.

"I said"—Fern drawled out each word and spoke loudly so that everyone had to hear her—"there's something I've been wanting to ask you."

"Yes?" Mads was plowing through his cake like a starving man, and Arlo wondered if he was really enjoying it that much or if he was trying to get them out of his office as quickly as possible.

"Do you think Haley's murder has anything to do with Mary Kennedy's disappearance?" Fern asked.

The room fell silent.

Mads stopped, seeming to contemplate the idea for longer than Arlo gave it credit for. "No."

"But I heard that Mary Kennedy's husband has recently been released from prison. What if he came back to finish his work at Lillyfield?"

Arlo gasped. "Where did you hear such a thing?"

"That's what I'd like to know," Mads muttered.

"It doesn't matter where it came from," Fern protested.

"I beg to differ." Mads placed his plastic fork on the edge of his plate and set it on Frances's desk. There was still half a piece of cake left, and Arlo suspected that he had been put off his celebration by Fern's meddling.

"Not if it's true," Helen added.

Mads gave the ladies a tight smile. The stern frown he saved for her. "We are in the middle of a police investigation. I can't comment right now."

"You've reopened the Mary Kennedy case?" Helen asked.

"No."

"Then the two cases aren't related."

Mads pinched the bridge of his nose with a sigh. "I didn't say that either."

"What are you saying then?" Helen pressed.

"I'm saying thank you very much for the cake and the birthday wishes—early birthday wishes—but I have a young man in jail and a murder to solve." He nodded toward Arlo as if she and she alone was responsible for removing the ladies from the police station. As if.

"Does that mean you don't think he did it?" Camille asked.

"He confessed," Mads returned.

"I watched a show about people who confess to crimes they didn't commit and are serving time in prison now and trying to get out." Helen nodded her head and looked around to see if anyone else had seen the show. No one nodded. Not even Arlo, who had sat next to Helen when she was watching it. Still, she agreed. There had to be something up with Dylan's confession. He just didn't seem the type. But wasn't that the way it was? The type of person that you thought would commit a murder wasn't the one who did?

And that should leave Joe in the clear for anything, if the type that didn't did and the type that would didn't. Or something like that.

"I can't discuss the particulars of the case. That's all I can share right now." Practiced words from a press conference, she was sure.

"Have you talked to Haley's family?" Camille asked.

"Now what do you think, Miss Camille?" Mads's voice was gentle and somewhat chiding, but still held a thread of steel. He wasn't backing down from his stance.

"Poor Courtney," Fern said. "She and Dylan used to come in the bookstore together. I think they were really good friends. She's probably beside herself thinking he killed her sister."

Arlo had to agree. Courtney and Dylan were good friends and shared books and time there in her store. Sometimes with Haley, sometimes not. It was bad enough to have a sister killed in such a way, but to have her killed by a person that you cared about seemed more than anyone should have to bear.

"All I can say is that he confessed." Mads picked up his plate once again as if the matter was settled.

"Which means as far as you're concerned, the investigation is over." Fern nodded.

"For the most part," he said around a bite of banana rum delight. "But we still have to gather any evidence we have for the DA's office."

"It could be that you'll find evidence against his

confession," Helen hedged in a tone that was part question, part statement. Or maybe that was just hope shining through.

"Anything is possible, I suppose," Mads said.

"I suppose you're right," Helen returned.

"But if you're not investigating Haley's murder as thoroughly as before, you should have ample time for Mary Kennedy," Camille added.

Mads sighed, and Arlo knew he wished he had told them he had tons more investigating to do. But it was out now, and the ladies wanted to find who killed the piano teacher. Whether Mads helped them or not, Arlo was sure they would do it.

"I'm sorry." The timid voice came from the doorway of the police station. Courtney Adams stood there looking as if she was about to dart away like a scared rabbit at any moment. Arlo supposed they did all look a little odd, in their party hats and eating birthday cake.

But this was more of a frightened look than a perplexed one. "I'll come back." She started to turn to leave, but Mads stopped her.

He set his plate on Frances's desk once again and made his way around it, toward the young girl. "Can I help you?"

Courtney stopped. She looked at the book club ladies and Arlo all in their silly pointed hats. Fern even had cake suspended on her fork halfway between her plate and her mouth. Courtney had something she wanted to say, that much was apparent, but it seemed as if she didn't want any of them to hear. Then she closed her eyes, took a deep breath, and opened them again. "You need to let Dylan go. He's innocent." Tears started to well in her eyes.

Arlo couldn't imagine the pain it was causing her to stand there and plead for him.

Mads sighed. "I don't really think he's guilty," he said. "But do you know what this town would do if I let a confessed murderer loose?"

Courtney dashed away her tears. "Surely you could—"

He shook his head, effectively cutting short whatever she had been about to say. "I can't let him go until I have the real murderer."

"I understand." Courtney nodded, then turned and fled from the station.

12

"ARE YOU SURE YOU'RE UP FOR THIS?" CHLOE ASKED Courtney the next day.

Arlo stood next to the coffee counter and watched the young girl. She didn't seem quite ready, but she had assured both Arlo and Chloe that she could return. And after yesterday's show at the police station, Arlo couldn't help but wonder if Courtney knew something that the rest of them didn't.

"I can do this." Courtney nodded and swallowed hard.

"If you're certain," Arlo asked. Sort of. It was mostly a question.

Courtney tried on a smile. "I'm just ready for everything to return to normal."

Aren't we all?

But what Arlo would really like was for the book club to return to normal. Or become normal. They couldn't exactly *return* to a place they had never been.

As usual, they had gathered at noon with their picnic lunch and some sort of history of Sugar Springs book that looked like it came from a fairytale. It was huge, leather bound, gold embossed, and Arlo had no idea where Camille had found it. She wasn't sure she wanted to ask either. Some things were better left a mystery. And keeping to herself might just keep her out of the witness stand one day.

Chloe came around the counter and stopped next to Arlo. She glanced back at Courtney, who was wiping down the espresso machine. Tears had started to leak from her eyes. She wasn't sobbing, just crying silent tears.

"I'm not so sure about this." Chloe lowered her voice so only Arlo could hear.

"We need to keep an eye on her."

Chloe gave a quick nod, her blond curls bouncing. "Of course, but I don't feel right leaving. I think I'll go to the back and check inventory. It may only take an hour or so, but that might be an hour we can use to gauge how she's going to do."

"Aye, aye, Captain." Arlo gave Chloe a small salute.

Her best friend smiled in return and headed for the storeroom.

Arlo looked back to Courtney. She hadn't stopped working, hadn't stopped wiping down the espresso machine and cleaning all the little pieces, and she hadn't stopped crying. Arlo glanced toward the book club and caught Helen's gaze. She knew the look on her guardian's face well. *Poor darling.*

Fern looked from Helen to Arlo, then over to Courtney. Before anyone could say anything at all, the woman was on her feet and marching toward the coffee bar.

"Courtney, dear," Fern started when she stopped at the bar's straight edge. "I'm not quite sure you're ready to come back to work."

Arlo was not exactly surprised by the caring tone of Fern's voice; she knew Fern had it in her. It just wasn't often people got to see the kindness firsthand.

"I'm okay," Courtney said. "Really."

Fern shook her head. "I don't mind working," she parried, still using that same gentle voice. "After all, I learned to make the coffee drinks for this very reason."

"I heard it was so you could get free coffee," Courtney said. The words almost came across as a joke, and maybe they would have, had her face not been shiny with tears.

"Well, yeah. Coffee and times just like this when somebody needs to leave for something important."

Whether it was the tone of Fern's voice or the fact that one of the town's grumpiest residents was being so kind to her, the week seemed to catch up to Courtney all at once. Her face crumpled, and her tears fell with a force. Her breath caught on a sob, and her knees buckled. Fern was behind the counter in a shot, supporting the girl with one arm across her shoulders as she urged her toward the barstools on the other side of the counter.

"What happened?" Chloe was at the door of the stockroom, somehow having heard Courtney's breakdown.

"I'm okay," Courtney said. Her voice sounded anything but. "I'm fine, really." Only someone with a heart of ice would've believed what she was saying. She could barely speak, she was crying so, and she couldn't seem to catch her breath.

Arlo moved toward her, laying a hand on her back and rubbing reassuringly. "It's okay if you need to go home, Courtney. In fact, I think I must insist that you do."

"I said I would come in."

"You can change your mind," Arlo said.

Courtney grabbed a napkin off the stack on the counter and wiped at her face. It was a futile effort, seeing as how the minute the tears were gone, they were replaced with others. She grabbed another napkin and blew her nose, then laid her head down on her folded arms. Sobs shook her shoulders, and she was saying something, though no one could figure out what it was. Arlo looked around the group, but everyone shook their heads. Arlo smoothed a hand down the back of Courtney's soft blonde hair.

"Let me call your mom," Arlo said.

Courtney wailed something that sounded a lot like no but didn't bother to lift her head.

"I can run you home," Chloe said.

Courtney finally lifted her head. "No," she said. "I'm fine." No one dared contradict her declaration, though Arlo suspected Fern had wanted to. Thankfully the lady kept her tongue and allowed Courtney her time.

"It's just… It's just everyone talks about him like he's really guilty," Courtney said. "But I know better. I know he didn't do it. Dylan didn't kill my sister."

Helen caught Arlo's gaze over the top of Courtney's head. Her guardian raised her eyebrows in question, though said nothing. It was the same thing she had been telling Mads the day before.

"You seem so certain, love," Camille crooned. She rubbed one of Courtney's arms through the sleeve of her blouse. "How can you be so sure?"

"I just am." Courtney's whole demeanor had changed as Camille had asked the question.

What made her so certain that Dylan Wright was

innocent? Arlo had no idea, but she could tell that Courtney believed what she was saying. Whether or not it was true was another story altogether.

"There has to be some reason," Fern prodded.

"He's innocent," Courtney said. Her voice had started to rise in tone and a few people peeked out from between the bookshelves see what was going on.

Arlo shook her head and motioned for everybody to go back to what they were doing, but she didn't say anything to alert Courtney to everyone's interest.

"Well, I think it's marvelous that you have such faith in him," Camille started. "Especially with all the witness statements coming in saying otherwise."

Arlo started to ask Camille what she knew about witness statements, then remembered that the woman was a retired high school English teacher. And a master manipulator. She was trying to get Courtney to reveal what she knew through the art of complementary persuasion.

Courtney seemed to think about what Camille said for a moment, and she blew her nose again and turned to Arlo. "You're right," she said.

It wasn't often a woman was told that. "I'm right?"

"Yes." Courtney slid from the barstool and started untying the back of her apron. "You're right. It was too early for me to come back."

"Take all the time you need," Chloe said.

Though Arlo wondered how they would get through. Fern's coffee could launch rockets into space. Arlo wasn't sure how much longer the good people of Sugar Springs would have to be subjected to the black sludge that she herself made and called coffee.

"Thank you," Courtney said. Instead of hanging her apron on the hook just inside the door next to the coffee bar, she wadded it up and set it on the counter. "Maybe next week," she said, and she started for the door. She paused there before actually leaving. "Dylan's paying penance for... well, he says he's got to pay for his sins. But he didn't kill Haley. That much I know for a fact."

Arlo, Chloe, and the book club ladies watched her head out into the warm Mississippi sunshine. Though the day looked cheery and bright, she knew that Courtney was dying inside. But hopefully some of the beautifulness of the day would rub off on her and lift her spirits. Just a bit would be nice; any part of it would be good.

"Poor dear," Camille said.

"Poor dear's right," Fern said.

The ladies made their way back to the reading nook.

"Gimme a kiss," Faulkner chirped.

Helen obliged him, bending close to the cage and pursing her lips so he could nip them as was their usual custom. Arlo had grown tired of warning her guardian against the action. She supposed if Helen wanted to kiss the bird, who was she to stop her?

"She just seems so positive that Dylan can't be the one," Fern said.

"I never taught him," Camille said, albeit a little unnecessarily. She hadn't taught in years. "But I did teach his father. He was a right nice fellow."

Arlo supposed "right nice fellow" was as good a description as any for Dr. Robert Wright, Dylan's father. He kept half the citizens of Sugar Springs in good health, doing everything from delivering babies to giving flu shots. Everyone had been hopeful that Dylan would take his place whenever Dr. Robert decided to retire. Of course, Dylan couldn't do that if he was behind bars for killing his girlfriend. But still Arlo agreed. She was with everyone else who seemed more than skeptical that Dylan Wright was guilty of killing Haley Adams. It just seemed so out of character for him.

"They said Ted Bundy was very polite as well," Chloe said. All heads swiveled to her. She shrugged, then checked her watch and gasped. "I gotta go," she said.

She took her apron off and grabbed Courtney's as well and hung them both by the door. She ran her fingers down each one to knock out any unnecessary wrinkles. Chloe's apron would be there tomorrow when she came back to work, and Courtney's would be there for whenever she decided she could get her life back on track. But Arlo and Chloe would give her as long as she needed in order to make that happen. Even if they had to keep drinking Fern's jet fuel coffee.

Arlo checked her own watch. "Go?"

Chloe shook her head and blew her bangs out of her face. "Jayden's teacher wants to talk with me. Evidently, he's been acting out a little this week. I feel it's due to the move."

"The move?" Fern asked. "He hasn't moved yet."

Chloe shot her a look. "Not helping." And she went to the back to get her purse. Arlo waved goodbye to Chloe as she made her way out the door, then turned her attention to the customer who needed ringing out at the cash register.

"I think we should call Sam," Camille said. That got her attention.

"Why do you need to call Sam?"

Camille smiled in a self-satisfied, yet private way that

made Arlo think she should duck and run for cover. "He's just so knowledgeable about such things."

Arlo thought back to the last thing they were talking about. It had been Dr. Wright and Dylan, but apparently in saying goodbye to Chloe and ringing out a customer, she had missed a quantum leap to a different subject.

"About what?" Arlo asked.

"Murder and things. He seems very knowledgeable about that sort of thing. Dead bodies and science." Camille flicked one delicate hand in a gesture Arlo supposed was meant to encompass dead bodies and science all in one.

"You mean forensics," Fern said.

Camille snapped her fingers. "That's it. Forensics. Forensics. Forensics. Sam is good at forensics."

"What are you doing?" Fern asked.

"Sam is good at forensics," Faulkner squawked. "But the butler did it."

"I heard that if you say something three times and use it in a sentence that you'll always remember it."

"I'm not sure that's the kind of sentence they mean," Helen said gently.

Camille sniffed delicately. "I'm sure it's not. But it's the only one I have that I can use forensics in that I know is correct. Forensics. Forensics. Forensics."

"Sam is good at forensics." Faulkner flapped his wings from this place atop his cage. "The butler did it, but Sam is good at forensics."

"Who taught him that?" Sam asked.

Arlo whirled around. She pointed one finger at her ex–high school sweetheart, who seemingly appeared from nowhere once again. "Bell," she said.

He had the audacity to chuckle.

"We were just talking about you," Camille chirped.

"Really?" Sam asked.

"Were your ears burning?" Camille continued. "Is that why you came down?"

"Sorry to disappoint you, but no. I got a text from Fern."

Everyone turned toward the curmudgeon-turned-gardener. Fern gave a small shrug. "Seemed the easiest way to get him down here since you wanted to talk to him."

"You have to do something," Arlo said where only he could hear. "They're going to run you ragged."

Sam gave her that same sweet smile she knew so well. "I don't mind."

"You are a flirt, Samuel Tucker," Arlo grumbled.

He shrugged, and his smile deepened and showed off his dimples. Even more than before. "What can I say?"

She shook her head. "You are a stinker. I think you're enjoying all this attention."

"You know what they say, if you can't get attention from the girl you want, then take all the attention from all the girls you can get." He tapped on the coffee bar behind him, then made his way over to the reading nook.

"Sam is good at forensics," Faulkner squawked.

Arlo could do nothing but stand and stare at the place where he had been as Sam walked away. What did he mean by the girl that he wanted? That didn't make a lot of sense. Unless... She turned toward Sam, but he was actively engaged in a conversation with Camille over how the police knew that Haley had been hit in the head with an object instead of just falling down the stairs to her death.

Arlo half-listened as she moved over to straighten the

comic books. The after-school rush had departed, and it would be another day before tiny little hands came in and disrupted Archie, Superman, and Batman and Robin. "All they can tell was that she was pushed because of bruise marks on her arms that are consistent with someone grabbing a person and perhaps manhandling them a bit. That would account for that theory."

"But if a statuette was missing, how do they know that's the murder weapon?" Fern asked. "Couldn't it just have easily been with someone, like an employee; who knows? Maybe even Anastasia. Everyone in town knows how she is."

Everyone in town did indeed know that Anastasia Whitney was the poster child for Generation Entitled. Thirty-five, still living at home. She flounced around as if the world owed her more than she was currently getting and she wasn't pleased with the results. But Arlo couldn't imagine Anastasia stealing a statuette from her grandmother. Why? To sell it? Who even knew how to sell something like that? Who even knew if the statuette was worth that much? For all Arlo knew, it could be some off-brand reproduction.

She moved to the other side of the comic book stand before Sam could answer. "I thought you guys were talking about Mary Kennedy?" she asked.

"We were," Fern said.

Helen's mouth twisted into a thoughtful frown. "We started off there anyway."

"You shouldn't be bothering Sam with any of this," Arlo reminded them.

"Yes, yes, we know. 'Book clubs should talk about books.'" Fern sat back and crossed her arms over her chest. She shifted her gaze to the coffee bar across from her seat.

"And baristas should barista." She pushed to her feet and headed for the coffee station.

"We were talking about *Missing Girl*," Camille defended.

Arlo purposely didn't look at Sam. She knew what he was hiding behind the hand that was pinching the bridge of his nose. That rattlesnake smile. Traitor.

"We started off talking about *Missing Girl*," Helen said. "Then we started talking about how it reflected the murder of Mary Kennedy."

"We don't know for a fact she was murdered," Fern called from the coffee bar. Arlo resisted the urge to close her eyes and wish they would all go away. The only problem would be that she would open her eyes, and they would all still be there. Not that she didn't want them. She did. But sometimes she just wished...

Sometimes she just wished they didn't holler "murder" across the floor of the bookstore while the before-dinner crowd of parents and such were still milling around.

"Anyway," Helen started again. "Mary Kennedy took us to Lillyfield, and Lillyfield took us to—"

"Haley Adams. I know." How could she argue with that logic? She couldn't, which was why she simply shook her head and went back to stocking books.

She hated to even think it, but with any luck, Dylan Wright would be guilty, and Haley Adams's murder would be solved. Then the girls would only have to worry about Mary Kennedy. And hopefully with a little more luck, Arlo could keep them contained for that one.

13

ARLO OPENED THE DOOR TO HER EMPTY HOUSE AND ONCE
again contemplated getting a pet. A cat was out of the question. What if she got another Auggie? And dogs? Well,
what if she got a dog, and it ended up insanely large like
Mads's dog? Dewey was a good twenty pounds over what
an Airedale should weigh and was about as rambunctious as
a two-year-old on a sugar high. So, she had settled for a bird
and gotten Faulkner. Heavy sigh. It seemed her luck with
pets was not going to hold out, so for now she would just be
coming home to an empty house.

She slipped on the kitchen light and set her purse on the
table as her phone began to ring. She hadn't even gotten her
shoes off. She slipped out of her flats and fished in her purse
for her phone.

Mads. Had he somehow known that she'd been thinking
about him? She shook her head and swiped the screen to
answer the call. "Hey, Mads. What's up?"

"I need to talk to you about something."

Arlo's stomach sank, and she eased down into the nearest kitchen chair. "What have they done now?"

"What? Who?"

"My book club. I'm guessing this call is about them?"

His deep, warm chuckle came to her through the phone line. It was rich and familiar and nostalgic all in one. "I'm not calling about your book club girls."

Arlo smiled at the thought of him calling them girls. Kind like the Golden Girls. But a little more rambunctious and determined to solve crimes whether there was one or not.

"Then what is this about?"

"The movie premiere."

Of course.

"The producer talked to Helen about rooms, and I blocked off some stuff at the hotel."

Arlo frowned. "You're the chief of police. How did you get saddled with all this?"

He sighed. "How do I get saddled with anything?"

"True," Arlo said with a small nod. "Absolutely true. So you blocked off some rooms at the hotel and…"

"I'm wondering if we should do some sort of Sugar Springs experience, like a lock-in at the gym?"

"Did you come up with an idea?" Arlo plucked an apple from the fruit bowl at the center of her table and took a huge bite. She wasn't crazy about the peel, so she took the piece from her mouth and started nibbling on the white part as he explained.

"It was Frances's idea. I told her I didn't think it would be what people would want when they came to a movie premiere, but you know Frances."

That she did. "I see."

"Do you?" Mads asked.

"Keep going," Arlo urged him.

"I told her I would think about it, so now I'm calling you see what you think about it."

"Is the problem here that we don't think we'll have enough room to house everybody?"

"That's right."

"Okay…" Arlo continued to feast on the fleshy part of the apple. "Let me think a sec."

"Take all the time you need. They only want me to get back to them by tomorrow morning."

"Tomorrow *morning*?"

"I've been sitting on this awhile."

"I'll say." She managed another bite of apple. "So not having enough room. We can't make enough room, and people who are coming all the way here for a movie premiere do not want to sleep on the hard gym floor, Sugar Springs experience or not. So why not check into one of those bus tour companies? Maybe we can get someplace in Memphis to work with us or even Tupelo. Heck, maybe even Corinth. Just depends on how many people are coming in. We can have the tour company running routes and give tours of the city, if you want to be generous and call Sugar Springs a city."

"Good enough for me," Mads said.

"They give the tours, and when everybody's ready to go back to their hotel, they hop back on the bus."

"Bus?"

"Come on, Mads. You played for the NFL; you know what a luxury bus is like."

"Luxury. Got it." She could hear scratching in the background. She supposed he was writing all these ideas down.

"That help any?"

She could almost hear his grin on the other side of the phone line. "That helps a lot, actually."

"I think I should warn you," Arlo started. "The girls, as you call them, are pretty determined for you to reopen the Mary Kennedy case."

"Mary Kennedy?"

He didn't even remember. "The piano teacher who went missing like forty years ago. Helen, Fern, and Camille are convinced that Mary Kennedy's disappearance and disappearance of the girl in *Missing Girl* are one and the same. Just kind of dressed up for fiction."

"I've read *Missing Girl*, and they are not the same."

"I still can't believe you actually read it." Arlo tossed the apple peel toward the trash and missed. Not even a bank shot.

"Why? I read."

"Of course." And that was a new development. Mads had never been a reader before. At least not while they were in school. Back then, Arlo could barely get him to look at the *CliffsNotes*. He had been more interested in making out and football. Not necessarily in that order.

"The woman who's missing in the book comes back to town," Mads continued. "From everything I've heard about Mary Kennedy, she's still missing."

"Well, you're right about that, but they still say there are a lot of similarities. The mansion and some other stuff to do with the Whitneys and Lillyfield."

Mads sighed. Heavy enough that she could hear it all the way into her house. "I know they mean well," Mads said. "But please try to keep them on some kind of leash. I mean

I know it's not your job. But we're still trying to gather evidence on Haley Adams's death."

"I understand. And I'll talk to Elly about it. She's usually reasonable."

"Usually," he agreed, but they both knew that the last few weeks Helen had been much more interested in murderers and books and life outside the Inn than she had ever been before. Arlo was glad that the book club gave Helen something to get out and do, but at the same time, Arlo was a little leery since it made Helen start to think she could solve mysteries. At least she and the others weren't driving around in a van with a dog, but Arlo would never admit that out loud. They might hear and take up a collection for a Mystery Machine.

"I'll do what I can," Arlo said. It was weak as far as promises went, but it was the best one she could make.

....

"Guess what everyone was talking about at Dye Me a River today," Fern demanded as she and Camille breezed into the Books and More the next afternoon. "Go on. Guess."

It was Friday, beauty parlor day.

"You went to the beauty parlor *again*?" Arlo asked, peeking around to get a full look at Fern's hair. Camille and Helen went every week, but Fern was another matter altogether. That she had shelled out the money to have a professional work on her hair once was odd enough; that she had done it twice was more like a miracle. "Two times in a row."

"Yes," Fern huffed. "Now focus."

"Okay," Arlo said. "I'm going to go with Haley." A person

couldn't get killed in a town the size of Sugar Springs and not be the talk for at least a couple of days or weeks, maybe even years. It all depended.

"More than that," Fern said with a grin.

"Where's Elly?" Arlo asked.

"Oh, she had to stop and charge her car or something," Fern said. She might have just gotten back from the beauty parlor, but she had already smacked on her floppy straw hat. Though Arlo had previously witnessed that a mere hat couldn't destroy a "'do" from Teresa at Dye Me a River.

"My car does not run on electricity," Helen said, coming into the bookstore and shooting Fern a chastising look. "One of my tires was low and needed air." She plopped her handbag down on the couch. "See if I treat you to a Friday at Dye Me again."

Which explained why Fern was willing to have her hair professionally colored and set again.

Fern sniffed. "If you want me to get it right, then learn to text better. The garbled mess that you sent me wasn't enough to go on."

Arlo had been patiently explaining to Helen that simply removing the vowels from words did not make any sort of text code. Apparently, her lessons had been falling on deaf ears.

"Anyway," Camille started once again. "Half of Dye Me a River says that someone from Lillyfield told Mads that they had seen Dylan and Haley arguing earlier in the morning on the day she was killed."

"My vote goes to that Pam," Fern said.

Arlo would not tell them there had to be more than that to go on. She would not engage in this talk. If she did, it would only lead to more talk and probably action, and no one wanted action. She had promised Mads that she would do what she could to keep the girls in check.

"And," Helen drawled, picking up the story as Camille paused to draw breath, "CCTV shows that Dylan was indeed in the mansion. That afternoon."

"But there are no cameras where Haley fell so it's not like they can put him at the scene. The scene-scene." Fern said.

Arlo was beginning to think her head was spinning. "And all this came out of the beauty shop today?"

"I keep telling you, you got to get your hair cut more than once every couple of years, and you'll be able to find out all sorts of things in this town," Helen said.

Arlo didn't bother to point out that only half of it would be true. Who even knew how much of this was the gospel? "You have no evidence to back up any of this. I mean, it's all a rumor. You know that, right?"

"All rumors and legends start with some grain of truth," Camille said sagely.

"I don't think I would believe it until I heard Mads say something, and you are not going down there." She added the last as the ladies turned, no doubt to march down the police station to question the chief about the whole deal.

"It's that Pam," Fern said. "What do we really know about her? Suppose she's got a lot to hide."

"What do you mean?" Camille asked.

"Just that it might be a gauge of whether or not she's telling the truth. If she has something to hide, then maybe she's making all this up."

Helen shook her head. "Why would Pam want to make stuff up? She's a cook."

Fern shook her head. "Pam isn't a cook; she's a nutritionist. And a nurse, I think. Dutch is the cook, remember?"

Arlo remembered. Dutch with the many colorful tattoos standing at the grave site, head bowed, expression solemn.

"Whatever she is, she could have something to hide. And she could be telling lies to hide it. Whatever it is," Fern continued.

"If she even said these things," Arlo said. This conversation was getting a little out of hand. "Which we don't know that she did."

"There's only one way to find out." Fern started for the door to the third floor, even as Helen and Camille headed toward the reading nook.

Arlo seemed torn between the two of them. "You're having a meeting now?"

"Of course," Camille said. "Friday's a little bit of a challenge. We have to wait until we get all our appointments in, then have the meeting."

"Fern will be making drinks here in a minute or two." She smiled and waved at Chloe who had managed to keep silent during this whole exchange. Arlo was certain she was sniggering behind her hand and hiding her face so Arlo couldn't see her laugh. It was something she would have to talk to her best friend about later. Arlo needed backup in these situations. Chloe may not have been involved in the investigation of Wally's murder, but she definitely needed to help Arlo with this one.

"Where are you going?" she called after Fern.

"Up to talk to Sam. Anyone know Pam's last name?"

"I don't reckon I heard anyone say," Helen mused.

Camille shook her head. "Me either."

Fern shrugged as if it was no big deal at all. Like last names were for amateurs. "I'm sure Sam can figure it out."

Still trying to form the words of protest to keep Fern on the first floor and out of Sam's office, Arlo watched her disappear into the stairwell. Then she looked back to the two remaining members of the Friday-night-turned-everyday book club. Not exactly what she had planned. Not at all actually. No hipsters, no coffee drinkers, no guys with beards and black-framed Buddy Holly-esque glasses boasting cardigans and man buns.

Okay, if she were being truthful, there weren't many cardigan-wearing hipsters in Sugar Springs. But she expected at least a few more people. Maybe having it on Friday night had been a mistake. Maybe a Sunday afternoon. She could open for that, she supposed. Though she liked to have her Sundays off.

She moved toward the book cart as the bell sounded over the front door. She turned to see a young man step into the bookstore. He wore a gray cardigan and rusty-brown jeans with flat skater shoes. He had a man bun but no beard and no black glasses.

As soon as he came in, he spotted her and started in her direction. Either he knew who she was or he knew she could help.

"Arlo Stanley?" he asked.

"That's me," she replied.

"I'm Andy," he said. "Sam's nephew." When she didn't reply, he continued. "He told me you might need some help."

Arlo smiled. Andy was perfect. This was the kind of guy she was looking for to be in the book club, but he also seemed to be a great candidate for employment. "Let me get you an application."

"Thank you." He moved toward the dogleg coffee bar where old-fashioned metal stools waited. When he wasn't looking, Chloe flashed her a thumbs-up. Arlo smiled and gave a quick nod, then ducked back into her office for the stack of blank applications she had there. It was a standard form just to know what a person did and if they had been convicted of any major crimes. Other than that, she went with her gut. So far, her gut was telling her that Andy would be a great addition to the Books and More. Even Chloe thought so.

She returned with the form and handed it to him along with a ballpoint pen. "Take your time," she said. "We can talk when you're finished."

. . . .

"So what about the guy?" Chloe asked a little while later. "Sam's nephew."

"You like him?" Arlo asked.

Chloe nodded. "I do."

Arlo smiled. "Good. I'll call him next week and tell him he got the job."

"Next week?" Chloe asked.

Arlo gave a small shrug. "I don't want appear too eager. He'll think he can run all over us. Otherwise I think he'll be great help. He can lift the heavy boxes and"—she cut her eyes toward where the book club ladies sat, lounging in the reading nook, still discussing whether or not Mary Kennedy actually had a necklace when she left Lillyfield that fateful night—"he might be able to help us with other things that get away from us around here."

Chloe chuckled. "Very well put, bestie." She slipped off her stool and went around to the other side of the coffee bar.

"Why don't you go ahead and go home?" Arlo asked. "I have Fern here if anyone needs coffee."

Chloe frowned a bit, and Arlo knew she was torn with indecision. "It would be good to get a jump start on moving everything around. I've got to get the new dresser moved back into the bedroom. Thank goodness it's already painted blue in there. I don't think Jayden could take a lavender- or peach-colored room."

"You still feel good about this?" Arlo asked.

Chloe sighed and grabbed her purse from underneath the counter. "Yeah, I do. I feel like it's the right decision and the right time to make it. It's going to be a big adjustment for the both of us," she said.

Arlo smiled. "Trust me. It'll all be great in the end."

14

SOMEONE'S GOING TO GET HURT!

Arlo read the note, then laid it on the coffee bar. She looked to Chloe, who bit her lip, her agitation practically tangible. "And this was taped to the door when you got here this morning?"

Chloe nodded. "What do you suppose it means? Who's going to get hurt? How are they going to get hurt?"

"Good questions. But I wish you would have called me when you first got it."

Chloe had given Arlo the note as soon as she had arrived at the Books and More.

SOMEONE'S GOING TO GET HURT! Big red letters, block print, with an exclamation point for good measure.

Someone was scared. About what? Haley's murder? The Mary Kennedy case? Or maybe she was reading too much into the whole thing. Maybe it was just a senior prank, someone trying to stir up emotions when the town was already on high alert.

"What have you got there?" Sam asked, coming up behind her.

Arlo shoved the paper to the other side of the counter where Sam couldn't see it. "Nothing."

Chloe shot her a look and handed the paper to Sam. "This was on the door when I came in this morning."

Sam studied the note, lines of worry starting to form as he did so.

"What do you make of it?" Arlo asked.

He shrugged and handed it back to Chloe. "Could be that someone here might be stepping on toes that don't like to be stepped on. Or it could be a joke. Not a very funny one, but still a joke."

"I think she should take it to Mads," Chloe added.

Arlo sighed. The very last thing she wanted to do was add more to his already heaping plate. "Mads has more important things to do than run down the kids who taped this to the window for giggles."

"What kid would be up at six thirty for something like that?" Chloe asked.

Arlo frowned. "What do you mean?"

"If it was a kid or a high school prank," Sam said, taking up the explanation, "the funniest part would be seeing the face of the person finds it. In this case, Chloe. If they left the note, they would want to see her face."

"At six in the morning," Arlo finished.

"Exactly."

"But Chloe hasn't done anything," Arlo protested. Chloe hadn't even been with them when they went out to the mansion or on one of their harebrained trips to find clues.

"But they knew she would show it to you." Sam looked from one of them to the other. "I don't mean to scare you, but I think Chloe's right, Arlo. You should take this over for Mads to see."

She picked up the note and read it again. It was clear, not threatening, and a little on the cryptic side. She looked at it a moment more, then tucked the missive into her pocket. "I'll think about it," she said. Though she had no intention of bothering Mads with such things.

....

Arlo was more than surprised at all the things one little boy could have. That Saturday after the Books and More closed, the moving crew, which consisted of everyone they could finagle into helping, filled the back of Fern's car, as well as her trunk, Arlo's back seat, every available space in Chloe's SUV, and the bed of Sam's truck, as well as the one belonging to Chloe's father, with boxes, bags, and baskets of toys, clothes, and assorted boy paraphernalia.

"What's going on over there?" Fern nodded her head toward the lake that sat on the edge of the Lillyfield property.

That wasn't entirely true. The lake sat *mostly* on Lillyfield property. It was man-made, and no one at the time that it had been created ever dreamed that the prosperous Lilly family could have so much as a nickel's worth of financial trouble. Even then, someone down the line, maybe even Weston Whitney himself, had sold off a chunk of the estate. And some of that chunk just happened to contain some lake water.

"It looks like they're dredging out the lake," Sam said.

"For what?" Helen asked.

The whole moving procession was stalled, watching the

goings-on as the group tried to figure out exactly what was happening at Lillyfield Lake. All sorts of equipment had been brought in, including something that looked like a large pump, along with a couple of generators to keep everything going.

"No idea," Camille said. "Let's get these boxes inside." Of everyone, she was the one most interested in getting the work done. She hadn't said as much, but Arlo figured she had a date with Joe tonight.

"Yes!" Jayden said, standing the doorway of the little cottage and waving them in.

Scratch that. Camille wasn't the most focused on getting the move accomplished. But she was a close second to Jayden.

"I'm going to go find out what's going on," Fern said. She ducked into the little house, then started her march down the hill to where the lake was located.

"I'll go with you." Helen rushed to put her box down and headed off after her.

Not willing to be left out, Camille did the same.

"Where's everybody going?" Jayden wailed.

Arlo looked from the boy to the three elderly women heading down the hill clearly on a mission. She shook her head.

"Go on," Sam said. "We men got this." He winked at Jayden, who seemed a little relieved that Sam, the strongest of them all, was still by his side.

"And Pops is here now." Chloe nodded her head toward the Dodge truck that had just pulled in behind Sam's red Chevy.

"I'll be right back," she said. Then with a sigh and an

apologetic look to Jayden and Chloe, she trailed behind her Friday night book club.

Fern went straight to Jason as the other ladies beelined after her.

"You are never going to guess," Fern said when Arlo finally caught up. Jason had moved away to talk to one of the workers. At least that's what he acted like he was doing. Arlo was fairly certain he was merely trying to escape before Fern could ask him any more questions.

"They're draining the lake."

"Draining it?" Arlo squeaked. "Why?"

"Jason believes Pam's statement is true." Helen nodded as if that explained everything.

"Hold on." Arlo shook her head as if trying to get her thoughts rattled back into place. "What did Pam say?" And when did she say it?

"Pam recently told Jason that she saw Dylan Wright out here and that he tossed something into the lake." Camille looked to the other ladies for backup. They nodded accordingly.

"So, they're draining it," Arlo almost asked. Even with all the equipment confirming Camille's story, she wanted to hear it once again.

"Apparently they've been out here all day," Helen started. That explained the crowd, Arlo supposed. "They sent divers down, but since the lake bed is so muddy, they weren't able to see much so they decided that draining it was the best option."

"They say it could be the murder weapon." Fern's eyes were wide with intrigue. Or maybe just a morbid kind of fascination.

Arlo looked back over the water. The machine on the far

side of the lake was sitting on the back of a flatbed, a large, cloudy-white hose attached to the back end.

One of the workers called something to the truck driver, and the racket that followed was deafening.

A few chugs and a gurgle later, the water splashed from the hose and over the hill.

"Let's go back to the cottage." Arlo had to yell to be heard over the noise of the water pump.

"What if they find something?" Fern hollered in return.

"It'll be a while, and we'll be close enough to see." She pointed to the cottage where everyone was still visible. It looked as though they were making progress on the move.

"Arlo's right," Helen yelled. "And I can't hear myself think."

Camille nodded, and the four of them headed back to the cottage—to help Jayden move and give their ears a little rest. Though Arlo knew the respite wouldn't last long. Not if there was a murder weapon to be found.

"When did Pam tell Jason all this?" she asked when they were far enough away they could talk without screaming at one another.

Camille shrugged. "A couple of days ago. When she was at the police station."

"I thought she said that she saw Dylan and Haley arguing."

"I guess she saw this too. Anyway, she told them what she saw, and Jason got a warrant to drain the lake."

"Just that quick?" Arlo asked.

Fern nodded. "Amazing, huh? I wonder if he thought up the idea himself…"

"Wait." She said the word but kept walking. "If Pam saw

Dylan throw something into the lake, that would have been days ago. Why is she only coming forward now?"

"Who knows?" Fern said.

"Maybe she only now remembered that she saw him," Camille mused.

But to Arlo that was a long shot. A person you work with is killed, and her boyfriend tosses something into the nearest lake. Well, that seems sort of suspicious. Or was she reaching for it?

"I thought Jason said that Dylan was seen a day or two later at the lake," Camille added.

"Like he knew he was going to get into trouble, so he had to get rid of the evidence?"

Arlo shook her head. They were almost at the cottage now, and she stopped. She didn't want Jayden, or even Chloe's father, to hear what they were talking about. "If he was going to confess, why would he bother getting rid of the evidence?"

"How should I know?" Fern grumbled.

"Maybe he didn't plan on confessing," Helen pondered. "Maybe he thought he was going to get away with it, so he tossed the statuette, then his conscience got the better of him, and he had to turn himself in."

"Maybe," Arlo said. "But if that's the case, why didn't Dylan himself tell Jason where the statuette could be found?"

. . . .

The thought stayed with Arlo the rest of the evening as they unpacked boxes, made the bed, and hung Jayden's sports posters on the walls.

He was in his room rearranging things to his satisfaction and otherwise basking in his new living quarters. Sam and Pops had left earlier when their truck services and lifting muscles were no longer needed. Now Camille and Chloe lingered in the kitchen, making tea and discussing the true differences between Earl Grey and oolong, while Helen and Fern stared out the front window. Until they had started removing all the water from it, Arlo hadn't realized just how big the lake was. The lake level had seriously dropped, and a large mass of dingy white was slowly becoming visible toward the middle of the lake. The ladies watched in awe as the mystery was revealed.

"I think it's a refrigerator," Fern said with a decisive nod.

"Why would there be a refrigerator in the middle of the lake?" Helen asked.

"There are lakes with whole towns underneath the water," Fern returned.

"Towns, yes," Helen said. "Refrigerators, no. That doesn't make any sense."

"Well, it's something," Fern replied.

They lingered at the window just waiting for the object to surface, if even just a bit more. Enough to show what it really was. Camille and Chloe finished their conversation, or put it on hold, and moved into the living room to look out the window with the others.

For Arlo, watching the water being pumped from the lake and waiting to see what it revealed was a little like watching paint dry, but she found herself staring at it all the same.

"It's some kind of ball," Camille said. "A big metal ball. Or maybe plastic."

"What kind of ball has holes in it?" Fern demanded.

"A Wiffle ball," Helen replied with a shrug.

"Well, that's a darned big one if it is." Fern frowned. "Wiffle ball," she grumbled.

"Wait a minute…" Camille said.

Arlo turned her attention to the woman. She had moved to the other side of the room to the second window that looked out over the Lillyfield property. She held a pair of binoculars to her eyes as she gazed through the glass. "It's not white," she said slowly. "It's baby blue." Her voice grew with each word she spoke, until she finally exclaimed, "That's a car!"

"What?" Helen and Fern screeched. Neither one asked where she had gotten the binoculars—they had obviously come from Camille's mysterious, magical white handbag—or if they could look through them. Helen wrenched open the door, and she and Fern rushed out into the fading sunlight.

Left with no other choice, Arlo started after them. She heard Chloe call behind her for Jayden to stay in his room and that she would be right back, but Arlo herself kept jogging down the hill toward what was left of Lillyfield Lake.

For three women well past retirement, the book club ladies were spry. They must have been fueled by a strong, nosy curiosity, she supposed—not allowing herself to think that she had to be in really bad shape if she couldn't keep up with them any better than this—and Arlo didn't reach them until they were almost to the lake.

"It's Mary Kennedy's car," Camille exclaimed, jumping up and down in apparent glee. "We found it! We found Mary Kennedy's car!"

15

"I STILL CAN'T BELIEVE WE TOOK A WHOLE WEEK TO GET
me moved into that little room," Jayden complained the
next morning.

Chloe shot Arlo an apologetic look, but Arlo just
shook her head. She had arrived early—well, early for a
Sunday—to Chloe's bungalow with a box of doughnuts,
sausage rolls, and cups of coffee and hot chocolate to go
around.

There had to have been more of the little cottages, built
sometime after the war to house the paid servants, but now
only one remained. It was tiny with only a bedroom and a
bathroom off the main, living, dining, and kitchen area. It
suited Chloe and was cheap enough that she could afford it
and their start-up business, and still maintain some of her
independence.

"Honey wanted you to stay with her last week, remember?" Chloe asked.

"Yeah," he said. "I remember." He slid from his barstool
and wandered over to the window to check on the car still

there in the mud. It was perhaps his fifth trip to look at it since Arlo had been there. To a nine-almost-ten-year-old boy, a car sunk in a lake recently drained to find a murder weapon was a pretty cool thing to see.

"Awesome!" Jayden exclaimed.

"What is it?" Chloe asked.

Arlo and Chloe moved to the window to see.

Workers had arrived at Lillyfield Lake-turned-mud-pit and were assessing the small vintage car stuck in the middle.

"Are they going to pull the car out of the mud?" Jayden asked.

Arlo was amazed at how enthralling the idea was to him. It seemed everyone could find something interesting in the discovery of the car. In fact, several people had already gathered at the scene once again.

Last night, after the lump in the water could be identified as a car, the police made everyone clear the scene. Not that there was much to look at, just half a lake and part of a car, but apparently they needed some measure of privacy to continue draining all the water. Or maybe Mads and Jason were simply tired of holding back the masses in order to get a little police work done. Though in the bright light of a new day, looking out the window at the tiny car still plopped in the middle of a lake of mud, Arlo had to wonder how much of anything was accomplished in the dark hours.

Jayden turned to his mother. "Can I go? Please, please, please! Can I go look?" He took her hand in his and jumped up and down.

Chloe hesitated.

Then Arlo spotted a familiar floppy hat among the townspeople who were milling around at the edge of the mud.

"I can take him if you want to finish unpacking." Arlo gave a pointed nod toward the crowd, but Chloe wasn't paying attention to that. She was too busy trying to determine if she should give in or hold her ground. It seemed full-time parenting was going to be a bigger adjustment than either of them thought.

"Please." Jayden pulled her arm harder, like he was ringing a bell for the servants to come.

"We'll all go," Chloe finally relented. "Get your shoes on."

But Jayden was already seated on the tiny bench by the door, pulling on his rain boots. "Come on, Manny." He whistled for his dog.

He-Man, the snow-white bichon frise, was immediately at his side, and the pair were out the door before Chloe and Arlo even had time to breathe.

"Maybe this wasn't such a good idea." Chloe chewed on her lower lip. "Manny needs to be on a leash. And sometimes I think Jayden does too." She slipped into her garden clogs as Arlo tied her running shoes.

"He's just excited," Arlo soothed. "And there are enough townspeople down there that one dog in the mix shouldn't cause too much ruckus." She stood and looped arms with her best friend. "Full-time parenting is tough. It's gonna take a little time."

"I hope you're right," Chloe fretted as they walked from the cottage arm in arm.

The expanse of the Lillyfield estate was lush and green. Given the Mississippi heat, Arlo wondered what the water bill was. Probably more than her mortgage. And it surely cost a mint to keep the kudzu curtailed at the edge of the property.

It looked as if half the town had gathered on the public

side of the lake. Huge security guards in black suits with sunglasses and earpieces shielded the property line and kept any would-be strays on the correct side of the water. Arlo had never known Lillyfield to have its own private security. She figured Baxter must have hired them out of Memphis after the murder investigation was underway.

"Arlo!" Helen caught sight of her and waved.

"You watch them," Chloe murmured with a small laugh. "I'll keep an eye on Jayden."

Divide and conquer.

"Isn't it exciting?" Camille eyes sparkled like sunlight off glass.

Arlo wasn't sure *exciting* was the right word, but it was something to see.

Murphy Jones, the town's one and only salvage man, had brought out his tow truck. It was parked with the bed toward the lake edge, even with the spot where the car rested. Unfortunately, that was on Lillyfield land, and Arlo was certain someone would be getting a bill to resod the grass where his big tires had already chewed it up.

Murphy Jones himself stood talking to Mads and Jason and a couple of volunteer firemen in full uniform. They had even brought out the truck for this special occasion. That was Sugar Springs—one fire truck and a handful of volunteer firemen. Heaven knew what they would do if two places caught on fire at once. But she wasn't about to ask the question and jinx the town.

The men seemed to be in a heated discussion on the best way to hook up the car and pull it from the mud. Arlo figured since that was Murphy's job and his dad's before him, everyone should just let him do his thing.

"I didn't expect so many people to be here," Arlo said. Truth be told, she hadn't expected anyone to be there. Then again, what had she been thinking? Not much happened in little bitty Sugar Springs. This was better than a free matinée.

"Wonder what the problem is?" Helen asked, using her height to peer over the crowd at where the men stood still debating.

"It's the mud," Fern said. "There's a lot of tricks to pulling a car like that out of the mud. Plus this one's been in there for fifty years. You'll have to raise the chassis, and Lord knows you can't pull it out from the bumper. That will just pop right off."

Arlo, Helen, and Camille stared at Fern with their mouths practically hanging open.

"How do you know all that?" Helen asked.

That's what Arlo wanted to know.

"I used to date a mechanic." Fern shrugged as if it were no big thing.

"You dated?" Camille asked.

"A long time ago." Fern frowned at her friends' obvious interest. "About a year or so after Charlie died." She waved hand around as if to dispel their curiosity.

"I bet you're right though," Helen said. "That makes a lot of sense."

"How are they going to get it out?" Arlo asked. If it took as long as Fern's explanation seemed to indicate, the crowd would be out there for the balance of the day.

"Dated," Camille mused. For some reason the thought of Fern dating totally discombobulated the woman.

"You're dating," Fern countered.

Camille sniffed and shifted her purse to her other arm. "I believe that's different."

"I don't see how." Fern propped her hands on her hips.

"It just is." Camille raised her eyebrows as if daring Fern to continue. Arlo figured it was time for some intervention.

"So where is your guy, Camille?"

"He has some business to attend to today."

And that wasn't suspicious sounding at all.

"So when are we going to get to meet him?" Helen asked.

"Soon. Maybe. I don't know." Camille shifted her purse again. It was obvious she was uncomfortable. Arlo didn't know if it was from being put on the spot or if she understood how worried her friends were going to be when they caught sight of this new man in her life. Arlo wasn't even sure if she herself was over the shock.

Maybe she would call Sam today. He might have some more information on Joe Foster.

"I know I would like to meet him," Fern said. Her tone clearly indicated that she thought he was a figment of Camille's imagination.

"That would be fantastic." Helen nodded enthusiastically. "Maybe we could all go out one night."

"After you've already cooked and cleaned for half the bachelors in the county?" Arlo protested. Not to mention whatever guests she had at the inn.

Helen patted her on the cheek. "I can count on you for help, right?"

"Of course." What else was she supposed to say?

"It's all settled." Helen smiled, Arlo was certain in pride over her brilliant idea.

"Bowling," Fern said. "We should go bowling."

"Joe would like that," Camille said with a small nod. Arlo wasn't sure if she was telling the truth or trying to appease her friends.

"And Arlo could bring Sam," Helen added.

Arlo sighed. If it wasn't Mads, it was Sam who Helen was trying to set her up with. Arlo wasn't sure how she felt about it either way except to note that she had ruined it for all of them so long ago.

Manny reached them first, barking and running around between their legs as Jayden tramped up. Chloe trailed behind. She looked tired, most likely from the move and adjusting to having an almost ten-year-old underfoot.

"They're gonna start trying to pull it out!" Jayden said. He practically jumped up and down in place. "It's going to be so awesome."

Fern looked over to where Murphy Jones had waded out into the mud. He was feeling around the car at the back wheels.

Behind him, on the other side of the lake, a group of townspeople watched. One of them in particular caught Arlo's eye as he moved through the scene. Joe! At least it looked like Joe. Maybe it was Dutch, the cook. But what would Dutch be doing on that side of the property? He would more likely be standing at the edge of the small stone wall that surrounded the back gardens of the mansion. Surely it was Joe. She scanned the crowd for the man she had seen, but he was there one minute and gone the next. She looked back over to the group of Lillyfield staff. No Dutch in sight.

"That's never going to work," Fern said with a shake of her head. "Murphy Jones couldn't pour water from a boot with the instructions on the heel." Her criticism brought Arlo out of her own thoughts. Maybe she had just imagined that she had seen Joe. After all, he and Dutch couldn't be the only bald men in the area. Could they? "Men," Fern muttered.

"If you have so much experience, why don't you tell him what to do?" Camille said. The two were definitely at odds today. Although Arlo didn't know exactly what it was about, she suspected this whole deal with Joe was making Camille a little bit edgy. And if he was indeed among the crowd watching…

"You know what? I think I will." Fern started toward the group of men still standing next to the tow truck. Then she stopped and turned back around. "Come on, Jayden."

Jayden's eyes lit up like fireworks on the Fourth. "Really?"

Fern nodded once and motioned for him to follow.

Jayden took off running like only a young boy in galoshes could do, Manny nipping at his heels.

Arlo, Chloe, Camille, and Helen watched the boy and dog approach the men who were doing their best to get the little Volkswagen out of the mud.

"Do you really think she dated a mechanic?" Camille asked.

"I think she was a mechanic," Helen whipped.

Arlo chuckled. "I wouldn't put it past her."

It was true Fern was a different soul, but that's what made the book club so special.

Okay, Arlo had finally admitted it. As much as she wanted her book club to be filled with hipsters and young, up-and-coming citizens of Sugar Springs, she couldn't imagine not having these three ladies in her life. Not that they wouldn't have been. They all lived in a tiny little town in Mississippi. But they might not have been as much of a part of her everyday as they were now. Sometimes it made her feel exhausted. Most times it made her feel blessed.

As they watched, Fern gestured this way and that while Manny ran around the men, barking to get someone to chase him. But the men paid the little white dog no mind, and Jayden was too enthralled in the conversation to either. Arlo kept one eye on them and the other on the crowd, unable to stop herself from searching for the man she thought she had seen. Joe or Dutch or some other bald figure with scary tattoos.

Fern gestured with her arms wide and then made another gesture like she was playing tug of war with an invisible rope.

Mads nodded even as Murphy Jones shook his head. Both men turned to the volunteer fireman, no doubt to break the tie between them.

From the distance they couldn't hear what was being said, but knew Fern had won her argument when she clapped her hands together.

"Oh, brother," Camille muttered.

"If it works, there will be hell to pay next week." Helen shook her head, her long braid falling back behind her shoulder.

"For heaven's sake," Camille exclaimed.

Arlo turned to see Fern standing at the edge of the mud, shouting and gesturing to Murphy Jones. Once again, he had waded back into the mud. He was doing his best to work a chain through the open windows of the Beetle.

"I guess that explains how someone got that Beetle to sink," Helen said, gesturing to the open windows on both sides of the car. Arlo hadn't been paying much attention to that when they walked up. "I wonder if there's still water inside," Helen said. "Those things are practically watertight."

They watched as Fern continued to instruct. Once Murphy Jones had pulled the chain through both sides of the car, he secured it in the back. The chain looping through both windows would allow it to be pulled from the water by the car body, not the bumper or the chassis as Fern had been talking about.

As half the town watched, Murphy Jones then tried to make his way out of the mud. Arlo had to admit it was a lot like watching a Laurel and Hardy slapstick comedy routine as every step he took sucked the boot from each foot, forcing him to backtrack into his shoe again. He finally made it out of the mud by holding onto each boot with one hand and walking like some sort of duck until he got to the grass. Fern nodded and gave him a boost up, then dusted her hands on the seat of her overalls. She waited at the edge of the mud pit for him to get into the cab of the truck and start the engine.

A small cheer went up in the crowd as he started to pull the Volkswagen from the mud. But it was a short-lived triumph. After only a couple of inches, the bogged-down car stalled. Dirt flew in all directions as Jones revved the engine. He pressed the gas, popped the clutch, and did everything in his power to work the car out of the mud.

"Oh my!" Camille said.

Finally, with a large sucking sound, the truck found traction, and the Beetle slipped from its fifty-year-old resting place. Murphy Jones engaged the towing mechanism and pulled the car the rest of the way from the mud and onto the now dirt banks of what had once been Lillyfield Lake. One of the firemen went over to the car and opened the door. Water poured from inside, and a lone fish flopped on the grass. The firemen picked it up and tossed it back into the mud.

"Manny!" Jayden's voice rose above all others. It was closely followed by Chloe's exclamation of "Jayden!"

The ten-year-old stood at the edge of the mud watching as his dog plunged through the muddy lakebed. Each step the canine took looked to be harder than the last. Manny seemed to be sinking further into the mud. And suddenly, he stopped. Struggled. He was stuck. And the harder he tried to escape, the farther down he sank.

Jayden took off into the mud, holding onto his boots much the same way that Murphy Jones had. Right before Jayden reached his dog, he fell face first into the muck.

"Jayden!" Chloe hollered again.

Arlo took off toward her best friend. Fern beat her there by a split second.

"I'm going to go get him." Chloe looked around as if trying to find something that would help her. But there was nothing, not a stick or a branch. Maybe Murphy Jones had some rope in his truck, but someone was going to have to wade out into the mud to retrieve the boy and his dog.

"I'll get him." Tyler Blake, one of the volunteer firemen, nodded at the three of them, then trudged into the muddy lake bed. By the time he reached him, Jayden had managed to push himself into a sitting position. He seemed mortified that he had to be rescued.

"You get the dog," Mads said. "I'll get the boy."

Until Mads spoke the words, Arlo hadn't realized that the Chief of Police had waded out behind Tyler.

Jayden's face crumpled, and his embarrassment seemed to double. "I didn't fall," he said, even as Tyler picked up Manny. "Honest, Mads. I didn't fall. I tripped."

"I know, buddy," Mads said in a soothing voice.

Beside Arlo, Chloe nearly wilted in relief.

"There was something in the mud." Jayden said.

"Of course. Probably a tree branch or some kind of log," Mads assured him. "The main thing is you're okay."

"But I didn't just fall," Jayden wailed as Mads set him on his feet next to his mom.

Chloe knelt beside him and wrapped her arms around him, smearing mud all over herself as well.

Tyler appeared a second later, placing an incredibly muddy Manny next to the two of them.

"There is not enough soap in the world," Fern said.

"Thank heavens," Camille gushed as she and Helen made it to their side. Manny started to bark happily. He braced his legs up on Helen but she grabbed him up and held them away from her. Like that was going to help. Somehow even being held away up in the air, Manny managed to shake himself and sling mud on everyone around. The action seemed to break the spell that Jayden was under. He laughed.

"But I want you to know I didn't fall," he said. "I'm not clumsy. But there was something in the mud."

"I know, baby." Chloe smoothed a clump of hair back from his forehead.

"And I'm not a baby," he reminded her.

"I'm sorry. I know you're not."

Arlo watched as Chloe swallowed down her emotions.

"But I think we're gonna need a bath."

Jayden chuckled and looked at his dog. "All three of us."

"Would you look at that!" Fern pointed to where Tyler had trudged back out into the mud. He was standing close to the same spot where Jayden had tripped, and in his hands he held up very muddy object, but even then, it was unmistakably some sort of small statuette.

16

"It's all anybody can talk about," Helen explained sometime after noon the following day.

Mondays on Main Street were normally a quiet affair. Most of the shops were closed on Sunday, and Monday was all about getting back into the work week. The Books and More was no exception, though on this particular Monday the rule had been shattered. Main Street was abuzz with the events at Lillyfield the day before.

After Tyler Blake pulled the muddy statuette from the lake bed, Mads had rushed over to where Tyler stood, grabbing the statuette and putting it in the back of his city SUV.

Then he yelled for everyone to clear the scene, and the fun was over. Everyone returned to their regularly scheduled lives.

Arlo knew what Helen said was true. It was all anyone could talk about—the discovery of the Volkswagen and Tyler finding the statuette in the mud. Well, it had really been Jayden who found it, but Tyler was getting all the credit for digging it out.

"I know," Camille said. "If I hear one more person say DNA, I think I might scream."

"Here, here," Fern said. "All anybody cares about is that statuette."

"Which is allegedly the murder weapon that killed Haley Adams," Arlo pointed out.

"Well, yeah," Helen said. "But it's as if no one remembers Mary Kennedy at all."

"Well, you have to admit Haley is fresher in everyone's mind."

"I suppose you're right," Camille acquiesced.

And now that they had the murder weapon, or what they believed to be the murder weapon, then justice seemed within their grasp. Everyone was talking about DNA and wondering if fingerprints could be found on the statuette. It was a hideous-looking thing even covered in mud, a bronze woman standing tall and proud, her skirt swishing around her and a bouquet of flowers behind her back. Arlo supposed it might have been a pretty statuette once upon a time, but beneath the shadow of Haley's murder, it now appeared tainted.

"So how is Mads going to get all that dirt off of it and find DNA as well?" Helen asked.

"Yeah," Camille added. "It's not like he can wash it. That would wash away blood and fingerprints, right?"

"I think so," Arlo said. She got up from her perch on the edge of Helen's chair and made her way back to the bookcase she had been working on when the ladies had arrived.

"I don't think it's possible to wash away all the blood," Camille said. "Is it? I mean, what if it was already dried on there?"

"What about that stuff they spray on blood to make it glow under a blue light? Some sort of magic stuff," Helen said.

"Luminol," Fern replied with an emphatic nod.

Arlo wondered if she should be worried that the lady knew the word so readily. How many times had luminol come up in a normal conversation? Not many, she was certain.

"It picks up protein traces," Fern continued. "And it glows under a blue light. You can scrub and scrub and scrub, but it can still pick up traces of blood. Of course, sometimes it depends on how much blood there was to begin with."

"And you know this how?" Helen asked.

Fern shrugged. "You just pick these things up along the way."

Arlo stifled a chuckle and went back to work.

"I for one want to know about the car," Camille said.

"I'm with you," Fern agreed. "Though I don't know if they would be able to pull any fingerprints off the vehicle since it's been in the water for fifty years."

"Probably not," Helen said. "More's the pity. It seems like a really good clue to finding out what happened to Mary Kennedy."

Fern nodded. "It just proves foul play."

"Agreed." Camille pressed her lips together and gave a nod of her own. "A car that floats sunk in a lake with the windows down on the property belonging to the number one suspect in the murder case."

"Wait," Arlo said, setting aside her vow to not get involved. "Weston Whitney wasn't the number one suspect. He never even went to trial for it. Her husband did. Jeff, right? Jeff Kennedy?"

"I suppose you're right," Fern said. "Maybe he wasn't the number one suspect, but we all think that Weston did it. You read his diaries, how he was going to plant the necklace on her so that everyone thought she stole it."

"But that's not the same as murder," Arlo protested.

"Close enough for me," Fern grumbled.

"So if he is guilty...was guilty, that means an innocent man was wrongly accused and spent over a decade in prison." Arlo looked at each of them in turn to see if they were still in agreement.

"It wouldn't be the first time." Helen nodded.

As much as she hated that fact was true, it was true. But there was still no proof that Weston Whitney had anything at all to do with Mary Kennedy, and it certainly had never been proven that she was murdered. How her husband got railroaded for the crime was anybody's guess, but the justice system was a mite different in the seventies than it was in the twenty-first century.

"I don't think Weston had it in him to kill anybody," Helen said.

"He must've grown himself a pair," Fern added.

Arlo gasped at the language. Behind her, she heard Chloe stifle a chuckle. Yes, it was all fine and dandy if you weren't the one responsible for the crazy lady.

"Fern," Arlo admonished.

Fern shrugged. "I calls 'em like I sees 'em. And Weston Whitney was a sweet, sweet man."

"Not that there's anything wrong with that," Helen added.

"All I'm saying," Fern began again. "If Weston Whitney, and not Jeff Kennedy, did indeed kill Mary, then Weston must have found some gumption some other place. Because he sure wasn't born with it."

"That sounds a little bit better, thank you." Arlo turned back to her books.

"He just never seemed the type," Camille mused.

It was a typical day for the book club ladies despite all the excitement. They were the same as ever. Fern in her overalls and big floppy hat, Camille and her pearls, matching pantsuit, and running shoes. Helen and her bedazzled everything. Yet there was a different vibe in the air, a new kind of electricity. Arlo wasn't sure if it was from the upcoming storm the weatherman kept calling for or if it was merely the excitement of the biggest clue in a fifty-year-old murder being found.

"We really need to look at that car."

"It's still there on the grass," Chloe said.

Arlo shot her best friend a *shut up now* look.

Chloe just shrugged.

"Just right there on the grass?" Camille asked.

"Yeah."

"And no one's watching it? No one is guarding it?" Fern looked from Helen to Camille.

"Don't even," Arlo said. "If Mads is reopening that investigation, you need to let him work."

"But if he left a clue right there out in the open—" Fern countered.

"You are a book club," Arlo informed them. "Why not talk about a book?"

Chloe sniggered as all three ladies turned to stare at Arlo as if she had lost her cotton-pickin' mind.

Arlo sighed and went back to shelving cookbooks.

"I'm not as worried about the car as I am the journals," Camille said.

"That's because you were an English teacher. They always want to read everything," Fern scoffed.

Arlo shook her head and told herself she would not comment that they were a book club, and book clubs should read, and even if Camille was the English teacher, that didn't mean she wanted to read any more than Fern. Because if Arlo actually said the words, they would just be white noise to the three ladies.

"I don't know," Helen said.

"She might be onto something here. There's got to be all sorts of stuff in his journals. And it seems to be the way, doesn't it? A killer commits a crime and writes all the details down in a journal or an email or a letter to his mother… Maybe we just haven't run across it yet."

Fern shook her head. "You have been reading way too many crime novels."

"Is there such a thing?" Helen asked.

"There is if you think every killer's going to outline their confession in a monologue somewhere," Fern scoffed. "Besides, I've been through the journals we have…twice. We already know what's in those."

"I suppose you're right," Helen said. "But I would like to find the rest of them."

"You and me both," Camille said. "They have to be somewhere at Lillyfield."

"My guess is the attic." Fern gave a confident nod. "Where else would you keep something like that?"

"The basement?" Helen countered.

"The library," Camille breathed. "If these journals came

from the donations they more than likely came from the Lillyfield library—"

"Then the rest of the journals should be in the library too." Fern's nod was even more confident than before. And Arlo hated to, but she agreed with their logic.

"Not that it matters," Helen said. "How in the world are we supposed to get into the library at Lillyfield?"

"I've got it," Camille said. "We knock on the door and say that we had a flat tire and our cell phones are dead and that we need to use their phone. And when they take us to use the phone, we sneak into the library and look for the books."

Fern turned to Helen.

Arlo's guardian shrugged.

Fern turned back to Camille. "That has more holes than Swiss cheese."

"It's better than your idea," Camille countered. "Because you didn't even come up with one."

"We could go by Chloe's and then somehow manage to wander onto the estate. With a house that big, they can't keep every door locked, can they?"

Arlo cleared her throat. "Yes. Yes, they can." But the ladies were too far gone into making their plans to give her much notice.

THANKFULLY, MONDAY PASSED WITHOUT ANY MAJOR events concerning Lillyfield. The book club continued to discuss ways to get into the mansion, but Arlo let them talk. As long as they were *discussing,* they weren't *doing.* She supposed it was the rain that kept them at the store instead of running off to Lillyfield, but she still said a small prayer to whatever god might be listening and thanked her lucky stars while she was at it.

Sam came down on Tuesday morning, and they made plans to go bowling on Friday night, the big night when everyone would get to meet Joe. Arlo tried to not make it weird, but somehow it was more than strange. She couldn't decide if it was something between her and Sam or the fact that they had already seen Joe. Even though they hadn't technically met him, they knew the others were in for a big surprise.

"Check this out," Fern said. She reached into her bag and pulled out a Ziploc baggie filled with something milky white, though at this angle and distance Arlo couldn't tell what it was. "What you think of these?"

"I'm not sure I can say until I know what *these* are," Helen said.

"Ditto for me," said Camille.

Fern looked positively heartbroken. "Really? Neither one of you know what these are?" She turned her eyes toward heaven. "Lord, save me from the idiots in my life."

"I'm going to ignore the fact that she just called us idiots," Camille said. "And I'll ask you again, what are they?"

"Glow-in-the-dark stars," Fern gushed.

"Whatever for?" Helen asked.

But Arlo knew.

"You put them on things and they absorb the light during the day. Then when you turn off your lights they glow. All the little boys like them."

Helen began to nod. Arlo's guardian had caught on quick. "And you think we should go decorate Jayden's room with these?"

"Exactly," Fern said. She turned to Camille.

"At the cottage, of course," Camille said.

"Naturally," Fern added. And the cottage was on the Lillyfield property and right next to a muddy field where a VW Beetle that had been pulled from the lake bed sat sadly ignored by law enforcement. At least according to these three, it had been sadly ignored. They might not have found a way into Lillyfield, but they were still exercising their meddling muscles.

"Chloe?" Fern held up the bag for her to see. "Can we go and decorate Jayden's room with these? I thought it would be fun to hang them on the ceiling. Then at night it'll almost be like looking up at the stars."

Chloe smiled. "I think he would love that."

Fern stood. "It's settled then. Who wants to go with me to Lillyfield, er, I mean, who wants to go with me to Chloe's cottage?"

Helen and Camille's hands shot into the air.

"Little cottage," Faulkner squawked. "There's always a little cottage. Right at the woods. Don't go in the woods."

Seriously, Arlo was going to have to watch the patrons and the attention they paid to Faulkner. It seemed his vocabulary was growing stranger by the day.

"I think you should tag along," Chloe said as Arlo made her way to the coffee bar. None of the book club ladies heard. They were too busy discussing whose car they were going to take, which route they were going to drive, and how exactly they were going to hang the stars in Jayden's room. Their conversation was a little too loud and a little too animated for her to believe it real. Which meant the whole deal was a cover-up to get out to Lillyfield and dig around inside the little Beetle.

"I suppose you're right."

. . . .

And that's how Arlo found herself standing in Jayden's room in Chloe's cottage half an hour later.

She hadn't made any sort of excuse as to why she was tagging along with the ladies, just told them that she was going. They had cheered like they always did and made room for her in Fern's Lincoln.

Now as they bickered back and forth and hung the stars, she just wondered when the ladies would make a break for the Beetle.

"Don't you find it terribly interesting that that poor little car is just sitting out there?" Fern asked.

All three ladies turned to her.

Arlo sat up a little straighter in her chair. "Me? Why would I find it interesting?" But she knew the expedition had begun.

"You're a literary person," Camille started.

"The connection to Wally's book. Uh-huh."

"If you're so sure there isn't a connection, then put your money where your mouth is," Helen said.

Here it comes.

"A bet?" Fern clapped her hands in excitement.

Helen shook her head. "We go see what Mary Kennedy left in her car. Maybe there's a clue there as to how she disappeared." She gave a delicate shrug. "Who knows what's out there."

"We'll never know if we don't go look in that Beetle," Camille continued.

Stars hung, the ladies had been biding their time to get to now.

Arlo sighed and stood. "Look at this." She motioned them into the living room and over to the window. "See the lake there?"

"I see a mud pit," Fern grumbled.

"I can't see anything," Camille said.

"Fine," Arlo led them to the front door and out onto the lawn. "Now you see the lake?"

"Again. Mud pit," Helen said. She crossed her arms, a sure sign she was growing irritated with the whole thing.

"Well that mud pit is half on the Lillyfield property and half on public lands."

"We know this." Fern frowned.

"See the marker at the edge on both sides?"

"I see them," Camille said cheerfully.

"And look at what side the Beetle is sitting on."

It was clearly on the Lillyfield land, but none of the ladies wanted to admit that.

"I'm fairly sure that Judith Whitney is already having a fit that the car is on her land to begin with. Not to mention all the memories that it has to be dredging up for her."

"I suppose," Helen agreed.

"I don't think it would be a good idea to push our luck and go trespassing on her land to find clues to a mystery that may or may not be there." Arlo held her stance.

"We were invited here," Camille said. "And we have a friend here."

"That's right," Fern agreed. "That friend invited us, and we came over, so we can't be trespassing."

"Good enough for me." Helen started toward the car.

"Elly, wait!" Arlo took off after her guardian with Camille and Fern gleefully trailing behind her.

"We can't all go digging in this car." Helen slung her braid over her shoulder when she reached the Beetle.

"You and I can look for clues," Fern said. "And Camille and Arlo can watch for security."

Arlo looked at the car, back to the cottage, and over to where Lillyfield mansion towered like a watchman over the land.

It wouldn't be long before somebody came out. If she was guessing right, whoever it was would not call police because that would just be extra publicity. She was also fairly certain that extra publicity was something they didn't want. If so, they would probably just ask the ladies to leave. Maybe the best thing she could do would be to allow the ladies to have their look, let them be told to leave by the mansion's security, and they could all tromp back to the Books and More.

Arlo checked her watch, interested to see just how long it would be before someone from the mansion came down and forcibly escorted them from the property.

"I don't see a purse or anything," Helen said.

"A purse would be brilliant," Camille chirped. "Lots of clues. If she was murdered, it might still be here in the car."

What else would a killer do with his victim's handbag?

"Are the keys still in the ignition?" Fern asked.

"Good idea," Camille said not willing to be completely left out of the investigation. "Maybe there's something good in the trunk."

A second passed. "Nope," Helen replied.

"We'll have to pry it open." Fern's voice was emphatic.

"No," Arlo returned. "It's one thing to be out here digging around in it. And another thing altogether to vandalize it."

Fern deflated like a week-old party balloon. "I guess you're right."

Helen braced her hands against the top of the car. "Wait. The trunk is in the front of the car. It think it would be awkward if she put her purse there. I think she took it with her."

"Why would she put her purse in the trunk anyway?" Camille asked.

Helen shrugged. "I put my purse in the trunk all the time."

"Do you even have a trunk?"

Helen shot Fern a withering look. "Ha, ha. Very funny."

"Well, unlike your car, this car has a back seat, so if she didn't want to set it in the front seat next to her, she could put it behind her. Not like a two-seater." Camille nodded.

"The point?" Fern asked.

"If she took the purse with her, then she left of her own accord," Helen surmised.

The ladies were about to debate the topic when two burly men in military black and dark sunglasses headed down the hill.

"Gather your things, girls," Camille said.

"I'll handle this," Helen said.

Thank heavens. Arlo was scrambling to find the right explanation to give to the security guard, and she would gladly let Helen handle it. Especially considering the fact that Helen was about the same height of the men coming after them. Nothing like a little physical intimidation to brighten the day.

"Should I shut the door?" Camille asked.

Arlo shook her head. "This is how we found it."

Camille and Fern waited next to her as Arlo watched Helen walk up to meet the security guard. They were half-way between Lillyfield and the mud pit that had once been a pretty little lake. The trio was close enough to see but not close enough to understand.

They talked, gestured, pointed, and when Helen braced her hands on her hips, Arlo knew the conversation was over.

"It's time to go."

"I do hope this doesn't cause any problems for Chloe," Camille said.

Arlo hadn't thought about her friend's status as a

resident/tenant on the Lillyfield property. She was sure the Lillyfield budget didn't need the money they got from renting her a little cottage, and asking her to move out immediately would do no harm to their fiscal health. For Chloe, it would be nothing short of devastating. Especially since Jayden had just moved in.

Helen finished her conversation with the security guards, and Arlo considered it a good sign that they turned on their heels and started back toward the mansion.

"What did they say?" Fern called before Helen was even halfway back to them.

Helen shook her head, her lips pressed tightly together as she returned.

"They advised us to leave immediately," Helen said when she returned to their side.

"And that's exactly what we should do." Arlo pointed toward the side of the cottage where they had left the Lincoln. "We don't want to give them any excuse to change their minds."

"I guess," Camille said. But the two words held such dejection. She sounded like a little boy who dropped his ice cream and lost his dog all on the same day.

"I guess Judith Whitney can see the car from her bedroom window," Helen said.

"What makes you say that?" Fern asked as they trudged up the hill toward the cottage.

"He said that lady of the house requested that we leave."

"He was just saying that," Camille said.

"Or it was Pam. Maybe he thinks she speaks for Judith," Arlo put in.

"Or Anastasia," Fern added.

"Maybe. But I got the distinct impression that Judith was spittin' mad to have the car sitting on the grass and even madder that that we were out here," Helen explained.

Fern shrugged. "Understandable."

"Which is the exact reason why I thought we shouldn't do this," Arlo reminded them.

"I'm sure I didn't raise you to be a wet blanket," Helen said. But neither one reminded the other that *raising* only included sixteen until now.

"But the funny thing," Helen continued, "is I got the impression from the guard—the big, hunky one—that even though she can't walk or talk or even write, her mind is sound."

Fern looked back toward the spot where the guards had disappeared. "They were both hunky."

"Focus," Camille snapped at Fern, then to Helen, "Like she's trapped in a body that doesn't work?"

"Exactly," Helen said. "He didn't come right out and say it, but it seemed like that's what he was implying."

They all slipped into Fern's Lincoln, and she started the car.

"Lock the cottage?" Helen asked.

Fern nodded as she pulled the Lincoln out onto the short drive. A few moments later they were back on the road to the Books and More.

"I wish we knew if what you think about Judith is true," Camille said.

"What difference does it make?" Arlo asked.

"Wet blanket," Helen singsonged.

Arlo sighed and sat back in her seat. She supposed trying to be the voice of reason was getting her nowhere, so at least she should be the person who did her best to keep them all from getting arrested. She didn't know what such a person was called. According to Helen, a wet blanket.

"There's only one way to know that," Helen said. "And that's to get back into Lillyfield."

"No," Arlo said. "You call me a wet blanket until the cows come home and dance with the chickens, but you are not going to force your way into Lillyfield and bother Judith Whitney."

"But—" Camille started.

"No." Arlo said.

"It's okay, girls," Fern said. She shifted in her seat as they started through town. Only a few more minutes and they would be back at the Books and More. "We still have to figure out what this means." She held up her hand, and dangling from her fingers was a diamond necklace.

18

"I still can't believe you took that necklace without telling anyone," Camille huffed half an hour later.

"And the key," Helen added.

"Too bad we can't go see if it works," Fern lamented. Someone—Mary Kennedy, they presumed—had rented a room at the Moonlight Motel and left the keys in the glove box of the Beetle.

In the seventies, the Moonlight was something of an embarrassment to the town. The seedy motel rented rooms on the short term and was situated next to the old highway. Arlo had even heard once that the local madam had run her business from one of those rooms. But when the new highway went in, the Moonlight was taken down, leveled to make way for future businesses.

Along with the key, they found a leather pouch with a few papers stuffed inside. Lucky for them, the glove box on a Volkswagen was about as sealed as the car itself, but the pages hadn't survived for years underwater without some trauma. As soon as the ladies got them back to the Books and More and Fern had explained that she had found those in addition to the diamond necklace, Helen had grabbed the pouch, opened it, and started spreading the damp papers out on the coffee table in the reading nook.

"You have a hairdryer, don't you?" Helen asked.

"At home," Arlo said.

Helen looked like Arlo like she had somehow committed a grave offense.

"Why would I have a hairdryer at the bookstore?" Arlo asked.

"I don't know. I just thought maybe you would." Helen gave a negligent shrug.

"I have one." Sam.

Arlo closed her eyes for a brief moment and spun around to face her ex-sweetheart. "Why do you have a hairdryer?"

"Hey, Sam. Good to see you." He quirked a brow at her but otherwise his expression remained the same.

"Yeah, yeah," Arlo said.

"Can I borrow it?" Helen gestured toward the papers spread out on the coffee table.

"What have you got there?" Sam walked over to investigate.

"Papers," Fern said triumphantly. "I'm hoping they're journal pages or love letters from Weston Whitney to Mary Kennedy."

Sam propped his hands on his hips. "Interesting stuff."

"Found them in the car this morning." Fern gave a self-satisfied nod. "Along with this." She held up the necklace for Sam to see.

He whistled low and under his breath. "That's some rocks."

It sure was. The necklace looked like something Marilyn Monroe might have worn in the "Diamonds are a Girl's Best Friend" scene. It consisted of single strand of stones that circled and swirled at the center with teardrop-shaped sapphires dangling in the space each loop created.

And it was obvious that no one in Sugar Springs save the Lilly-Whitneys could have afforded a necklace like that. If it truly was made from real gemstones.

"We don't know. It could be rhinestones," Arlo reminded them.

"We should try using it to cut a piece of glass," Camille said.

"Absolutely not," Arlo said as Fern started toward the front window. "Glass cuts glass. You may not use that on my window. Please and thank you."

"I can take it down to Henry Wilson and see what he knows about it," Fern said.

They had already decided that if anyone in town sold the necklace to Weston, it was Henry Wilson at Wilson's Jewelry Store. Whether Wilson would remember it or not was another matter altogether.

"If nothing else, someone there should be able to tell us if the diamonds are real or not," Fern continued. She looked ready to do just that, rush outside and down the block without giving a thought to the questions the other jewelry store employees might ask.

"And where are you going to tell them you got it?" Arlo asked.

Fern shrugged. "I don't know. Somebody's got to be able to check it."

"Rumor was that Mary Kennedy stole the necklace from

the Whitneys and used the money to disappear," Helen reminded her.

"But the journal we found suggested that Weston planted the necklace in Mary's car so he could claim her a thief afterward," Camille added.

"Then Mary didn't have any money if she only stole one necklace," Fern said. "As I got this one right here." And she didn't have to remind them all that it had been underwater for nearly fifty years.

"There's some interesting stuff here," Sam said, ignoring their chatter while perusing the wet parchment in front of him. "What I can read of it."

"And that would be a lot easier if they were dry," Helen hinted.

"Mmhmm," Sam continued, drawing closer to the papers on the table.

"The hairdryer?" Helen repeated.

"Oh, right." Sam jumped up, startled, and crossed over to the door that led upstairs. A few moments later he returned with a hairdryer.

"Do I need to ask why you have a hairdryer in your office?" Arlo asked.

Sam handed the device to Helen. "If you want," he said. "But I'll not give away all the secrets of the trade."

"What should we do about this?" Fern asked, her voice raised to nearly a yell to be heard over the roar of the hairdryer. She held up the necklace.

"Put that down," Camille said. "You don't want any customers over here." Though Camille's voice was almost as loud as Fern's.

"Why don't we discuss that after Helen gets the pages

dry? After all, there may be a clue in there." Arlo bit back a sigh. What was she saying? Once again, the ladies had sucked her into their vortex of mystery solving.

Helen shut off the hairdryer, though the pages were nowhere near complete. It was obvious to Arlo that she was ready to join in the discussion.

"Then I think we should take everything down to Mads," Arlo continued.

Helen shook her head as if disgusted. "Why would we take it to Mads? He doesn't care a thing about Mary Kennedy."

"If you hand him these items, he would probably consent to reopening the case." Arlo looked at each of her book club ladies in turn. They looked back at her, then at one another.

Finally Fern spoke. "Probably?"

"I'm not sure I like those odds," Camille said. "Sam?" She turned to the resident PI.

"I don't have a dog in this fight."

"But you do have a learned opinion. What do you say?" Helen asked.

"As a law-abiding citizen of Sugar Springs, Mississippi, I would tell you that you should take any and all evidence of any crime to the chief of police."

"Well said." Arlo smiled at him.

"But," he continued, "I don't believe that Mads is interested in solving the case of who killed Mary Kennedy. There's no one around much who cares about the case at all."

Judith Whitney was the only one who had any sort of connection to Mary Kennedy's disappearance. If half the rumors in town were true, Judith was the reason Mary Kennedy had disappeared to begin with. The other half believed that Weston was responsible. And still more blamed Mary's husband. Now Weston was gone, Mary Kennedy was gone, Jeff Kennedy was gone. There was no one around to care much one way or another if a killer or kidnapper was brought to justice.

"You are not helping," Arlo said. She shot him a stabbing look.

"I wasn't aware that I was supposed to be." He grinned at her.

Arlo shook her head. "Now you know."

The rat had the audacity to chuckle. "You know these ladies are going to do what they want regardless of what you or I say." He had lowered his voice so that only she could hear.

"I do, but I swear they're out to make the gray before we're done."

"They don't seem to talk about books much," Sam commented.

"They talk about *Missing Girl* all the time."

Helen switched the hairdryer back on as Fern and Camille perched on the couch and waited for the pages to dry. Dan the grocer came in the shop to get a coffee, and Sam pulled Arlo a little closer to the door to the third floor so they could be heard over the drone of the hairdryer.

"And they still believe that Mary Kennedy and the girl in *Missing Girl* are the same?"

"They feel Wally made the changes to the story to make it fit better into fiction, but otherwise, yes, for all practical intents and purposes, Mary Kennedy is the missing girl."

Not that it mattered. There were enough changes to the story that it hardly resembled the original. Only to three little old ladies who had lived through the time themselves.

Sam tilted his head from one side to the other as if weighing the theory balanced against itself. "I suppose it could've been."

"I don't see how they can even prove it. And I would much rather go back to talking about *To Kill a Mockingbird* than getting kicked off the Lillyfield property by security. Again."

"Live a little, Arlo. You used to like having a little fun. When did you turn into such a stick in the mud?"

She pulled back, a little offended from his words. "I'm not a stick in the mud."

"So, where's the girl who broke into the school with me and replaced all the cans of whipped cream in the lunchroom with shaving cream?"

A small bit of laughter escaped Arlo. She tried to hold it in, but she couldn't. "That was funny."

"I still can't believe they didn't notice the difference until they started eating it."

"People always see what they want to see, right?"

He nodded. "I suppose you're right." He smiled down at her, and Arlo got that warm, fuzzy feeling again.

"Eureka!" Helen shrieked as she turned off the dryer. She held a paper high in the air.

Fern and Camille were on their feet in an instant.

"You are not going to believe this."

Sam gestured for her to go first, and he trailed behind her as she looked over to where Helen stood in the reading nook.

"What is it?" Fern asked. "What is it we're not going to believe?"

Helen held up the paper toward them triumphantly. She pointed to the greeting at the top of the page.

Fern and Camille both squinted and leaned closer to the paper trying to read what was there.

"My dearest M," Fern said. "But I can't read the rest of it."

Camille adjusted her glasses. "Are you sure that's an M? It looks a little like a J to me."

"It has to be an M," Helen said. "If it was a J, it would mean that the letter was written to Judith. Why would Mary have a love letter that Weston wrote to Judith?"

"Are you sure it's Weston Whitney's handwriting?" Fern asked. "That's very important for our case."

"Why are you so sure it's a love letter?" Arlo asked.

"No adventure," Sam said close to her ear. That was the second time today that someone had basically called her boring. What was happening to her? Being a homeowner and a business owner…was it making her… No, *old* wasn't the word. The ladies in her book club were elderly. Was her life making her…boring?

"This one's typed." Helen held it up so they could see it. Most of the words were smeared, including the name half of *dearest* and whatever else Weston had wanted to say to his dearest.

"This one's not." Camille pointed to one in the center of the table. "More than one. Most of them here are handwritten, in the same handwriting as Weston Whitney's journals."

"Here's the receipt for her room," Fern said. "Single occupancy. But that's about all I can tell."

Arlo started to say something else about them minding

their own business, but Sam calling her boring once again rose in her thoughts. She didn't want to be boring. And she supposed that if the book club was analyzing fifty-year-old papers found in the glove box of a once-submerged VW Beetle, then they weren't at the mansion in the way of the real investigation—who killed Haley Adams.

Other than the ones that were typed, it was the same handwriting. Though some were not signed, the ones that were seemed to be in the worst shape of all. Sometimes Arlo could make out *sincerely*; sometimes there was nothing at the bottom of the page but a smear. There were at least thirty pages in all, different sizes and shapes, and all worse for wear from their time in Lillyfield Lake.

"I know someone who knows what Weston Whitney's handwriting looks like," Helen's eyes sparkled in that way they did when trouble was brewing. Every time she got that look on her face, Arlo suspected she needed a hobby. Other than the book club and trying to solve mysteries that might not even be mysteries at all.

"You do," Arlo said. "You have three of his journals." But the ladies weren't listening.

"Judith Whitney," Fern said with a firm nod.

"Righto."

. . . .

"I still think you should have brought the necklace back," Arlo said later that afternoon.

When Jayden had arrived at the bookstore after school and got his snack and started his homework at the coffee bar, Arlo decided it was better to get the ladies out of the bookstore and out of earshot of the impressionable youngster.

"We will," Fern said. "Just as soon as we finish our investigation." She knocked on one of the large double doors of Lillyfield mansion. She seemed to think about it a moment, then rang the bell for good measure.

Arlo started. "What are you going to do? Take her fingerprints?"

"Ha, ha. Very funny." Helen shot her a look. But Arlo was not about to be dissuaded. She may have agreed to come here to the Whitney mansion with them again under the guise of bringing food to poor Mrs. Whitney, but that didn't mean she wasn't going to try everything in her power to talk these ladies out of harassing the residents and staff of Lillyfield.

"We brought food," Camille said. "Isn't that what you're supposed to do?"

"Most people make it themselves at home," Arlo said. "Not buy it at the grocery store bakery and put it in their own pan so it looks like they baked it at home."

Fern scoffed. "What difference does that make? We needed to get out here quickly, and we needed to have an excuse. There you have it."

"I still don't think they're going to let you in. They're going to take one look at the four of us, take the cake, and then shut the door in our faces."

Camille snickered. "Take the cake. If we were at the store, that's what Faulkner would be saying."

It was true, but Arlo couldn't acknowledge it. She knew what Camille was doing, trying to get her off track so she wasn't concentrating on getting them out of the mansion before they even got in.

Suddenly the door in front of them opened, and a small maid stood there. She wasn't the one they had met before—Sabrina—and Arlo once again wondered how many maids were working there total. And if perhaps this young woman took Haley's place in the household. The young woman looked hesitant, as if she wasn't sure she should have opened the door in the first place.

Great. Just the kind of girl to be manipulated by these book-reading amateur sleuths.

"Hi," Helen gushed, stepping forward even though it was Camille who held the cake. "We are concerned friends and neighbors of Mrs. Whitney, and we wanted to come by and offer our prayers and well wishes. Just to check on her, you know?"

The girl nodded mutely.

"May we come in?" Helen asked. She still used that keeper of the inn voice that was strong and friendly. The young girl was no match for its power.

She stepped back so they could enter the house.

Arlo had no choice but to file in behind the three ladies.

The mansion looked pretty much the same as it had when they had been there before. The only differences were that the tricolored gladiolus had been changed out for two shades of purple ones, lavender and grape, and some-one had placed a bust of Beethoven on the table closest to the door. Last time they had been there, the table had been devoid of decoration. Well, its decoration had been moved, leaving only a dust ring as proof that it had ever been there. Most likely it had been the statuette of the young girl with flowers behind her back, the same object used to kill Haley Adams.

Arlo pulled her thoughts back into line. She wasn't there to do anything about Haley's murder. She was supposed to keep the book club ladies from aggravating Judith Whitney and ending up in jail. That was the only reason.

"Hi, love. I'm Camille. These are my friends—Arlo, Fern, and Helen. Did you work with Haley?" Camille must have been reading her mind, though Arlo would have never asked the question outright.

The girl swallowed hard. "I did."

"She was a nice girl, that Haley," Camille continued.

"Yes." The one word was so quietly spoke it was almost drowned out by the ticking of the grandfather clock.

"We brought this cake. We just wanted to check in and see if there's any more information about Haley's murder, she was such a sweet gir—"

"It was me," she said, cutting through whatever Camille had been about to say next. It was more than obvious that the knowledge had been a great burden to the young maid. "I was the one who saw them arguing. Dylan and Haley."

"You don't say?" Fern asked. "Was it a bad argument?"

The girl cast her eyes downward and gave a short shrug. "I don't know."

"You don't remember?" Camille asked.

"It was just an argument. I told the police that." But she looked everywhere except at four of them. Arlo glanced up and caught Helen's narrowed gaze. And she knew her one-time guardian was thinking the same thing she was. The young girl was lying.

But why?

19

"Just an argument," the maid continued. Her voice grew shakier with each word she said, as if she had started to regret saying them at all. "Maybe it was that day. Maybe the day before, but it was just an argument. The kind boys and girls have when they're dating. Now if you'll excuse me." Before anyone could utter another word, the maid disappeared down one of the many corridors, leaving them standing at the foot of the staircase. Cake still in hand.

"Do you think we should just go on up?" Camille said.

"Of course," Fern said. "Judith's got to be up there somewhere. The third floor is a ballroom, and the fourth floor is the attic, so surely all we have to do is cover the rooms on the second floor."

Piece of cake, Arlo thought. It was just twenty or so of them.

"I don't know," Helen said. "I think that would look a little suspicious."

And surely land them in jail.

"Let's go," Arlo said. She started for the front door when different voice stopped her.

"I'm sorry," a girl's voice interrupted. "Was no one here

to greet you?" She seemed distressed by the very idea. It was Sabrina, the maid who had let them in before, that same day when Haley had been murdered.

"One of the maids let us in, then she just left us here," Helen said. "We came to see Judith. We're friends of hers."

"Really?" the girl said. And Arlo wondered if she recognized them as well. Maybe. Maybe not. It had been a pretty traumatic day. "I didn't think she had any friends."

Arlo wasn't sure what to say that, so she didn't say anything. But she could tell Fern was dying to ask more.

"Can you take us to see her?" Helen asked.

"Of course," she started up the staircase, hooking one arm over her shoulder to motion them to follow behind. "I remember you from before. The day Haley died." Sabrina's voice lost its happy edge. She stopped in the middle of the staircase and turned to look back down at them. Her brown eyes were clouded with sorrow. "It's just so sad."

"I agree," Fern said.

"And then that Andrea." She made a face.

"Who is Andrea, love?" Camille asked.

Sabrina flicked one hand in no particular direction. "She's the other maid."

"I take it that you two don't get along?" Fern asked.

"No," Sabrina said simply. Then she turned back around and trudged the rest of the way up the gleaming staircase. When they got to the landing, she waited on them before heading down one side of the hallway. "She didn't like Haley at all, and I think she's lying."

It had to be the same girl who let them in.

"Lying about what, love?" Camille asked in that gentle teacher voice with her Aussie-gone-southern accent.

"She said she saw Dylan and Haley arguing. But they never argued. They were so much in love. Perfect for each other. And Haley was such a sweet person. Did you know that she was helping look after Judith since her stroke? She was premed, you know, so she had medical knowledge, and she was trying to help."

Sabrina tapped lightly on one of the doors about midway down the hall and entered without waiting for permission. She held the door open and allowed them to step inside before closing it behind them.

Arlo looked around. They stood in an antechamber to the bedroom. Maybe a lady's sitting room, or maybe a dressing room, though she wasn't sure exactly what to call the space. It was filled with antiques—tables, chairs, couch—and more of those gilded frame portraits. This time on walls of pale salmon.

"Let me see if she's awake." She placed one finger to her lips and quietly walked to the door opposite them. She eased it open and slipped inside, shutting it behind her without a sound.

She returned a few moments later.

"She's awake. But you can't stay long."

They didn't need to stay long. They didn't need to be there at all.

Camille nodded, and Helen started toward the door of the inner room, Fern trailing behind. Camille patted Sabrina's arm. "If you think they've got it wrong, you should contact Mads and Jason, the police chief and his officer. They'll know what to do."

"It's just—" She stopped, her eyes focused on something behind Camille.

Arlo turned around to see the maid standing there. The young maid that had let them into the house. Andrea.

Sabrina pressed her lips together. "Yeah, whatever." After that she clammed up, and it was so obvious to Arlo: she didn't trust anyone in the mansion. Least of all Andrea.

Fern, Camille, and Helen marched into the room with more confidence and purpose than Arlo had ever seen, leaving Andrea behind standing in the doorway. Arlo simply followed behind wondering how they had managed to get this far.

Even as nice as it was, the room had been converted to a quasi-hospital space. There was a hospital bed and other hospital equipment that only someone with Judith Whitney's money would be able to afford in their home.

"Judith, love," Camille crooned at the lady in the bed. If Arlo had been shown the woman and not told who she was, she would have never guessed it to be the once-vibrant, if not flat-out mean-spirited, Judith Whitney. Her normally coiffed blond hair was mashed on one side and sticking out on the other. It clearly hadn't been set in several weeks, and judging by the amount of gray showing through the gold, nor had it been colored. At least it looked clean. Marginally, anyway. Her green eyes were dull and reminded Arlo of a fish. They stared ahead but appeared unseeing. A shiny glob of spittle glinted in one corner of her mouth.

"You brought her a cake," Pam said, entering the room behind them, her tone surly. She was as intimidating as ever. Head and shoulders taller than everyone except Helen, she glared at them as if she could make them leave by her scathing look alone. She was dressed like anyone you might meet on the streets of Sugar Springs but seemed to hold herself up higher than that.

"Well, of course we know Judith can't eat it, but surely someone in the household might find it tasty," Fern said.

It was obvious to Arlo that she was trying to bait Pam, but the younger woman just sniffed.

"I suppose you've seen her now and know that she is unable to truly entertain guests," Pam said, looking down her nose the entire time. There was something familiar in her manner, a snobbery that shouldn't have been there given her station in life. Not that there was anything wrong with being in home health care or being a nutritionist. It was just that not many of them carried themselves like royalty.

"She can't entertain, and the whole town is coming out here in a couple of weeks for the barbecue." Fern tsked as if to say, *What a shame*.

"We thought it would be better to go ahead and host it this year. We didn't want to offend anyone." Pam sniffed again.

Arlo wondered about the *we*. Had Judith been in on that decision? Or had it simply been made for her? From the look of her now, she was incapable of coherent speech, much less discussion about the annual barbecue. Arlo had expected her to be alert at the very least. According to the security officer she had talked to, Judith was more like a fine, whole person trapped in a body that merely didn't work, instead of both physically and mentally incapacitated. Was she drugged?

"Time to go." Pam pulled a silk cord similar to the ones used to hold back the drapes around the bed.

"But the cake," Camille protested.

"I'll take that." Pam stepped forward, hands outstretched.

"I just bet you will," Fern grumbled under her breath.

The door opened behind them, and Roberts appeared, surely to make certain they left.

So they did.

....

"Let's think about this logically," Helen said forty-five minutes later.

The ladies had all gathered back in the reading nook, at least for a time. Helen would have to go cook supper at the Inn soon. "Wally's heroine, Darlene," Helen said. "She came back to her town pretending to be someone else. In fact, I don't even like to call her Darlene because her real name wasn't Darlene. It was Millicent."

"The only reason Darlene-slash-Millicent even came back to town was to exact her revenge." Camille nodded.

Arlo was at once happy that they were talking about the book instead of Haley, Lillyfield, and everything else going on in Sugar Springs.

"Kind of like *The Count of Monte Cristo*," Fern said dramatically.

That made two books to make it into the discussion. It was a banner day, Arlo thought. Then she waved goodbye as Chloe and Jayden left with their promises to be at the cottage later for the house rewarming party.

"It sounds logical enough," Helen said. "But there's no one in town like that."

"There has to be," Camille protested. "Somebody had to have left and come back."

"Lots of people leave and come back. Lots of people just flat out leave," Fern said.

"No," Helen said. "This is something different. This is someone who left and came back, but they're not the same person."

"Hmmm, I guess Sam's not the missing piano teacher suddenly returned then, huh?" Arlo chimed in.

"I wish she would take this just the least bit seriously," Helen complained to no one in particular.

Arlo held up both of her hands in surrender.

Helen turned back to Fern and Camille, purposely leaving Arlo out of it. "No. It's not Sam. This is someone else. Someone who left, then came back and didn't tell us they were the person that left. Someone that just came back out of the blue."

"What about Debbie Hatfield?" Fern snapped her fingers. "She just showed up one day with no warning."

"Debbie Hatfield has lived in this town for over forty years," Arlo said.

"I rest my case." Fern gave an emphatic nod.

"I don't think it's Debbie Hatfield. She doesn't seem to have any kind of beef with anyone. This would be someone trying to outdo everyone else. Debbie is a nurse at the hospital. She works double shifts for her grandkids. She is not our count."

Camille stood, her purse still hooked over one arm. "This is fun and all, but I must be going."

"Another date with Joe?" Fern grumbled.

"As a matter of fact, yes." Camille picked up her book bag and started for the door.

"You should bring him by Chloe's," Helen said. "The more the merrier."

Arlo almost choked. They had their bowling plans all

lined out, but she wasn't ready to have that confrontation tonight. And definitely not at Chloe's.

"Yeah," Fern said, her voice gravelly. "You should bring him over."

"And if I didn't know any better, Fern, I would think you might be jealous," Camille said.

"Jealous." Fern scoffed in reply, but Arlo noticed it was after Camille was already outside.

"I must be going too. I've got to get dinner on and then work out something for in the morning for breakfast. I'll see you ladies tonight at Chloe's," Helen said.

"I wouldn't miss it for the world," Fern said.

"Don't mind her," Arlo joked. "She's just coming for the mini quiches."

Fern slung her book bag over one shoulder and headed for the door. "See you then," she said.

"See you then."

....

"Want to make a bet on whether or not Camille brings this Joe?" Chloe asked sometime later. They were standing in the tiny living room in the cottage, milling around with other friends who had come by to wish Chloe and Jayden well.

"I don't think she'll bring him."

"Why not?"

Arlo hadn't told a soul about seeing Camille and Joe at the steak house last week. There been so much going on, she hadn't really had an opportunity to say anything to anybody. It was a little shocking that she hadn't told her best friend.

Times change, she supposed.

"He's not someone you would expect Camille to be dating." How was that for diplomacy?

Chloe took a sip of the sparkling apple cider they were serving instead of champagne or wine. It wasn't hard cider, so Jayden could partake. This was a family party, after all.

"What's wrong with him? Is he badly scarred or like the Hunchback of Notre Dame? What?"

"He got quite a few tattoos." Arlo said.

"Define quite a lot."

Arlo picked up a cheese cracker and busied herself eating it so she could to figure out exactly how to answer her friend. Or try to, anyway. "You want a number?"

Chloe shrugged. "How about a body percentage? Would that be easier?"

"He was wearing clothes, so I can't say what was under them, but from what was exposed—"

"Head, neck, and arms?" Chloe asked.

Arlo nodded. "Maybe seventy-five percent."

"Seventy-five percent!" Chloe screeched.

She drew the look of everyone standing around. There wasn't a lot of room in Chloe's little cottage, so they had decided to have a come and go party. People were invited to drop in, stay for a while, then head out. There hadn't been any more than five people there at one time, minus Helen and Arlo, of course, since they had been there most of the evening.

Fern had buzzed in a little bit later, then buzzed right back out again, and Arlo wondered if she was simply trying to avoid Camille tonight for whatever reason. Arlo was fairly certain that reason was Camille's crack about her being jealous.

Arlo didn't think Fern was jealous that Camille had a boyfriend. She was upset that Camille was spending time with someone other than Fern. The two had gotten close since Arlo had started the Friday night book club.

"Well I guess if I was dating a guy and seventy-five percent of his body was tattooed, I wouldn't bring him here either."

"That's not very fair. Seventy-five percent of what was showing isn't a great deal of tattoos. He might be perfectly untattooed on the rest of his body." Arlo sighed. "Besides, it's not really the tattoos that are a problem."

"Oh, Lord," Chloe said. "What now?"

"I saw Camille and Joe when I was out with Sam."

"Yeah. I got that."

"Sam said that he thought Joe's tattoos were ones he'd gotten in prison."

Chloe's eyes widened in shock. "That doesn't mean anything," she said when she had pulled herself back together. "They may not be. And anyone can go to prison. I'm sure there are even innocent men in prison."

"You're right," she said. "It just worries me. I know she's old enough to be my grandmother, but Camille just seems so innocent. Maybe it's that accent."

"Definitely the accent." Chloe laughed. "But you have to trust that Camille can take care of herself."

"You know how people prey on the elderly when they're on the internet. They don't know how to work everything. Heck, I don't even know how to work everything."

"I know. We'll just have to watch out for her. So do you think it's serious between the two of them?"

Arlo shrugged. "I have no idea. She seems like she's

happy, and he seemed to be having a good time. But anytime the book club ladies crook their fingers, she's there, trying to find clues and necklaces and breaking into a car that has been sunk in water for fifty years."

"Yeah," Chloe said thoughtfully.

How serious could it really be between Camille and Joe if she still spent more time with Fern and Helen than she did her boyfriend?

"Have you seen Jayden?" Chloe asked Sam as he approached.

"I think he's outside with Manny."

"Let me go make sure they don't get in the mud again."

Arlo laughed and grabbed another cheese cracker. "I'll stay here and guard the refreshment table."

Chloe shook her head but smiled. "You do that."

"I never really realized how small this place was until we got five people in here." Sam laughed.

"I figure she'll eventually take some of Wally's money and buy a house in town. It would get her closer to everything, and it would be a lot easier."

"And she'd have room for her cat?"

"She doesn't need room for the cat. She doesn't have a cat. You've got a cat, remember?"

Sam looked down at the healing scratches on the back of his hands. "I remember."

"Ouch," she winced. "He still attacking you?"

"Only on days that end in Y." Sam shook his head. "That's not true. He has settled down pretty good. These are all starting to heal finally. But that cat does have a mean hook."

Arlo nodded. "Yes, he does."

"I noticed Camille isn't here with Joe tonight."

"They could still show up."

Sam shot her a look. "You really think she's going to bring him here?"

"You're the one who said that anyone can go to prison for any reason."

"And I stand by that." He took a sip of his own apple cider and swallowed before continuing. "It's just that Sugar Springs is a small town, and she's lived here a long time."

"Maybe she's just going to break down social barriers," Arlo said.

Sam chuckled. "You just keep telling yourself that."

Arlo wanted to come back with something snappy, but she couldn't think of anything to say. Mainly because Sam was right. Demanding social change in a town the size of Sugar Springs was no light undertaking.

"Uh-oh," Sam said. "Here comes Mads."

The Chief of Police was indeed headed their way, with a scowl of determination marring his handsome features. There could only be one reason why. "Don't you dare leave," she told Sam.

Sam tossed back the contents of his drink, then looked down into his empty glass. "Oh, look. I think I need a refill."

"Sam."

But he was already on his way for more apple cider.

"Arlo." Mads gave her a stern nod.

"Hey."

"I need to talk to you a minute."

Arlo feigned innocence. "Oh, yeah?"

Mads's frown deepened, a feat she didn't think possible. "I've had a few complaints from the brand new Lillyfield security."

"You don't say."

"Seriously, Arlo. What in the world were you doing snooping around the car?"

The split second after he asked the question, a half a dozen excuses,—er, reasons—and made-up lies floated around inside her head. Thankfully she didn't have to settle on one as Mads closed his eyes and held up one hand. "No. Never mind. Don't tell me."

"Okay, I won't."

"Just do me a favor." He opened his eyes and pinned her with a hard stare. "If they try to go out there again, stop them. And if you can't stop them, then for heaven's sake, don't go with them. I can only do so much to keep you out of jail."

"That seems a little chicken," Arlo said. "Leave my friends to take the heat."

"Not at all," Mads said. "You need to stay out of jail because they'll need someone for bail."

"That sort of makes sense." But it stung a little. Was she supposed to be fun loving or logical?

"And three elderly citizens of Sugar Springs have better defense for doing stupid things than a smart and savvy business owner."

Arlo wasn't sure exactly how to take that. So she decided to skip over it altogether. Mads wasn't one for throwing around compliments. "You really need to go up to the mansion," she said.

"Are you just completely ignoring what I'm telling you?"

"I heard you. And I have noted it."

He shook his head. "Good."

"Now about Lillyfield... There's a maid out there I think you should see."

"Why? Do you think she's my type?"

"Ha. Ha. She's young enough to be your daughter." Well maybe not, but it sounded good. "She thinks that the other maid, Andrea, is lying about seeing Haley and Dylan arguing."

Mads closed his eyes and pinched the bridge of his nose between his thumb and forefinger. "Why is everyone determined to be an armchair quarterback on this case?"

"I don't know about all that," Arlo said. "But she talked to me for a bit when we were there this morning."

Mads sighed. "I know."

"So you heard."

"Let's just say that Judith Whitney is the last person who needs the welcome wagon to come bringing casseroles to her door."

"I wouldn't call it the welcome wagon," Arlo corrected. "One of the lady's church auxiliaries, maybe. And it was a cake."

"Don't push me, Arlo. It's been a long day."

She felt a little sorry for him, just about. Even if he'd almost threatened to take her to jail. "You're trying to keep the girls out from behind bars, and I'm trying to keep the girls out from behind bars."

"Then we should work this together, don't you think?"

She supposed he was right. "Go over to the mansion," she said. "Talk to the other maid. Not the one who gave a statement against Haley and Dylan. See what she has to say."

"I'll put Jason on it."

Arlo opened her mouth to say that she wished he would check it out for himself, but she knew what his plan was for Jason and this investigation. Still she would've felt better if Mads had gone out himself.

"But now you have to tell your book club not to mess with Judith Whitney."

"I'll do my best."

Mads gave a quick nod. And she knew that he understood how hard it was to keep three headstrong elderly ladies in check. It sounded like an easy feat, but in practice it lost all of its logic.

"I just don't need any more complaints, Arlo," Mads said. "Sooner or later I'll have to take them seriously."

20

"THIS IS GOING TO BE MARVELOUS FUN," CAMILLE SAID
Friday night just after six o'clock.

Camille, Fern, Helen, Arlo, Sam, and Joe were all meeting at the bowling alley to have a fun night out. She hadn't
been bowling in years. Though she knew that the first
hurdle was not in the 6–10 split, but Joe himself.

"I think so too." Helen smiled.

Arlo certainly hoped so. After spending what seemed like
half the day in the beauty parlor with her book club to glean
any and all gossip from the many conversations around her,
Arlo found herself with her hair a good two inches shorter
than it had been when she went in and her brain no more
knowledgeable about the goings-on in Sugar Springs.

Leave it to her to pick the least gossipy day to actually
get her hair cut.

And two inches might not mean a lot to some folks, but
Arlo felt practically naked. Her head felt too light to be on
her shoulders, and she suspected that Teresa took off more
than she needed to just to say she cut Arlo's hair.

Or maybe she was being a tad overdramatic and paranoid.

"Oh, there he is," Camille squealed like a schoolgirl and clapped her hands together.

"Sam?" Helen asked. Arlo was certain she meant it as joke. Though Sam was expected at any moment. Everyone knew it was time to meet Joe.

Even over the crack of the balls hitting pins in the many lanes around them, Arlo was certain she could hear a pin drop as Camille rushed over to her new beau.

Arlo had been holding out some hope that Joe wasn't really as tatted up as she remembered. That he wasn't quite as scary looking in person as he was in her memory. Surely time had sharpened all those edges instead of sanding them down, and once she saw Joe again, she would realize that he was not as bad as she had originally thought. But she didn't even have to look at him to see that wasn't the truth. Her own concerns were mirrored in the faces of Fern and Helen.

Camille rushed over to Joe, her voice so high Arlo was certain only a few dogs were able to hear it. She fussed about him, brushed her hand down his arm, kissed the side of his bald head, then tucked her arm into the crook of his elbow before escorting him down to where they waited.

"Fern, Helen, Arlo." Camille looked at each of them in turn. "This is Joe. Joe, these are the friends I was telling you about."

Arlo had to hand it to Helen and Fern. They recovered quite well.

"Joe," Helen greeted him, coming forward with one hand outstretched. "It's so good to finally meet you." They shook hands.

"Yeah," Fern said, though Arlo suspected she was having

trouble finding words. A unique situation for Fern, to be certain.

"Joe." Arlo shook his hand as well.

By now Fern had managed to push herself to her feet, and she walked over to where they stood. "I'm Fern."

Joe smiled. He really had a nice smile. Tattoos and everything else aside, he seemed to be a happy fellow. His blue eyes twinkled merrily as he looked at each of them, greeted them, and commented on how much Camille had talked about all of them.

"Sorry I'm late." Sam loped down the stairs where they waited next to the lanes.

"Joe, this is Sam Tucker."

"Oh, the private dick from upstairs."

Sam shook his hand with a smile. "I usually don't go around telling people that." Then he winked at Arlo.

She shook her head.

"It's nice to finally meet everyone. I was beginning to think Camille was trying to keep me a secret."

Camille blushed, the color of her cheeks completely complementing her rose-colored pantsuit. "Oh, Joe." She patted his arm, and he smiled lovingly at her.

"Let's get this party started," Fern said. She had rolled up the legs of her overalls, and the effect with the multi-colored, well-worn bowling shoes of the Stardust bowling alley, Sugar Springs, Mississippi, was a sight to behold.

"Get up there and see what you can do," Helen said.

"Highest pin goes first?" Sam asked.

Helen nodded as Fern knocked down seven pins on her first try. She hit reset. "Always." And she grabbed her ball and headed for the lane.

Sam scooted a little closer to Arlo. "I forgot how serious she was about this. If I had remembered, I never would have agreed." He said the words where only Arlo could hear.

"Same here," she whispered in return.

"It might still be fun," he said. But she couldn't read his eyes or his expression; even his body language seemed incredibly neutral. How was she supposed to know what he was thinking and if he wanted this to be a real date-date if he kept himself so vague?

"Beat that." Helen dusted her hands and looked to Camille and Joe to meet her challenge. Of course she'd made a strike.

"Why don't you just go ahead and go first," Joe said with a chuckle. "I don't mind."

"Don't you want to throw a couple balls first?" Camille asked him.

"We all get to have a turn, don't we?"

They nodded.

"What difference does it make who gets to go first?"

He had a point, though Arlo knew firsthand when it came to bowling Helen did not share his philosophy.

"Suit yourself," Helen said. And she sat down at the desk and began writing everyone's names in the blocks. "I say we're having teams," she said though she didn't wait for anyone to answer before grouping them together. Her and Fern against Joe and Camille against Arlo and Sam.

Then she tossed her braid over her shoulder and stood once again, making her way to the air blower to dry her hands. On her right wrist she sported a custom wristband for support that had *Elly* stitched on the back. A present from Arlo a few Christmases back.

Helen's first ball knocked down nine pins, and her second picked up the spare. Fern knocked down six on her first try and two on her second. Helen gave her a short coaching session on keeping her wrist tight and straight as Joe prepared to throw his first.

The crack of pins drew everyone's attention.

"You're a bowler, I see." Helen said.

Camille smiled prettily, as if she'd been holding in the secret all along.

"I've always been an avid bowler," Joe said.

Sam leaned in close. And the smell of his aftershave tickled Arlo's senses. So different than high school and yet so much the same. "That didn't come up in my investigation," he whispered near her ear.

"I spent some time inside," Joe said. "Those of us who had proven that we were there to serve our time and not cause any problems were given a few special privileges." He gave another one of those charming smiles. "Bowling was one of those."

Camille patted his cheek as she went to retrieve her ball.

"Nor did that come up in my investigation."

Arlo scooted a little closer to Sam, just to make certain no one else could hear. And that reason only. "That means he's come clean with her."

"It would seem so."

"And it doesn't seem like he's trying to hide it from anyone else either."

"He's got a cross on the back of his hand." Arlo allowed her gaze to drift to where Joe's hand rested on his knee. Indeed there was a cross tattooed there. It appeared as if there was a cloth draped around the symbol and what looked to be a tear. Or maybe a drop of blood. Arlo wasn't certain. She didn't know enough about such things to make a guess as to its significance.

"I suppose he found God on the inside?" Sam asked.

"It looks that way." And Arlo was somewhat relieved. It appeared that Joe was exactly who he said he was and perhaps even exactly who they thought him to be. And she was beginning to believe that it wasn't him that she had seen that day at Lillyfield, the day Haley was killed.

When it was Arlo's turn, she managed to pick up a spare before taking her seat again.

"I still can't believe they brought you in for questioning," Camille said.

Sam stopped on his way to the line.

"They brought you in for questioning?"

Joe shrugged as if it was no big deal. "Just standard stuff, I guess."

"I for one find it disgraceful that they would ask you to come in when you don't even know Haley Adams. Have you even been to Lillyfield mansion?" Camille asked.

"It happens." Joe shrugged.

If Arlo was reading them correctly, he was trying to make it less of it so Camille wouldn't get angry. Arlo had a feeling he was called in anytime anything happened in whatever small town he happened to be in. But she couldn't imagine. Seeing as how they had no record of him anywhere except for Memphis six months ago. Her thoughts warred with each other. He seemed like a big teddy bear; he doted on Camille and had obviously turned his life around. He hadn't said what he'd gone to prison for, and Arlo wasn't about to ask. But she had an idea that as soon as Fern thought about it she would. But it was so suspicious that he had no past.

No one doesn't have a past. He just had a hidden one. And why would someone want to hide their past? If they didn't want anyone else to know.

The real question was why?

"It's not worth getting upset over," Joe said.

"I still think it's shameful," Camille said.

"You said disgraceful," Fern agreed.

"It's both." Camille nodded emphatically.

"Where are you staying while you're in town?" Helen asked. Ever the business owner.

"I have an apartment in Corinth," Joe said.

"And that's how you found Camille?" Fern asked. Like she didn't already know.

"Golden Years." He smiled at Camille, and she returned it, beaming. Arlo had never seen her happier, and the idea was both sweet and unsettling. To fall in love that quick, that fast, it just seemed that heartbreak was inevitable.

"Jason is a little zealous," Fern said, turning the conversation back to Joe being called into the police for questioning.

"Amen to that," Sam said, having just returned from executing a perfect strike. It seemed that the teams were a little more well balanced than Arlo had originally thought.

"Where'd you learn to do that?" Arlo asked.

Sam grinned. "Wouldn't you like to know?"

"Jason's just trying to make sure he does right," Helen said.

"I don't blame him," Joe said. "Now let's talk about something else."

The conversation immediately turned from Joe and his police woes to the merits of nachos versus pizza.

Arlo caught Sam's gaze.

Did Joe want to change the subject because he had more to hide than what he was letting on, or was he simply tired of being the main focus of the conversation?

There was no way to know.

21

"WOULD YOU LOOK AT THIS." FERN BUZZED INTO THE Books and More shortly after Arlo unlocked the doors and turned the sign from CLOSED to OPEN. She wielded a yellow file folder high over her head as she marched over to where Arlo stood next to Faulkner's cage.

"Good morning, honey," Faulkner said, climbing up the inside of his wire cage as Arlo folded up the canvas cover.

"Good morning," Fern replied.

"What am I looking at?" Arlo asked, holding out a hand for the file.

"Help!" Faulkner called. "I'm being held prisoner. Help. Someone call the cops."

"Heavens!" Fern exclaimed. "Get him out first and then we'll talk."

Arlo laughed. "That's Jayden's influence. He's taught the bird all sorts of things this week."

"Perfect." Fern waited until Arlo had released Faulkner before handing her the files. "Mary Kennedy's medical records."

Arlo accepted the file and sank down into the couch.

"The butler did it!" Faulkner squawked.

"Mary Kennedy's medical records?" Arlo repeated.

"Yup."

Arlo shut her eyes briefly. "Do I want to know how you got these?" Arlo asked.

"Mary Kennedy is the piano teacher who went missing," Fern said.

"Missing! Missing!"

"I know who Mary Kennedy is," Arlo said. "I just don't know how you got her confidential medical records." She flipped open the folder and scanned the first page. "Are these even real?"

Fern crossed her arms in a self-satisfied way. "One hundred percent."

"And they came from?"

"The Sugar Springs Medical Clinic."

"You didn't break into the place to steal these records. Please tell me you didn't."

"I most certainly did not. I cut my finger." Fern held up the injured digit. "They were just lying there."

Arlo shook her head and tried to make sense of what Fern was saying. There was an explanation in there somewhere, she was certain of it.

"Okay, so you cut your finger and went to Sugar Springs Medical Clinic."

"That's right."

"And while you're there you snooped around and found Mary Kennedy's medical records?"

"They were just out in the open. It seems that the medical clinic is getting computerized, and they're putting all the old medical records into the system. They've hired temps and everything. I thought about maybe getting a job. Anyway, they were just laying out there."

It was perfectly plausible yet hard to believe all in the same moment.

"How did you cut your finger?"

"Opening a can of refried beans."

"This morning? Never mind."

Only Fern would cut her finger on a can bad enough to need stitches.

"Then I went to the medical clinic," Fern continued. "While I was waiting, the girl went to the back, and I just happened to see them lying there."

"Out in the waiting room?"

Fern gave a small shrug. "Maybe I went behind the glass. But I was getting bored, and there were no magazines, and I don't know where everyone else is today…"

Truth be known, Arlo was shocked but not surprised that Fern had actually taken the files.

Fern gave another one of those negligent shrugs. "I figure since us girls are the only ones who seem to be interested in what happened to Mary Kennedy and bringing her killer to justice, she wouldn't care if I took her medical file."

HIPAA be damned.

"And you know what it says in her file?" Fern continued.

"I'm sure you're going to tell me," Arlo replied.

Fern plowed on, undeterred. "Mary Kennedy was pregnant when she disappeared."

"Really?" Arlo didn't want to appear too interested, but that did make things a little more…interesting.

"Just think about it. We found letters from Weston Whitney in her car—"

"We found a wet mess of papers that may or may not have been from Weston. For all we know, they could have been grocery lists."

But Fern was already on a tear. "And then there was the necklace that she was accused of taking from the mansion. That Weston assuredly planted in her car. Not to mention the car managed to miraculously stay covered up for fifty years in a man-made lake in Mississippi.

"I think this proves that she was murdered," Fern said.

"How so?"

But Fern didn't have a chance to answer as the bell over the door rang and someone came into the Books and More.

Arlo stood and handed the file folder back to Fern. "Hey there, Phil," Arlo said.

"No coffee today?" Phil asked.

"We got the self-serve if that'll do," Arlo said, coming around and out of the reading nook in order to fully greet him. "Courtney's still out. But Chloe'll be in later. Then we'll be back to normal on Monday."

Phil nodded.

Behind him, Joey from the dry cleaners slipped into the bookstore.

"Help yourself," Arlo said to them both, and Phil gave a quick nod.

Fern sidled up next to her as Phil moved over to the coffee bar and started brewing his cup from the Keurig, idly chatting with Joey about the weather and ring around the collar. "If she was pregnant and leaving her husband,

and she stole the necklace to finance her escape, then why would she have left it in the car?"

"I don't know," Arlo said. Too much at one time, and all the crazy thoughts and theories were starting to give her a headache. The last thing she needed on a Saturday.

"I'll tell you why. Because Weston Whitney found out that she was carrying his baby. See, the two of them were having an affair."

Arlo shook her head. "Wait, wait, wait. Where'd you get all that?"

"Just hear me out," Fern said. "This is a deductive reasoning at its finest."

Arlo had her doubts about that.

"Now, where was I?" Fern continued. "The affair. Right."

Arlo glanced around the bookstore to make sure her customers were all okay and no one needed any help before returning her attention to Fern.

"Weston and Mary Kennedy were having an affair. She told him she was pregnant. He killed her, put her and her car in the lake, placed the necklace in there so that she could be accused of stealing it, and the rest is history, as they say."

Or an unsolved mystery.

"Then why wasn't her body in the car?" Arlo asked.

"I don't know. Maybe she's out there buried in all that mud somewhere."

And that just didn't make sense.

"Weston Whitney couldn't have been the father of her baby," Arlo said. "Everyone in town knows that they couldn't have children. That's why Judith and Weston adopted Baxter."

Sam took that minute to come into the bookstore from

the third-floor door. At least this time he didn't scare the bejesus out of her.

"I thought you were taking today off," she said.

"Duty calls," Sam quipped.

"I bet Sam agrees with me," Fern said.

"About what?"

"You had to ask," Arlo said in return.

Fern explained to him her theory of the affair between Weston and Mary Kennedy, about the planted necklace, undiscovered murder, and a car that had been purposely concealed for the last fifty years.

"It does make some sense though," Sam said.

"Don't you start too." Arlo shook her head. "There's no way that Weston Whitney could be the father of Mary Kennedy's baby if she was indeed pregnant when she disappeared because he and Judith couldn't have children. And everyone knows that it wasn't Judith's fault."

Sam tapped his finger on his chin thoughtfully. "And how do you know that it was Judith's fault and not Weston's?"

How did she know? She knew because everyone in town knew. That was the kind of town Sugar Springs was. "The grapevine, I guess."

"And the grapevine is never wrong," Fern scoffed.

"All I'm saying is we don't have any proof," Arlo said. "As entertaining as this is, it's simply speculation."

Fern's eyes twinkled with a triumphant gleam. "That's why I took Weston's file too." She raised the other file into the air as if holding the Olympic torch of crime solving.

"I feel very confident in saying there is no way both of these files were out in the open; you went behind the glass." Arlo frowned.

Fern just shrugged "Weston Whitney's file claims that he is not sterile. The reason they couldn't have children was Judith. She was barren."

"Did you take her file too?"

"I didn't have to. But I want to take this to Mads." Fern held up both files, at least a little lower this time and not quite so triumphantly.

"Mads doesn't want to open this case again," Arlo said. As bad as the girls wanted Mads to, Arlo could see his point of view on the matter. This was a decades-old murder, and most everyone involved in it was dead. It wasn't like they could bring Mary Kennedy's killer to justice. Not unless her killer was Judith; she was the only one left alive. A zing of something shot through Arlo. *What if...?*

"See," Fern said. "Now you're thinking. I saw the look on your face. You know it's true."

"Indigestion," Arlo lied.

"I'm going to take these to Mads." Fern indicated the two folders she held.

"You're going to take stolen medical records to the police chief with the hope that he will reopen a murder case?" Arlo asked. "Am I getting all this?"

Sam chuckled, and Arlo shot him a look. He immediately sobered. "Maybe that isn't the best idea."

She glared at him. "You think?"

"Fine," Fern huffed. She collapsed back to the sofa in the reading nook and set the files down next to her. "But I'm not taking them back either."

"Whatever does it for you," Arlo said.

"I doubt anyone will even miss them." Fern crossed her arms in a defiant gesture.

"She's probably right, you know," Sam said where only Arlo could hear.

"Don't you dare encourage her."

"Want to do lunch today?"

Arlo blinked at Sam. "I thought you were busy."

He nodded. "I am. But everybody has to stop for lunch. What say I run by The Diner and pick you up something?"

A warm and greasy hamburger compared to the cold peanut butter and jelly sandwich she had in her lunch box? No contest.

"I'll take you up on that, but I have to eat here. Chloe and Jayden are having an adjustment period."

"I wouldn't have it any other way." And with that, Sam gave her his patented carefree smile and made his way back upstairs.

Monday came, and everyone was talking again, but this time the conversation had shifted.

"Say that again," Helen instructed just after Fern had breezed in with her big announcement. It was early afternoon, the usual time for the book club to gather, except Fern was late, and Camille hadn't shown up at all.

Arlo couldn't decide if she should be sad or mournful. Was her book club experiment completely fizzling out?

"Courtney is at the police station telling Mads about how she and Dylan went to Corinth together on the day Haley was killed. She said there was no way that Dylan could be guilty because he was with her."

"They were together at the very time Haley was pushed down the stairs?" Helen asked.

"She wasn't pushed down the stairs. At least that's not what killed her," Fern reminded them. "But yes. At the very same time that she was conked on the head at the mansion with an ugly statuette, Courtney and Dylan were in Corinth."

"I don't understand," Helen said. "I thought they had him on CCTV at the mansion."

"Apparently the date was wrong."

Arlo and Chloe exchanged a look.

"Where's Camille?" Chloe asked. "Is she not coming?"

Helen shrugged. "Out with Joe, I guess."

"What were you doing at the police station?" Chloe asked.

"I went to take Frances some of my strawberries," Fern said.

Helen sniffed. "You haven't brought me any of your strawberries."

Fern shot her a look. "You haven't asked."

"So you went to the police station and overheard Courtney talking to Mads," Chloe reiterated.

"You got it."

"What do you think?" Chloe asked, looking to Arlo.

"It's possible, I guess," she replied.

"That I went to the police station or that I overheard the conversation I was just talking about?" Fern asked with a stern frown.

"Both," Arlo replied with a cheeky smile.

"What I want to know is why they went to Corinth together," Helen said.

"Let's go to Corinth!" Faulkner intoned. "Lots to do in Corinth."

"Well, it's obvious that he's never been there," Sam joked.

While they had been talking, he had come down the stairs to join them.

"Hey, Sam." Fern waved, then continued her story. "She told Mads that she and Dylan had gone to look at promise rings."

A moment of silence fell between them. Dylan had been about to pledge his love to his girl, and unbeknownst to him, she was being murdered at the very time he was picking out her ring.

"If they went at all, you mean," Helen said.

"You doubt it?" Chloe asked. "It seems like a logical enough reason to me."

Arlo turned to Sam. "You want to weigh in on this?"

Sam shrugged. "Not sure what I can add since I missed the first part."

Fern took a quick moment to fill Sam in on the details of how she had gone into the police station that morning and overheard Courtney supplying Dylan with an alibi.

"What she's saying can be easily checked," Sam said. "She most likely has a list of the jewelry stores where they went. All she'll have to do is give it to Jason or Mads, and they will go over to Corinth and ask around."

"Can they do that?" Fern asked. "They don't have any jurisdiction there."

Arlo had to credit Sam with keeping a straight face as he replied. "They don't need jurisdiction to ask questions. But I'm sure they'll contact the Corinth police before they go. Mads knows not to step on toes."

"So they go to Corinth and ask around," Helen said. "What then?"

"Hopefully they will find a jewelry store clerk who remembers Courtney and Dylan and can corroborate their story. Or if they purchased something, that would be even better."

"Because their receipt will have a time stamp on it." Fern nodded in understanding.

"You hope. Some of those stores in Corinth can be a little behind the times."

Fern shot Helen a look. "Yes, and Sugar Springs is an edgy metropolis."

"I'm just saying," Helen confirmed, "if they went downtown, there are a lot of older, family-owned stores there who still write hand receipts."

"She's right," Arlo said.

"The date might be enough," Sam said.

"Courtney's a pretty girl," Helen said. "Enough that most red-blooded American males would remember her."

She hoped. They all did. None of them wanted to see Dylan in trouble.

"What about his confession?" Arlo asked.

"How can he have a confession and an alibi?" Chloe wanted to know. "That doesn't make much sense to me." She turned as Phil came in from next door.

He gave her a quick nod, and she started his usual without a word exchanged between them.

"Confessions can be tricky. Especially if coerced," Sam said. He made his way around the sofa and perched on the edge of the chair closest to Faulkner's cage.

"The butler did it! He's guilty." Remarkably Faulkner made a sound similar to a gavel being banged.

Sam looked to Arlo.

She shrugged. She honestly had no idea where he picked up the things he did. When she had first gotten the bird, he'd known a few choice phrases, but since then, Arlo had managed to weed out most of his more questionable vocabulary. But it seemed as if he picked up words and phrases in his sleep.

"You think he was coerced?" Helen whistled low. "That doesn't mark good for Jason or Mads."

Sam held both hands up as if surrendering. "I'm not saying he was coerced. You were there when he confessed."

They all nodded. They had all been there.

"Maybe he's just impressionable?" Arlo asked.

"He's not even twenty years old," Sam explained. "You remember what it was like for you at nineteen?"

"No," Helen said with a shake of her head.

"Yes," Fern replied, a dreamy quality to her voice.

"Well, I do," Sam said. "I thought I knew everything. I thought I was grown, that I could make good decisions. I thought I had it all and a bag of chips."

Arlo had felt the same, but looking back, she realized just how dumb and immature she had been. But at the time she had been dang near bulletproof, chips and all. Yet she understood. Dylan had been questioned as an adult. He was legally that, but the scary truth was, he was nothing more than a half-grown kid.

"I would like to think that at his age I wouldn't have done anything like confess to a murder that I didn't commit, but I can't say that it's the truth. I did some dumb things when I was that age," Sam admitted.

Hadn't they all?

Sam looked up and caught Arlo's gaze. So many questions raised themselves, and none of them had anything to do with Dylan and Haley, and everything to do with her, Mads, and Sam. Oh, the mistakes she had made. Perhaps they had all made.

But a person couldn't go back. They couldn't change anything. And she knew for a fact that she wouldn't be the same person she was today had she not lived the life she had lived and made the mistakes that she had made.

Sam looked away, and Arlo did too, but her gaze collided with Chloe's. Her best friend raised a brow in question, but Arlo had nothing she could say about the matter. Nothing she could say here, in front of everyone, and in truth, nothing she could really say at all. Sam wanted to talk, but they had yet to do so. Maybe soon…

"What happens now?" Chloe asked.

She had given Phil his coffee, but instead of returning to his store, he propped one elbow on the bar and waited for the story to continue.

"I suppose the DA will look over evidence and see if he thinks there's enough to keep the charges against him."

"She," Helen corrected. "We have a lady DA now."

"You don't say," Sam drawled. "Northeast Mississippi will get into the twenty-first century yet."

"Don't count on it," Fern quipped.

"And if she doesn't think there's enough evidence?"

Sam shrugged. "She'll let him go."

Fern winced. "Jason is not going to like that one bit."

"Like it or not, that's what will happen."

"And it's certainly not right to keep an innocent person in jail," Phil said.

"Hear, hear." Chloe raised her water bottle in salute.

"If Jason still thinks he's guilty, then he'll have to find more compelling evidence against him," Sam explained. "But if he is innocent…"

"Then Jason needs to find another suspect," Helen finished for him.

"Or some more leads," Sam said.

"Against who?" Arlo asked. Who could have been angry enough or hateful enough to bludgeon a young premed student with an ugly, overpriced statue? What sort of enemies did a girl like Haley have? Arlo had no clue. But she wasn't the only one.

Sam shook his head. "I have no idea."

....

"I know who did it," Fern declared, sweeping into the Books and More the following day. It was noon, and both Camille and Sam had managed to make today's meeting, though Helen was running behind. She had called Arlo to tell her that she had a guest coming in and would need to be there when they arrived. Of course, that guest was running late, and when they got there, then she would be on her way.

"Who?" Camille said. She was on her feet in a second.

Fern eyed her coolly. "So good of you to join us."

"Jealous much?" Camille asked.

Fern waved away the words. "Guess," she said, pinning Arlo with an ardent look.

"Guess what?" Arlo asked. Somewhere between Fern coming in and shelving books in the religion section, she had lost the thread.

"Who killed Haley," Fern said impatiently.

"I got this," Chloe said. As usual, her friend and business partner was manning the coffee bar, preparing for the midmorning rush of toddlers when the mommy and me group let out a few doors down. "Who killed Haley?"

"Anastasia Whitney." Fern stopped, perhaps waiting for

applause. None was coming. Everyone around looked a bit stunned.

"Anastasia?" Arlo asked. "Judith's granddaughter?"

"Yes." Fern nodded so vigorously that she almost slung her hat from her head.

"Did I miss something?" Helen asked, coming into the bookstore.

"Yes," Fern said with a glare.

"I think we all did," Arlo said.

Fern gave them all a stern look as if they hadn't been paying good enough attention, and the confusion was their own fault and had nothing to do with her cryptic speech. "Let me reiterate," she said. "I believe that Anastasia Whitney, daughter of Baxter and Katherine, and granddaughter of Judith and Weston, is responsible for Haley Adams's murder."

"That's some accusation."

Fern shot Sam an indulgent smile. "Stay with me here. It'll all be clear in a sec."

"I sure hope so," Arlo murmured.

"What if Anastasia was written out of the will?" Fern asked.

"That's a mighty big what-if," Sam pointed out.

"I know," Fern replied. "But hear me out."

"Go on," Helen said. She took her usual seat in the over-stuffed armchair and waited for Fern to continue.

In fact, they all waited.

"Everyone in town knows that Judith is paying for Haley's education."

"They do?" Sam asked.

"Ditto," Arlo said.

"That's right." Camille nodded.

"And everybody knows?" Arlo asked.

"Everyone who goes to Dye Me a River more than two times a decade," Helen quipped.

Arlo supposed that it must be true, or at the very least it was a common belief in the beauty parlor circuits, for Helen did not dispute her.

"I figured she was grooming her to be her own personal doctor. You know," Helen said. "Like Elvis had. And Michael Jackson."

Arlo frowned. "I don't think anyone under the pay rate of Elvis or Michael Jackson can afford their own physician."

"You'd be surprised," Fern said.

Camille and Helen nodded.

"Her own physician how?" Sam asked.

"You know for constant care and drugs, maybe even for Botox," Fern grumped. "How am I supposed to know what the uberwealthy use their personal physicians for?"

"Valid point," Sam retuned, but Arlo saw the corners of his mouth twitching.

"So you're saying that Judith was paying for Haley to go to school for ten years or better so she could get free Botox?" Arlo asked.

"Don't get hung up on the details," Fern said.

"I thought she was paying for Haley's school because Judith and Haley's grandfather had something going on back in the day," Camille said.

Helen and Fern turned toward her, sharply, as if they couldn't believe what she had just said. "When and where did you hear that?" they both asked at the same time.

"Last time I was at the beauty parlor of course," Camille patted the perfect curls at the back of her head.

"We both go to the beauty parlor on Friday, and I didn't hear anything like that when I was there. And I was there the entire time you were."

Camille turned pink, not exactly a good color with her mint-green pantsuit. "Maybe I went another time too."

Helen looked positively betrayed. "When?" she asked. "When did you go?"

"I may have gone back on Monday," Camille said.

"May have?" Helen's tone was accusing.

"Yes. A girl has to look her best, you know."

From her place behind the bar, Chloe sniggered. Arlo shushed her, and thankfully none of the book club ladies heard.

"For Joe, I suppose," Fern grumbled.

"Of course." By this time, Camille had returned to her normal color, though Fern was turning a bit red herself now.

"I don't think that's the case at all," Helen said. "I don't think Judith wants her own doctor, and I don't believe for a minute that she had an affair with Haley's grandfather."

"So why would she pay for her school?" Sam asked. "Assuming that she is indeed paying for it."

"She's paying all right," Fern said.

"Maybe she's just trying to be kind."

Everyone stopped.

"Judith Whitney?" Fern scoffed once she had recovered.

"Judith Whitney has never done a kind thing in her life," Camille said.

"I don't know," Chloe put in. "She did adopt a child."

Baxter. Anastasia's father.

"Trust me, the woman had an ulterior motive for that one too," Fern said.

"But all of that doesn't add up to her granddaughter being slighted enough to kill someone," Sam pointed out.

"Maybe not for you or me," Fern said. "But these are the Whitneys we're talking about."

23

"What about Mary Kennedy?" Arlo asked a little later.

The ladies waved off her question.

"We'll get back to her," Helen said. "Right now, we're working on Dylan."

"If he's innocent, he needs to be let out of jail," Fern said.

"I couldn't agree more," Arlo said. "But finding the evidence of his guilt or innocence is up to Jason. And Mads."

"They're up to their elbows in calls and false leads." Fern scoffed. "That's why it's important for the citizens to do their part."

"Book. Club." Arlo said the words slowly and succinctly.

"That too." Helen held up her book, filled with little slips of paper and those self-sticking strips to keep the most interesting places marked.

Camille gasped, and all eyes turned to her. "What if this is all a setup?"

Arlo rested her forehead on the shelf in front of her.

Sam came up behind her and squeezed her shoulder. Even with her eyes closed, she could feel his silent laughter.

"OMG," Fern said. "You might just be right."

"And they're off again," Sam murmured.

"Just as long as they remain in the reading nook and aren't under Mads's feet," Arlo said.

"Or Jason's."

"Or Jason's," Arlo agreed.

"It makes perfect sense now," Fern was saying.

"What makes perfect sense?" Arlo asked, but none of the book club ladies were listening to her.

"Great," Sam said. "Now they believe that Dylan was framed, most probably by the person who killed Haley."

"Naturally," Arlo replied.

"And that's how a sweet kid like Dylan Wright got into such trouble," Camille intoned.

"What about his confession?" Arlo asked. That got their attention.

"I, for one, believe it was a coerced confession." Fern gave an emphatic nod. "You see it all the time these days. Police are under pressure to make an arrest, so they find their suspect and basically talk him into believing that he's guilty and the rest is history."

"Like the West Memphis Three," Helen said.

"You were there," Arlo reminded them. If anyone had coerced Dylan into confessing, it certainly hadn't been Mads or Jason.

"Do you really believe that Jason was under so much pressure that he found someone and made him think he was guilty? Made him confess? Who would put that kind of pressure on him?" Or Mads?

"The members of the First Baptist for one." Fern frowned. She and the First Baptist Church had parted ways before

Arlo had even moved to town, but she never missed an opportunity to blame them for whatever was wrong. From the heat of the sun to the price of gasoline, as far as Fern was concerned, the First Baptist Church had a hand in it.

"Fern, be serious," Arlo beseeched.

"I am." She gave Arlo an innocent look. "That's where poor Jason goes to church, and I imagine Madge Sanders had a thing or two to say about the matter."

Madge was one of the few over-eighty crowd who hadn't shown up for Friday-night-turned-every-day book club. Chances were great that she had heard that Fern was coming and opted out. Yes, their feud was that strong, though Arlo was certain neither one could remember what it was about.

Then again…Fern did have a mind like a steel trap.

And Madge did tend to be a little…strong at times. If she wanted something done, by God she got it done.

"Why would it be so important to Madge?" Arlo asked. Madge might be a force living in Sugar Springs, but she usually had to have a stake in whatever it was before she got involved.

"She lives next door to Dylan," Helen said. "I'm sure having a murderer so close was a little unnerving."

"Only if he's truly guilty," Arlo said. "If he isn't—and I don't think he is—then the real murderer is still out running around."

Everyone stopped.

"We have to do something." Helen was on her feet in a heartbeat. "We have to do something now."

"Like?" Camille stood, and Fern followed suit.

"We could go down to the police station and demand that Mads let Dylan go," Helen suggested.

"Please," Arlo begged. "Don't."

Chloe checked her watch. "I have to get Jayden from school." She shot Arlo a *forgive me* look but went to retrieve her purse.

Arlo waved her away. "Go. Get your boy."

The ladies started shuffling around the reading nook deciding what to take and what to leave behind when they walked down to the police station.

"I could go with them if you want," Sam said.

Arlo nearly wilted in relief. "Would you? I promised Mads I would keep them off Lillyfield grounds, but I have a feeling he really meant that I needed to keep them fully in check."

Sam chuckled. "Yeah, good luck with that."

. . . .

Jayden was seated at the coffee bar doing his homework when the ladies and Sam returned to the Books and More.

Sam's phone rang right as he walked into the door. He checked the screen, then shot Arlo an apologetic look as he motioned that he had to take the call. She nodded and he headed back out onto the presummer sunshine.

"That took a while," Arlo said as the ladies drew near.

"Well, you know Mads," Helen said. She settled down in the reading nook.

"Where's Sam?" Fern asked, looking around.

Arlo nodded toward the window, where they could just see Sam pacing back and forth as he listened to the person on the other end. "Phone call."

"What did you find out?" Chloe asked.

"They've already released Dylan. A clerk at the jewelry store where he bought a promise ring with Courtney's help confirmed Courtney's story," Camille said.

Arlo frowned. "What I don't understand is why he didn't tell that story earlier." It was almost as if he was willing to go to prison rather than tell the truth. And if Courtney hadn't stepped up, then that truth would still be unknown. The whole thing was strange.

"It's weird, I tell you." Fern settled back in her place on the couch.

"Weirdo! Weirdo!" Faulkner called.

"I agree," Helen said.

"And I stand by the theory that it's a setup. Dylan was a patsy for someone," Fern added.

"The question is who," Camille chimed in.

"It is not a setup," Arlo protested. "He's not taking the fall."

"So how do you explain the false confession and him not telling the whole truth when Mads arrested him?" Helen asked.

"I can't explain it. But things like what you're talking about just don't happen in places like Sugar Springs. Or in real life even."

"'Truth is stranger than fiction,'" Camille quoted.

"There you go." Fern gave a satisfied nod. "You can't argue with Mark Twain."

"Actually, it was Lord Byron," Camille said.

Fern frowned as if Camille had committed a grievous error. "You're an Aussie; what do you know about Missouri philosophers? That was Mark Twain."

"'Tis strange—but true; for truth is always strange;

Stranger than fiction; if it could be told, How much would novels gain by the exchange!'" Camille nodded in satisfaction.

"Looks like we've got a second Revolutionary War waging." Chloe chuckled softly.

"I know how to solve this." Arlo made her way over to the large quote book she had in the living section. But before she could even find the page the quote would be on, Helen spoke.

"'Truth is stranger than fiction, but it is because fiction is obliged to stick to possibilities; truth isn't.' Mark Twain said that." Helen held up her phone for all to see.

Fern gave a satisfied grunt. "See?"

"But Lord Byron said Camille's quote a few years before Twain was even born," Helen continued.

"Score one for down under!" Camille raised her hands in victory.

"I thought Lord Byron was British," Chloe said.

"I don't think it matters to them," Arlo replied.

Chloe nodded. "Right."

"Exactly." Arlo reshelved the book.

"Look at you, using your phone like a seasoned professional." Camille smiled, obviously still tickled at winning the quote war.

Helen stood and took a bow.

Arlo returned to the reading nook as the bell over the door rang. She turned toward the sound expecting to see Sam coming in after his call, but it was Joe Foster who stepped into Books and More.

"Joe." Camille stood. "What are you doing here?"

He jerked a thumb over his shoulder. "I was down at the police station."

"Is everything okay?" she asked, her voice heavy with concern.

"Yeah, just…you know. They wanted to question me about Haley."

Camille pressed her lips together and shook her head, her frustration evident as she asked, "Why would they need to talk to you again?"

"You know, just normal stuff."

"No, I don't know." Camille's agitation grew.

"You just went down there and told Mads that he had the wrong suspect," Arlo said. "What did you expect him to do?"

"Not bring my…friend in for questioning. Again."

"It's no problem, Camille." Joe wrung his hands, obviously uncomfortable with the whole situation.

"It is. The only reason they brought you in was because of how you look. And that's discrimination." Camille propped her hands on her hips as if daring anyone to disagree with her.

She was right, of course, but at the same time, Arlo wondered how men like Jason and Mads, Sam even, started a successful investigation.

"He's just kicking over rocks," Arlo said. "At least, that's what I've heard Mads call it." Or maybe it was Sam.

Camille turned to Arlo with a frown. "Rocks? What are you talking about?"

"He's investigating," Helen explained. "Leave no stone unturned."

"I suppose you want to credit that to Mark Twain as well." Camille shot a pointed look at Fern.

"Greek mythology." Helen raised her phone as if they could all see the screen.

"All I'm saying is he's probably looking at everyone and everything." Arlo replied.

"Then why wasn't I called in? Or Chloe? Or Helen?" Camille asked.

"Camille," Joe protested.

He really was a sweet man, prison tats and scary appearance aside. But the fact that Joe had been in prison, came to town, and then a young girl was killed was enough to warrant at least a little investigation into his whereabouts on the day in question.

"Really. I mean it. If he's questioning everyone, then he should be questioning everyone."

"He is," Joe said. His voice had turned strangely quiet for such a large man. "Everyone who happened to be at Lillyfield that day."

Camille whirled to face him fully. She turned so fast it almost made Arlo dizzy. "What are you talking about?"

"I was at the mansion the day Haley died."

Camille blinked as if that would better help her process the information.

"I knew it!" Arlo couldn't stop the words from escaping her.

"You knew what?" Helen asked.

"What were you doing at the mansion? You have no reason to go out there," Camille continued.

"I knew I saw Joe. Well, I thought it was Joe. Now I know for certain," Arlo said, turning to Helen.

"Joe?" Camille prompted.

"I was there on a personal matter."

And definitely not to tour the house and grounds.

"A personal matter?" Camille looked as if she had been punched square in the gut. "Can you explain that to me?"

Joe stared at his hands for a moment, then settled his attention back on Camille. "No." One word. Short, sweet, simple. Final.

"I see." Camille's voice turned cold, and Joe took the hint.

"I guess I should be going." He let out a nervous-sounding chuckle. "I'll let you ladies get on with your book club meeting." He leaned in to give Camille a kiss, but she turned her face, and his buss landed on her cheek.

For a moment, Arlo thought he might say something. Then that moment was gone. Another moment passed, and so was he.

Camille looked around at all of them, even the few customers who had witnessed the exchange. "Why do I feel like I'm the only one in the room who doesn't know the secret?"

"No one's got any secrets," Fern said. "You're just being overly sensitive. No wonder, since lover boy has been stringing you along."

"Stringing me along?" Camille looked to Helen to see if she felt the same about Joe.

"Maybe," Helen said with a shrug.

The door leading to the third-floor staircase opened, and Sam stepped into the shop. "Hey," he said, by way of greeting.

"I didn't expect you to come in that way," Arlo explained.

He nodded. "I needed my computer, so I went up the side staircase."

Something was wrong, really wrong judging by Sam's pained expression.

"What is it?" Arlo asked.

He sighed, then moved toward the reading area. Arlo

followed while Chloe came out from behind the coffee bar to join them. She leaned behind Helen's chair. Fern was still sitting, and Camille still hovered.

"You're going to want to sit down for this," Sam said.

Camille shook her head. "I don't think I want to know." But she sat anyway.

"Once you started seeing Joe, Arlo came to me and asked me to check into him."

"But you couldn't find out anything older than six months ago," Arlo said.

Sam took in a deep breath and let it out slowly. At least it seemed slow to Arlo. Why was he just sitting there breathing and not explaining? "I just had a lead that panned out."

"And?" Arlo asked. She seemed more anxious than anyone else to find out just who Joe was. Maybe because on some level she felt responsible for the ladies in her book club.

"Joe Foster is really Jeff Kennedy."

"Kennedy?" Helen muttered. "Jeff Kennedy?"

"As in Mary Kennedy's husband?" Fern screeched.

Sam nodded. "As in Mary Kennedy's husband."

24

"Wait, wait, wait," Fern said.

Camille sat still as a statuette.

Helen's mouth fell open. "Mary Kennedy of *Missing Girl*?"

"Mary Kennedy who disappeared over forty years ago," Sam amended.

Fifty, but no one bothered to correct him.

Fern rubbed at her temples. "I can't process this."

Camille looked as if she was having the same problem. "Joe is Jeff," she muttered. "Not who he said he was at all." She turned to Arlo and Sam. "Why would he lie about that?"

Sam shrugged. "Maybe he was concerned that too many people here would recognize his name."

"But he was on the dating site as Joe Foster. Why would he lie there too?"

"He had his name legally changed," Sam explained. "He really isn't Jeff Kennedy any longer. Legally, he's Joe Foster."

"Jeff Kennedy," Camille muttered. "I can't believe it." Suddenly she was on her feet. "Going out to the mansion on a 'personal matter.' Lying to me about his true identity. Who does he think he is?"

"Where are you going?" Arlo asked as Camille jerked up her book bag and marched toward the door.

"I'm going to break things off with this Mr. Kennedy-Foster."

"Don't you think you should think this through?" Helen asked.

"Can I go with you?" Fern asked.

"No and no." Camille was out the door in a flash.

Should she go after her? Or let her be? Arlo squirmed in place but managed to keep her seat.

"So that explains the tattoos," Helen said.

"He spent, what, four? Five years in jail?" Fern asked.

"It was more like three and a half initially," Sam said. "But he had a parole violation and went back inside. The second go-round he ran into some trouble and got another thirty tacked on."

"Thirty?" Fern gasped. "What did he do to warrant that?"

"He killed a man over a piece of corn bread," Sam said.

"Please tell me you're kidding," Arlo said.

"I'm not." Sam stared at his hands for a moment, then unclasped them.

"Corn bread?" Helen asked. "I'm glad we didn't go out to supper last week. That could have been disastrous."

Sam shook his head in that understanding way he had. "It was a territory thing between gangs. Basically, it was kill or be killed. Joe chose the first route. I didn't say anything before because, unfortunately, that's just prison. And he didn't have any more trouble after that."

"I suppose not," Fern said.

"That's terrible." Helen shook her head.

"And he was railroaded into jail in the first place." Fern let out an exasperated sigh. "A woman disappears, probably to start a new life, and his life is ruined because of it."

"He did hit her," Arlo reminded them.

"Yeah, but she could have just left him outright. She didn't have to go to all the trouble of sinking her car in the lake," Fern said.

"That's true." Helen nodded.

Sam leaned back and stretched one arm along the back of the sofa. Arlo sat next to him, back stiff as they talked around her. "What if she didn't sink her car in the lake?"

Arlo turned to Sam. "The object here is to not encourage them."

Sam the skunk smiled innocently at her.

"Then who did?" Helen asked.

"Top of my short list is Weston Whitney. In fact, he's the only name on my list," Fern said.

"That would explain why the necklace was in the car. And maybe his papers too," Helen replied.

"Exactly." Sam nodded.

"But what about the baby?" Fern said.

"I'd forgotten about that," Arlo breathed.

Mary Kennedy had been pregnant.

"I guess that depends on whether or not Mary's dead," Helen said.

"She would have to be," Fern decided. "Why else would she have left the necklace behind?"

"Do you think she really took the necklace in order to fund a do-over somewhere?" Helen asked.

"It's as good a reason as any," Sam said.

Arlo agreed. But Mary hadn't gotten to start over. She had most likely died that night. At the hands of her suspected lover? Her husband? It was anyone's guess.

"I'm still struggling with the fact that you can have a murder without a body." Arlo said.

"It depends if there is evidence of an attack or a struggle," Sam said. "A jury must have felt strongly enough about the evidence against Jeff—Joe—to put him in jail for years."

Years that had cost him more years. His life.

Now he was back. The question was why.

25

"I don't see any way around it." Fern looked from Helen to Camille, who picked at an invisible spot on her pale-blue slacks.

Arlo who should been moving a stack of books to a new display set them down and made her way over to the reading nook. As much as she said she wasn't getting involved, it seemed like she was dragged in again and again. But this time it was important.

"I know you guys mean well," she started, "but do not bully Camille into doing something she doesn't want to do." She expected Helen to bluster up and deny that she was bullying anybody, just as she expected Fern to wave away her concerns as being mother hen. But both ladies dropped their gazes to their laps, sheepish looks on their faces.

"But they're right," Camille said. "I do need to confront him."

"You didn't talk to him last night?" Arlo asked.

"No," Camille said softly. "He came by the house and knocked and hollered and called a hundred times, but I didn't answer. I needed time to think. And quiet," she added. "And it seems like since I found out, I haven't had either."

"I understand." Arlo perched on the sofa next to Camille. "You want to talk this through?"

Finally, Camille looked up from her lap. Her gaze met Arlo's, and she squeezed Arlo's hand, the gesture thankful. "I'm not sure there's much to talk through."

"Seems like a lot to me," Arlo said.

"I just want to know why," Camille said.

There was a lot of room for interpretation in that one. Why he had deceived her? Why he had gone to prison? Why he was back? There were a lot of *whys* to be uncovered, and Arlo didn't know which one Camille was referring to. And she wasn't sure she knew how to ask. But she delved in any way. "Why what?"

"Why he didn't tell me who he really is?"

"Maybe he wanted a chance to start again?" Arlo said.

"I think she's right," Helen said quietly.

"I agree," Fern was the calmest that Arlo had seen her all morning. "You can't start over if you keep telling everybody every detail of your past."

"And he did tell you had been in prison, right?" Arlo asked.

"He did, but…"

"But what?"

"I just don't think I can have a relationship with someone who can't be honest with me about who he is."

"If he was in the witness protection program? Would you expect him to tell you all then?" Fern asked.

When had Fern jumped on this Joe bandwagon? Yesterday she was ready to hang him up by his toes.

Camille was on her feet in a second. "I've got to go talk to him," she said. She grabbed her book bag; her purse was of course still hooked around one arm.

"Go get him, girl," Helen said.

"We'll be right here when you get back," Fern said. "We're not going anywhere."

Arlo stood as Camille bustled out of the Books and More. She just hoped her friend was making the right choice, and this wasn't a mistake to define her entire life.

. . . .

Two hours later Arlo's phone rang. She snatched it up and checked the screen. "It's Camille," she said.

"Answer it," Helen admonished. Like Arlo had no intentions of answering the phone. Like they hadn't been waiting for Camille to call for the last two hours.

"Camille?" Arlo greeted her after swiping the screen.

"Hello, love," Camille said. That lost puppy tone was gone from her voice, and that dreamy, *I'm so in love* vibe was back. "I just wanted to call and let you girls know that everything is fine. Joe explained it all, and I'm so glad I gave him the chance."

"So are you coming back to the Books and More?" Arlo asked. What a dumb question. It wasn't like the bookstore was an everyday sort of hangout. At least, it hadn't been until recently.

"Oh no, love." Camille chuckled. "Joe has some unfinished business, and I told him I would help him."

Arlo frowned. "Unfinished business?"

"Taking care of business! Taking care of business!" Faulkner squawked, drowning out anything Camille said.

Arlo motioned for Helen to try to keep the bird quiet.

"What did she say?" Fern demanded.

"Camille, can you repeat that?"

"Joe's daughter," Camille repeated. "That's why he came here. He wanted to find his daughter."

In a flash Arlo ran through any Kennedys that she knew in Sugar Springs or the surrounding area. She was certain there had to be a couple or so. After all, Kennedy wasn't that uncommon of a name, but for the life of her she couldn't think of even one. Or maybe the daughter would be a Foster...?

"He has a daughter?" Arlo asked.

"A daughter?" Fern echoed.

"Joe?" Helen asked.

Chloe whirled around as if trying to make sure she was hearing correctly.

"Yes, love," Camille said gently. "Joe has a daughter he's never met. And he came here to find her. It seems she works out at Lillyfield, and we're going out there now to talk to her."

"Joe has a daughter?" Arlo said, once more for confirmation.

"Isn't it amazing? One of those ancestry sites put them together. He found her birth certificate under her mother's name, and there you have it."

"But he's been in prison." Arlo hated saying it outright, but it was the truth after all.

Camille shook her head. "I didn't ask him all that. But I figure he did the math on it and knows that the daughter is his."

Incredible. Maybe that was why Joe was at Lillyfield

when Haley was killed. He said his business was personal; it didn't get much more personal than a daughter whom a father had never met.

"Okay," Arlo said. "I'll tell everyone that you won't be back today." The words made a rock of apprehension form in the pit of her stomach. Camille, sweet Camille, was out with Joe, who beat his wife allegedly. Who went to prison, killed a man over corn bread. And who had been nothing but kind to Camille as far as Arlo could see.

People change.

She could only hope.

She wanted this to be a happy time for Camille and Joe. There were no more secrets between them, at least Arlo didn't think so, and the two of them were headed to find his long-lost daughter. That sounded enough like a happy ending to her. Why did she feel as if it was all about to go sideways? Maybe because he still might be a suspect in Haley's murder? Or was her mother hen gene showing again?

"Thanks, love." Camille hung up, and Arlo looked at the phone screen trying to gather the wayward pieces of her thoughts. Why did it not seem like everything should be hunky-dory?

"Joe has a daughter?" Helen asked.

Arlo pocketed her phone and nodded, still unable to shake that uneasy feeling.

"Well, kiss a pig," Fern said. "Who would've thought that?"

"What's wrong, honey?" Helen asked.

Arlo shook her head but made her way back to the reading nook where Helen and Fern waited.

"Gimme some sugar, honey," Faulkner chirped.

"I don't know," Arlo said. "I mean, I should feel happy for Joe, right? He came here to find his daughter, and it seems like maybe he did."

"But?" Helen asked.

Arlo shook her head. "I don't know. Something about it just seems off. You know…with Joe." She didn't have to say any more. They understood.

"People change," Fern said with a shrug, echoing Arlo's earlier thoughts.

Lord, let it be true.

"Maybe it's all this talk of Lillyfield," Helen mused.

"I suppose." Arlo shrugged. "But if his daughter works at Lillyfield, who is she?"

"Wait." Helen's brow wrinkled into a thoughtful frown. "Who's the mom?"

"That's a good question." Fern nodded. "He went to prison right after Mary disappeared…"

"Maybe he met someone when he was out that first time?" Arlo asked.

"Mary Kennedy was pregnant when she disappeared," Fern said.

"But Mary was reportedly killed fifty years ago," Arlo reminded her. "Joe went to prison for it. So she couldn't have had a baby."

Fern shook her head. "No, Weston killed Mary to keep her from telling everybody that she was carrying *his* baby and that they were having an affair."

"This is beginning to make my head hurt," Helen said.

Chloe tossed her dishrag over one shoulder and made her way to the reading nook. "Let's break this down," she said. "Joe could have gotten married during his time out, but we don't know that for certain."

"Actually he wouldn't have had to have gotten married to have a baby," Arlo said.

"True enough," Fern agreed.

"But if he didn't get married or even start a new relationship, then it could be that daughter he's looking for belongs to Mary Kennedy."

"Which would mean that Mary Kennedy wasn't killed," Helen said.

"That's what I've been saying," Fern said.

"Which brings us back to Weston Whitney didn't kill her," Arlo started. "And Mary Kennedy faked her own death."

They all sat in silence for a moment.

"Perhaps Mary left because she knew that she wouldn't get any support from Weston, not even if the child was his and not Joe's. And if it was not Joe's, then he was certainly not going to welcome her back." Chloe looked around to see how this theory was taken.

"She could've simply let Joe believe it was his," Helen said. "I've known a lot of women in such situations."

"A lot?" Arlo asked. Seemed like Sugar Springs was the next Peyton Place.

"It's a relative term," Helen said with a wave of her hand. "All I'm saying is it's not totally out of the question."

"Maybe," Chloe said. "But the money belongs to Judith. If Weston left her, he would be penniless. If the baby was indeed Weston's, then Mary would be left with nothing."

Not unless she could convince Joe that the child was his.

"Holy cow!" Fern said. "It all makes sense now."

Helen nodded. "Mary knew that she would get no support from Weston if he left Judith. He would be penniless and unable to support her and the child."

"And Judith wouldn't exactly welcome her husband's bastard into Lillyfield," Fern continued. "So Mary couldn't go home, back to a violent husband, when she was pregnant with another man's child."

"It would have been fairly easy to convince Joe, or Jeff, that the baby was his. There were no DNA tests back in the seventies. Blood maybe, but that was too much of a gamble. She must've known that Jeff would know that the child wasn't his, and he would be furious when and if he found out."

"She couldn't risk that," Helen mused. "It was too dicey. Instead, she faked her own death and left town. Jeff was blamed and sent to prison, and that was that."

"That would mean that whoever this child is would be about forty-eight or forty-nine," Arlo pointed out. Most of the women they had encountered at Lillyfield had been young, all the maids. The older crowd consisted of Roberts and Dutch and—

"Pam," Arlo breathed. "It has to be Pam."

"But if Pam was that child, then she might not be Joe's daughter," Helen said.

If that came to light…

"Camille could be in danger," Arlo finished. Who knew how Joe would react to finding out that the child he had been looking for belonged to someone else?

"We have to get out there. Now," Helen said.

Fern was on her feet in an instant. "I'll drive."

"Are you sure about this?" Chloe asked as Arlo gathered her purse.

"Not at all, but I can't let them go by themselves. What if Joe and Camille are actually out there?"

"You don't think his daughter is dangerous?"

Arlo shook her head. "I have no idea. I don't even know if it's really Pam. But I know that Haley was killed out there."

"It doesn't have anything to do with it," Chloe said, her voice taking on a hopeful tone.

"It doesn't? You know this for a fact?" Arlo asked.

Chloe sighed. "No. But—"

Arlo nodded. "I know, I know. Things like this just don't happen in Sugar Springs. But they have now, and we have to deal with it."

"I'm not going to let you go by yourself," Chloe said, reaching behind her and untying her apron.

"Who's gonna watch the shop?" Fern stopped gathering her things and looked from Arlo to Chloe.

"Phil," Chloe said. Their neighbor next door picked that moment to walk into the Books and More for another cup of coffee.

"What?" Phil asked.

"We need you to stay here at the Books and More and watch the store," Arlo said.

"What about my store?"

"What do you get? Like two customers a day?" Fern asked.

"Never mind," Arlo said. "We're closing the store. If anybody comes by, just tell them that we'll be back as soon as we possibly can." She hated closing up shop, but what choice did she have?

"Sam," Chloe said with a snap of her fingers.

"We'll call him on the way."

They all filed into Fern's Lincoln and headed for the mansion.

"Call Sam," Chloe said. "Have him go downstairs and make sure that the Books and More is okay."

"And call Mads," Helen said from the front seat. "Make sure that he meets us at Lillyfield."

"And not Jason," Fern instructed. "I think Mads should be there."

"Stop giving me orders." Arlo's fingers were trembling so badly she could hardly thumb through her list of contacts to find the number she needed. She called Sam first. Then hung up before he could answer. Mads. She needed Mads to meet them at Lillyfield. And they already had a head start.

"Go," Mads answered the phone two long rings later.

"Mads, it's Arlo."

"I know. I've got a cell phone."

"I don't have time for that right now," Arlo said. "We're headed out to Lillyfield. We have reason to believe that Camille and Joe might be in trouble out there."

"Define *reason to believe*."

"I don't have time to explain right now," she said. "Can you just meet us out there?"

"Not without a little more to go on, Arlo. I am in the middle of a murder investigation."

"I know, but Joe Foster is really Jeff Kennedy. He was married to Mary Kennedy, who we believe had an affair with Weston Whitney. She was pregnant when she disappeared. The baby might be Weston's, but it could be Joe's. And Joe discovered that the woman he thinks is his daughter is working at Lillyfield now."

"Can you repeat that?"

"No!" Arlo said. "If you ever felt anything for me at all, just meet us out there. Camille could be in trouble."

"Fine," Mads said. "For you. But if nothing is going on, you owe me dinner."

Arlo stared at the phone for a moment and placed it back to her ear. "Okay. Fine. Dinner."

"See you in a bit." Mads hung up, and Arlo called Sam.

"Sam, it's Arlo. We had to leave the Books and More."

"You had to leave?" Sam's voice grew concerned. "All of you? Why?"

"It's too much to try and explain right now. But we're headed out to Lillyfield. Camille could be in trouble. Can you go down and reopen the store?"

"I'm over at Chloe's," Sam said. "I told her I'd look into having a doggie door put in for her. Well, for Manny."

Private dick and handyman.

"So if you're already out there, can you meet us?"

"Well, I'm close, but I've got Manny."

"Take him back to the house, and then go to the mansion," Arlo said. "We may need you."

"And you'll tell me what this is about then?"

She couldn't send him over without explaining; he could be in more danger than any of them if he didn't know what he was walking into.

"Camille and Joe are on their way to Lillyfield to find his daughter who works there."

"Joe Foster who is really Jeff Kennedy, whose baby is probably—"

"Mary Kennedy's daughter. But probably not because Mary Kennedy was having an affair with Weston Whitney when she disappeared."

"I'm pretty good at detangling puzzles and relationships, but it's gonna take a minute on this one."

"Just go to the mansion and make sure that Camille and Joe don't go inside. That's the main thing," Arlo said. "There's already been one murder there."

"You don't think Haley's murder has anything to do with Mary Kennedy?"

"Are you willing to take that chance?"

"No," he said. "No, I'm not."

"Are you going to the mansion?" Arlo asked.

"Let me take this dog back to the cottage, and I'll be over there as soon as I can."

"And Sam," she said. "Thank you."

Arlo hung up the phone and waited to be bombarded with questions from the ladies surrounding her, but no one said a word. Everyone was too worried about what they were going to find once they got to Lillyfield. Were Joe and Camille already out there? Would Sam get there before them? When would Mads arrive? And when would they? It seemed like the longest trip she had ever made.

When they pulled up in front of Lillyfield a few minutes later, Camille's car was already parked in the circular drive. Sam's truck was nowhere around, but he could've walked over from the cottage, Arlo was certain. It was simply a stone's throw from the Lillyfield back door. But they had no way of knowing if he had made it inside or was even there yet. He said had been walking Manny when Arlo, called and she had no clue how far from the house he had been when she reached him.

"Okay," Helen said turning in the seat to look at all three of them. "How are we going to do this?"

"We go to the front door and knock," Arlo said.

Chloe nodded. "Maybe I should do it," she said. "I mean, I'm a tenant, so it wouldn't be totally out of the question for me to come calling."

"With three of your closest friends," Fern quipped.

"I don't think the maid who answers the door cares about that sort of thing," Chloe said.

"Aren't you going to tell her she watches too much *Downton Abbey*?" Helen asked.

"Not the time," Arlo replied.

"Yeah," Helen said. "You're right."

"So I knock on the door, and the maid lets us in. That's the most important thing, right?" Chloe nodded, waiting for them to agree.

"Right," Arlo, Fern, and Helen said at the same time.

"Then what?"

"I have no idea," Arlo said. "I guess we just play it by ear."

"Let's do this." Fern slipped from the driver seat, then waited for everyone else to get out as well.

Chloe led the march to the front door with the three other ladies trailing behind. She was their ticket, and they were there to let her work her magic. After that, it was anybody's guess.

She rang the doorbell. They waited. It seemed like forever, but it had only been a few short seconds before the door creaked open. Andrea the maid stood before them. Andrea who had said she had heard Haley and Dylan arguing the day that Haley was killed.

"Hi, I'm Chloe." Chloe took a step forward, and thankfully the maid took a step back. Chloe plowed on. "I live in the cottage out back. I'd like to talk to somebody about putting in a doggie door and building a fence."

The girl blinked as if she didn't understand a word that Chloe was saying.

"Is there anyone I can talk to?" she asked. "The property manager perhaps."

Arlo had a feeling Chloe knew exactly who to talk to about some sort of alteration to the cottage, but that wasn't the point.

She took another large step into the foyer, and the three of them crowded in behind.

"I'll go find someone," Andrea said. If she recognized Arlo, she didn't say. She simply looked at them as if they had come to rob the place. Then she shut the door and bustled away.

"Now?" Arlo said. "Where do we go from here?"

Before anyone could answer, a piercing scream rent the air. It came from upstairs, the same direction they had gone trying to find Judith Whitney's room.

"There," Helen said.

"Let's do it." Fern started toward the staircase in a dead run.

26

ARLO, CHLOE, FERN, AND HELEN RACED UP THE STAIRS
with Andrea the maid hot on their heels.

"You can't go up there," Andrea cried.

Arlo wasn't sure if she was upset about the scream or the
fact that they weren't doing what she said. She turned toward
the maid. "Go back downstairs. See if you can find Sam Tucker."

"Who's Sam Tucker?"

"Never mind. Mads and Jason—the police chief and his
top officer—are on their way here right now. Go downstairs
and wait for them," Arlo instructed.

She hesitated.

"Now," Helen roared.

The maid scurried back down the stairs.

"I think it came from this direction," Fern said. She
rushed toward the end of the landing. A large mahogany
door gleamed, the barrier between them and...

Well, she didn't know what or who. Joe? Pam? Camille?
Judith? Maybe all of them. And why the scream? Who
screamed? Not Judith. Pam? Camille?

Fern raced to the door and flung it open. Nothing. No one was in the room.

Then voices came from next door.

Helen nodded toward the second mahogany door. It was cracked open an inch or two, but Arlo couldn't see anything inside.

Are we going in? Fern mouthed.

Helen nodded.

Chloe grabbed Arlo's arm. *Is this safe?* she mouthed.

Arlo shrugged.

Count of three, Helen mouthed. She held up one hand and ticked the count off on her fingers.

One…

Two…

Three…

They pushed their way into the room, and all eyes turned to them.

"Camille," Joe-Jeff drawled. "It looks like your friends are here."

Arlo wasn't sure what to make of the scene. Joe was standing in front of the large window that faced the front of the house. He looked the same as he always did. Bald head gleaming, tattoos marking him, jeans and motorcycle boots. Except today he had a gun. And it was pointed at Pam.

"Are you okay?" Helen asked Camille.

Their friend cowered in a corner with Judith Whitney. Actually, Camille was doing the cowering, Judith was strapped into a wheelchair. She didn't appear to be able to move her body, but those green, green eyes of hers were as sharp as ever. The stroke that had ravaged her body seemed to have only done damage to the physical. Her mind appeared to be in top form. It was a sight different than the last time that they had seen her.

"Do you think I would shoot her?" Joe asked in a stricken tone. "I adore Camille."

"There are two guns," Helen commented.

And there were.

Joe Foster, once known as Jeff Kennedy, was pointing a gun at Pam, who was pointing an even bigger one right back.

"I'm not trying to shoot anybody," Pam said. "I'm only trying to protect myself."

"From?" Fern asked.

"Crazy men busting in here and trying to tell me that they know who I am." Pam waved the gun in Joe's general direction. Camille ducked as if she had turned it on her.

"I've got an idea," Fern started, speaking slowly. She smiled at everyone in the room and inched closer into the fray. Arlo wanted to grab her arm and pull her back out of the line of gunfire. "Why don't we all put down the guns and talk this through?"

"Not a chance." Joe spit the words in disgust. Gone was the easygoing man who could easily bowl a 275, and in his place stood an angry man, eyes blazing with the resentment born from years' worth of lies come to light.

"Don't you find it much easier to talk to someone when they aren't pointing a gun at you?" she continued.

"No." Pam's one word was like a bullet.

"Okay, then," Fern continued. "Wouldn't it be easier to listen to someone if you weren't pointing a gun at them? You surely wouldn't have to worry about accidentally shooting someone in the room that you wouldn't want to shoot."

"Not when the person you're pointing it at ruined your life," Joe said.

"I ruined your life?" Pam scoffed.

"I came here to meet the daughter I never had. That I had just learned about. Instead I find walking, talking evidence of my wife's infidelity."

"You used to beat her," Pam said. "She told me. She told me everything."

"Then she lied. I knew what the talk was around town, but it was wrong. I never laid a hand on her. She was a little clumsy and managed to bruise herself up just walking to the mailbox. But I never laid a hand on her."

"And yet you killed her," Pam said.

Joe rolled his eyes. "How could I have killed her if you're standing here? I didn't know about you until six months ago."

"On the inside," Pam explained. "You killed her on the inside. You and Ms. Fancy Pants over there." She used one elbow to indicate Judith, all the while keeping her gun steadily trained on Joe. "I've heard the stories my entire life about the evil dealt to my mother."

"Your mother never could get the facts straight."

"Except for the one about who my father really was."

"I'm starting to feel dizzy from all this," Chloe said.

As far as Arlo could tell, they had gotten it right. Pam was Weston Whitney and Mary Kennedy's daughter. Though up until a few moments before, Joe thought that she was his own.

Sometime in between, they had started pulling guns, and now she just wished that Mads would get there. Or Sam. And she hoped Sam had a gun of his own.

"I came here to get revenge," Pam continued. She thought she had the upper hand and kept talking. "I didn't know I was going to get it twice."

"Twice?" Helen asked.

"I came for Judith, but it seems I can make my mother's rotten husband pay as well."

Chloe nudged Arlo. "Judith?" she whispered.

"If it hadn't had been for Judith Whitney, then my father would have left her and married my mother. I would have grown up in a house like this one." She laughed. "In this one actually."

"That's not true,"' Chloe said. She stepped forward, the same way that Fern had, and Arlo was beginning to feel a little cowardly at hanging back. Cowardice and intelligence. No sense in putting yourself in the crosshairs. "The money came from Judith's family. She was the Lilly. Your father had no money of his own."

Chloe was right. The fortune that Weston shared with his wife was only his because he was her husband. If he had left Judith for Mary, they would have been poor as church mice.

Pam looked a bit sucker punched. "But I—" she started. She shook her head. "But I came here to—" She stopped.

Arlo watched as the thoughts chased across her face. She had known, yet she hadn't put it all together until now.

"You came to get your revenge." Andrea stepped into the room.

"I thought I told you to go downstairs and wait for the police to come," Arlo said.

"But I know," Andrea said. She trembled as she said the words, but her long-lost-little-girl look was gone, and in its place, she blazed with a new confidence. "I know that you killed Haley, Pam. I was under the stairs when you hit her in the head with the statuette."

All the air was sucked from the center of the room in a collective gasp.

"You killed Haley?" Helen asked. Now it was her turn to advance, ever so slowly toward the nutritionist, if that was indeed what she was. Arlo had no idea at this point.

"So what?" Pam scoffed. "She got in my way. And she found about my secret."

"That you are Weston Whitney's bastard child?" Joe snarled.

"Sticks and stones." Pam laughed. "That I came here to kill Judith Whitney for ruining my life and my mother's life."

Where was Mads? Or Sam? One of them should have been there by now. Especially if Sam had been at the cottage when she called him.

"How did you go from killing Judith to caring for her?" Chloe asked.

The question had been on Arlo's mind as well.

"Caring for her?" Pam snickered. "How do you think she got like that?"

"She had a stroke," Chloe said. Though it came out more like a question than an answer.

"Yeah. See I was going to poison her. Just kill her outright. An overdose of her own blood-thinning medication." Pam gave them all an evil smile. "Did you know that warfarin is the same exact chemical compound as rat poison?"

"As a matter of fact, I did," Fern said.

That in itself was scary enough.

"A little too much, and bye-bye, Judith."

"But she's still here," Helen pointed out. She didn't bother to say that she had more limitations now than ever; the point was Judith Whitney was still alive.

"I may have miscalculated a bit. That's what caused the, uh—" She waved a hand toward Judith's poor body, crumpled up and strapped to a wheelchair so she wouldn't slide into the floor. "That's when I realized that it might be a lot more fun to play a little cat and mouse before I finished my work."

"I don't understand," Chloe said. "You became a nutritionist in order to come here and make her life hell?"

"No, stupid. I printed out a fake certificate from the internet to fool an old woman into letting me in."

"Which explains why a nutritionist was buying Cheetos at the grocery store," Fern mused.

Pam shrugged. "There's that."

"And what about Haley?" Arlo asked. "She just got in your way?"

"Collateral damage. So sad, such a bright young woman." But Pam didn't sound the least bit remorseful. "She started snooping around and questioning the medication I was giving Judy over there."

"She discovered your plan. And you killed her," Arlo said. "You killed her, then framed her boyfriend for the murder."

"Like I said, collateral damage."

"Dylan didn't throw anything into the lake," Fern mused. "You did."

Again Pam shrugged. Then she glanced around at all of them, and it took Arlo a moment to realize that she was counting. "How many bullets you got in that gun, convict?" she asked.

"Wouldn't you like to know?"

"At least two, I hope. I would hate for you have to take your own life by stabbing an old woman, then jumping out the window."

And Pam's plan became clear to Arlo. She was going to shoot them all, make it look like Joe had done it, and be the only witness left to say otherwise. They had to do something, and they had to do it fast.

But what? She looked across the room to where Camille still stood next to Judith's wheelchair. Camille looked a little worse for wear. Her snow-white curls stood on end, and the silk shell underneath her baby-blue jacket had come untucked from the matching slacks. Her pearls were askew, and she looked as if she was about to start chewing on her fingernails at any moment. But Camille wasn't looking at Arlo; she was looking at Fern.

If it hadn't been for that larger than large hat she wore, Arlo would have never seen Fern's nod. They were planning something; Arlo just wasn't sure what. But she knew she had to be ready too. She nudged Chloe. Her best friend nudged her back in acceptance.

On the count of three, they would move. At least she hoped it was the count of three. This would be a little deadlier than offsides in football. They had to get this right.

Yet despite her diligence, Fern and Camille moved first. Fern pounced on Joe and Camille on Pam, leaving Chloe and Arlo trying to figure out how to join the game.

Camille had jumped on Pam's back, and the woman was slinging her around like a dog slings a toy. Somehow Camille held on.

"Camille!" Joe cried when he saw his love in danger. His distraction gave Fern the upper hand. In no time flat, she had Joe disarmed.

"Looks like those jiu-jitsu lessons are paying off," Helen commented as Fern gave him one last kick. It landed on his knee and had him on the ground in a flash.

"Damn straight," Fern said.

But Camille was not faring as well. Arlo saw her opportunity to help her friend, but then the doorbell rang, breaking her concentration. Mads? No. He wouldn't ring the bell. Sam? Maybe Sam. She needed one of them, and ASAP.

"You should be answering that," Chloe hollered at Andrea, who hovered by the door.

The young woman wrung her hands.

"Go," Chloe roared.

Andrea fled from the room.

Pam continued to turn in a circle, trying to shake Camille off, but Camille held fast. The main problem was with every turn, the gun Pam held swung wildly.

Camille had her arms wrapped around the woman's throat, choking her in her efforts to remain in place. "Help," she squealed as she held on for her life. Quite literally.

Pam made gasping, gurgling noises as she tried to pry Camille's fingers loose with her free hand.

"Don't hurt her," Joe growled. Tears streamed down his craggy face. "You will not hurt my baby." He charged into the fray.

Arlo ducked again when Pam swung around in a circle. What was taking Mads so long? And Sam?

Joe grabbed at Camille's arms, trying to peel her off

Pam. To save Camille? Or Pam? She had only a moment to speculate.

Then a shot rang out, and the world seemed to grow still and dark.

27

"Give me that," Arlo heard Helen screech as the ringing in her ears subsided.

She looked down at herself. She appeared fine. She hadn't been shot.

Helen took the gun from Fern and motioned for the other woman to stand aside. Neither one seemed to be suffering from a gunshot wound.

Joe darted from one side to the other in his mission to bring down Pam, his charge not helping the chaos as Pam moved from side to side to avoid him.

Fern might be unarmed, but Pam still swung her weapon wildly as she tried to fend off Camille and Joe.

In what could have only been seconds but felt like an eternity, Chloe managed to break Pam's grip on the gun and remove it from her possession while Arlo unbalanced her. Pam was on the ground, still gasping for air, as Camille wasn't about to let go.

"Everybody freeze," Mads called.

Finally. Help, true help, had arrived.

....

"I still think I should have one of those shiny silver blankets." Fern was still fussing nearly an hour later.

Mads had come in first, followed by Sam. Jason had pulled up to the house seconds after Mads had Joe and Pam handcuffed. Mads put Pam in the back of Jason's car and sent him back to town with the prisoner. Jason called Officer Harve Lambert, one of the two regular officers of the SSPD, to come pick up Joe.

The biggest miracle of all? No one had been hurt. Arlo sent up a prayer of thanks to the deity who had helped them today. She would be forever grateful for small wonders.

"You do not need one of those blankets," Helen said. She drank coffee from the mugs provided by the Lillyfield household staff. "Those are for people who are in shock."

"I might be," Fern argued.

Sam smiled a bit and shook his head.

Arlo wasn't sure what to make of it all. Judith Whitney had been tucked back into bed and was currently being watched over by Andrea. Mads had talked to her a little after all the guns had been accounted for and it was confirmed that no one had been shot. Arlo had heard Andrea promise that she would come down to the station and give a full statement as soon as someone could be brought in to look after Mrs. Whitney.

Dutch, the cook, had called a temp medical service over in Corinth to send someone to help for a while until a permanent replacement could be brought in to care for Judith. Hopefully this one wouldn't have homicidal tendencies.

"Looks like you're going to be here for a while," Sam said.

Arlo took a sip of her own coffee and scanned the area.

People were still milling around everywhere. Jason had returned to the scene, leaving Harve to guard their two prisoners. Now the chief officer was helping gather statements. "Looks like." Arlo turned back to Sam. "What took you so long anyway?"

"Seriously?" he asked. He pointed toward his feet. In all the excitement, Arlo hadn't noticed that he was covered with mud from the knees down.

"Manny?" she asked.

He nodded. "Right after I hung up the phone with you, he got off his leash. I think the clasp is broken."

"And he ran right into Lillyfield Lake."

"You mean the sinking mud pit that was once known as Lillyfield Lake."

And Arlo could piece the rest together herself. He had to make the split-second decision between the happiness of a boy and his dog, and helping her. How could he have known that the situation would have turned that deadly? Potentially deadly.

"So is he safe?" Arlo asked. "Manny?"

"Yes, he's safe. Still covered in mud from stem to stern, but safe."

"I guess that's all that matters." Arlo smiled.

Sam returned the gesture. Then he snaked one arm around her shoulders, pulled her close, and kissed the top of her head. "And you're safe too."

....

It took three more days, but finally everyone had given their statement, and things settled down around Sugar Springs.

Just in time for Monday. Start of a new week. The book club met at noon as usual. Some things weren't about to change.

Arlo had tried not to give herself too much empty time to think about Sam and his sweet, but chaste kiss after the big hullabaloo at Lillyfield, but every time she let her guard down, those thoughts would sneak in. Soon, she told herself. Soon she would get up the nerve to ask him about it. What it meant to him. What it meant to them. If it meant anything at all.

"Joe will have to go back to prison because he had a gun," Helen said. "Is that right?"

Camille nodded. "It's a violation of his parole."

"Can't have a gun when you're out on parole," Fern said.

"But 'Don't hurt my baby?'" Helen scoffed.

"What can I say?" Camille beamed. "He adores me. He told you so himself."

"Well, now he's adoring you from Cell Block C," Fern joked.

Camille sniffed. "Be that as it may, he is a nice man."

Arlo couldn't argue with that. Joe was like the rest of the sad players in this tragic drama—Mary, Pam, perhaps even Weston before his death—a victim of money and power and the problems that come with both.

"And he said he was sorry about the note," Camille said to Arlo.

"Joe left that?" Arlo asked. She had almost forgotten with so much going on.

"What note?" Helen asked.

"We got a note saying, *SOMEONE'S GOING TO GET HURT!*" Arlo explained. "Though I wasn't sure what it was."

"He can't even write a threatening note right," Camille

said. "That just proves what kind of man he is. One that shouldn't have been mixed up in all this in the first place."

Arlo wasn't sure how to respond to that. So she sent up a small wish that Camille would get over this jailhouse crush, and soon.

"Now what happens?" Chloe asked. She leaned against the bookstore side of the coffee bar and waited for someone to answer.

"Nothing, I suppose. According to Pam, Mary Kennedy died of natural causes a few years back," Helen said.

"It's such a shame," Camille mused.

"What's that?" Helen asked.

Camille sighed. "Mary Kennedy. She had the perfect opportunity to start over. She had money—well, she would have if she had kept the necklace from the car."

"I don't think she knew the necklace was in the car," Arlo said. "At least that's what Pam told police. Mary left Lillyfield with plans of sinking her car in the lake and having Weston arrested for her attempted murder. Weston had wanted to have her arrested for theft. But she didn't plan on complications with her pregnancy."

"According to Pam's statement," Fern said, "by the time she would have been able to accuse Weston of anything, she was too embroiled in the life she had. If she had blown her cover and her plan had not been successful, she would have had nothing."

"So she kept what she had and grew more miserable by the day."

Camille shook her head sadly.

"Wait," Arlo said. "How do you know what Pam's statement said? Please tell me you did not steal her statement from the police station," Arlo begged.

"Would I do something like that?" Fern asked sweetly.

"Yes," they all answered at the same time.

But Fern was nonplussed. "Frances told me."

"Good ol' Frances," Chloe said.

"What about Courtney?" Helen asked.

As if on cue, Courtney walked into the Books and More arm in arm with Dylan Wright, her sister's once-boyfriend.

Greetings went up all around, and Courtney seemed happier than Arlo had seen her in a long time.

"I just wanted to let you know that I'll be back to work tomorrow. If that's okay?" Courtney looked from Arlo to Chloe.

"Perfect," Arlo said.

"Good for me," Chloe replied.

"And I wanted to be the first to tell you that Dylan and I are pre-pre-engaged." She held out her left hand, showing off the sparkling emerald there.

"Pre-pre-engaged?" Fern repeated. "What the heck is that?"

"We're promised to each other." Dylan smiled lovingly at Courtney.

"Isn't this a little soon?" Fern grumbled, but Arlo stepped in.

"No, Fern. No, it's not." And it surely wasn't going to be if they wanted Courtney to return to work. And they wanted Courtney to return to work.

"That's the thing."' Courtney turned a deep crimson color, one to rival State's maroon. "Dylan and I fell in love, but we didn't know how to tell Haley. Now that she's gone, well, we feel it only right that we share our love with the world. Otherwise it's like she died for nothing."

Arlo saw no profit in arguing the point and allowed Courtney to continue. "Mom and Dad are not so happy," Courtney continued, "but they'll change their minds."

"It's not me they have a problem with," Dylan hastily added.

Chloe caught her eye, and Arlo gave a small nod. They knew exactly what the problem was. Sisterly betrayal.

"Anyway," Dylan continued, "I couldn't tell everyone where I was when Haley was killed because I was in Corinth picking out a ring with Courtney."

"My ring," Courtney explained. "Not one for Haley." Like everyone had assumed.

This time as she mentioned her sister's name, her eyes filled with tears. "I just hope we can do her memory justice."

The love was young and already on shaky ground.

"What about the maid who said you and Haley were fighting that day?" Camille asked. "What was that all about?"

Dylan stuffed his hands into his jeans pockets and shrugged. "That was the day before. Haley knew something was up. Even though I hadn't told her yet. I went to the mansion to see her and talk to her."

"To break up with her," Courtney clarified.

"But I couldn't do it. Then we ended up in an argument. But it was the day before. Not the same day."

Which explained how the maid could have gotten it confused. Dylan and Haley didn't look like the kind of couple to argue, and when they did, people remembered. But Arlo knew as well as anyone, sometimes one day blended into the next.

Courtney and Dylan said their goodbyes and started out of the Books and More.